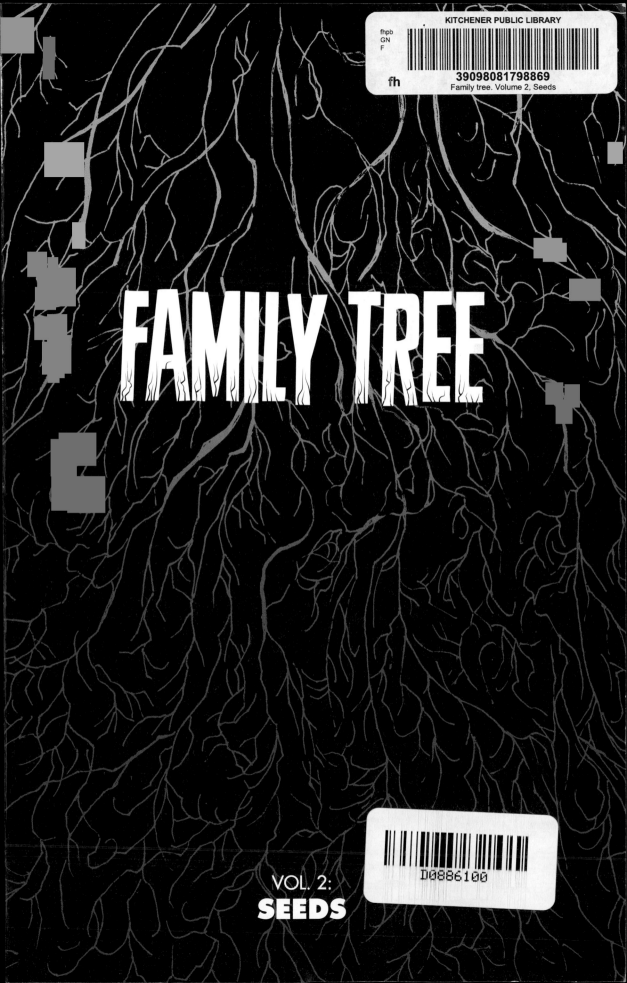

KITCHENER PUBLIC LIBRARY

fhpb
GN
F

fh

39098081798869

Family tree. Volume 2, Seeds

D0886100

FAMILY TREE

VOL. 2:
SEEDS

IMAGE COMICS, INC. • **Todd McFarlane:** President • **Jim Valentino:** Vice President • **Marc Silvestri:** Chief Executive Officer • **Erik Larsen:** Chief Financial Officer • **Robert Kirkman:** Chief Operating Officer • **Eric Stephenson:** Publisher / Chief Creative Officer • **Shanna Matuszak:** Editorial Coordinator • **Marla Eizik:** Talent Liaison • **Nicole Lapalme:** Controller • **Leanna Caunter:** Accounting Analyst • **Sue Korpela:** Accounting & HR Manager • **Jeff Boison:** Director of Sales & Publishing Planning • **Dirk Wood:** Director of International Sales & Licensing • **Alex Cox:** Director of Direct Market & Speciality Sales • **Chloe Ramos-Peterson:** Book Market & Library Sales Manager • **Emilio Bautista:** Digital Sales Coordinator • **Kat Salazar:** Director of PR & Marketing • **Drew Fitzgerald:** Marketing Content Associate • **Heather Doornink:** Production Director • **Drew Gill:** Art Director • **Hilary DiLoreto:** Print Manager • **Tricia Ramos:** Traffic Manager • **Erika Schnatz:** Senior Production Artist • **Ryan Brewer:** Production Artist • **Deanna Phelps:** Production Artist • IMAGECOMICS.COM

FAMILY TREE, VOL. 2. First printing. October 2020. Published by Image Comics, Inc. Office of publication: 2701 NW Vaughn St., Suite 780, Portland, OR 97210. Copyright © 2020 171 Studios & Phil Hester. All rights reserved. Contains material originally published in single magazine form as FAMILY TREE #5-8. "Family Tree," its logos, and the likenesses of all characters herein are trademarks of 171 Studios & Phil Hester, unless otherwise noted. "Image" and the Image Comics logos are registered trademarks of Image Comics, Inc. No part of this publication may be reproduced or transmitted, in any form or by any means (except for short excerpts for journalistic or review purposes), without the express written permission of 171 Studios & Phil Hester, or Image Comics, Inc. All names, characters, events, and locales in this publication are entirely fictional. Any resemblance to actual persons (living or dead), events, or places, without satirical intent, is coincidental. Printed in the USA. For international rights, contact: foreignlicensing@imagecomics.com. ISBN: 978-1-5343-1696-6.

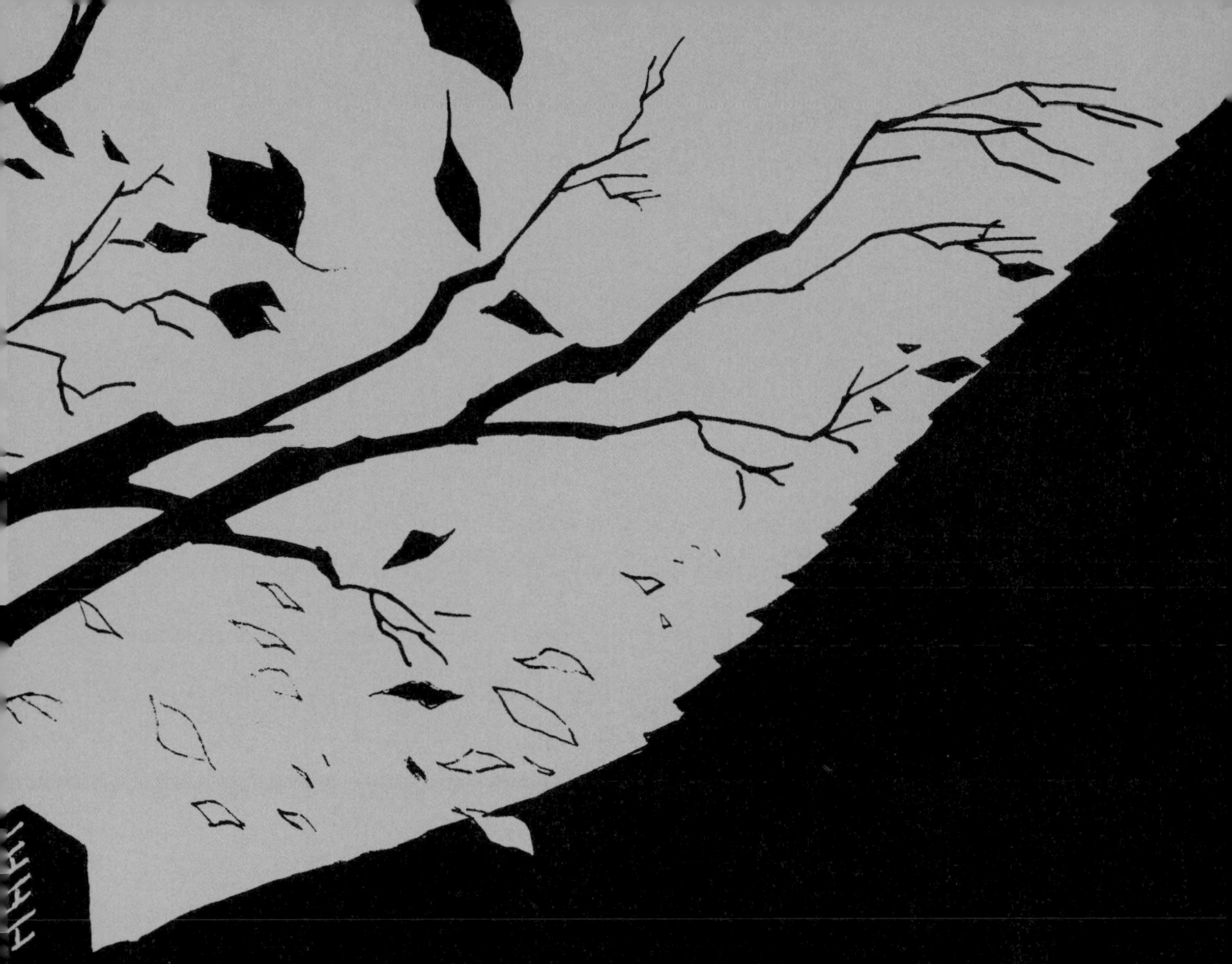

WRITTEN BY JEFF **LEMIRE**

ART BY PHIL **HESTER**
ERIC **GAPSTUR**
RYAN **CODY**

LETTERING BY STEVE **WANDS**

EDITED BY WILL **DENNIS**

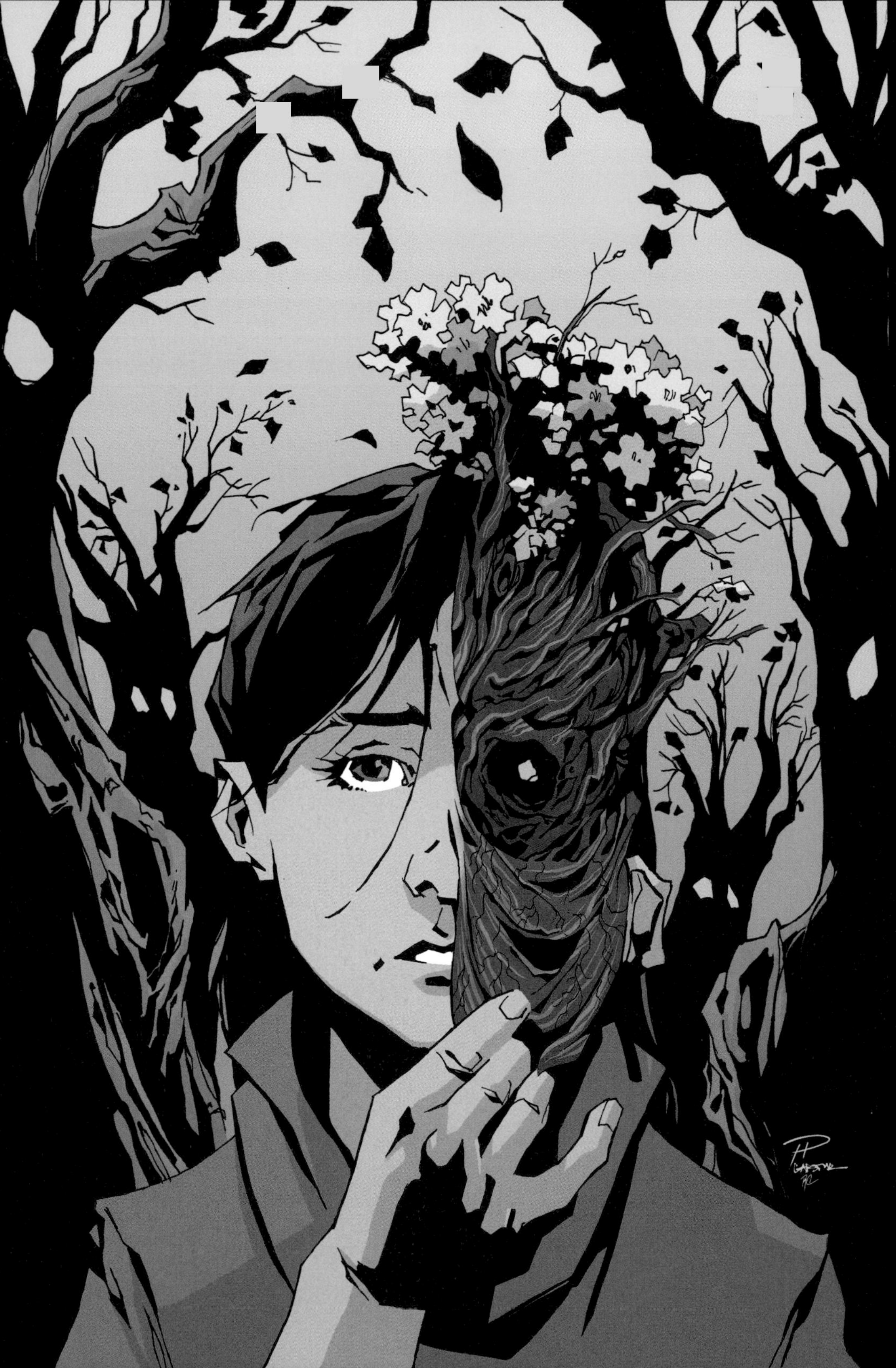

CHAPTER
FIVE

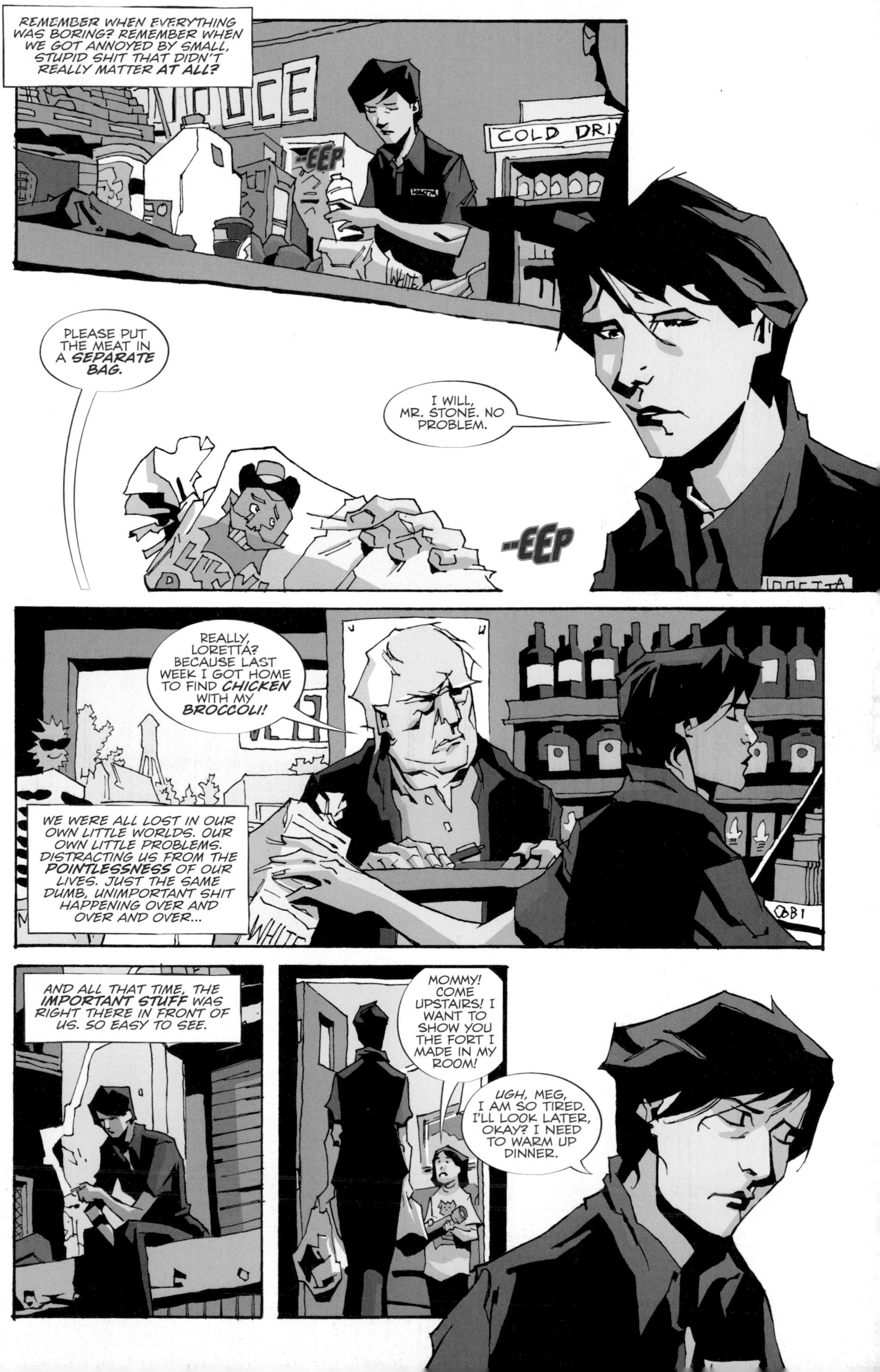
REMEMBER WHEN EVERYTHING WAS BORING? REMEMBER WHEN WE GOT ANNOYED BY SMALL, STUPID SHIT THAT DIDN'T REALLY MATTER AT ALL?
COLD DRI
--EEP
PLEASE PUT THE MEAT IN A SEPARATE BAG.
I WILL, MR. STONE. NO PROBLEM.
--EEP
REALLY, LORETTA? BECAUSE LAST WEEK I GOT HOME TO FIND CHICKEN WITH MY BROCCOLI!
WE WERE ALL LOST IN OUR OWN LITTLE WORLDS. OUR OWN LITTLE PROBLEMS. DISTRACTING US FROM THE POINTLESSNESS OF OUR LIVES. JUST THE SAME DUMB, UNIMPORTANT SHIT HAPPENING OVER AND OVER AND OVER...
AND ALL THAT TIME, THE IMPORTANT STUFF WAS RIGHT THERE IN FRONT OF US. SO EASY TO SEE.
MOMMY! COME UPSTAIRS! I WANT TO SHOW YOU THE FORT I MADE IN MY ROOM!
UGH, MEG, I AM SO TIRED. I'LL LOOK LATER, OKAY? I NEED TO WARM UP DINNER.

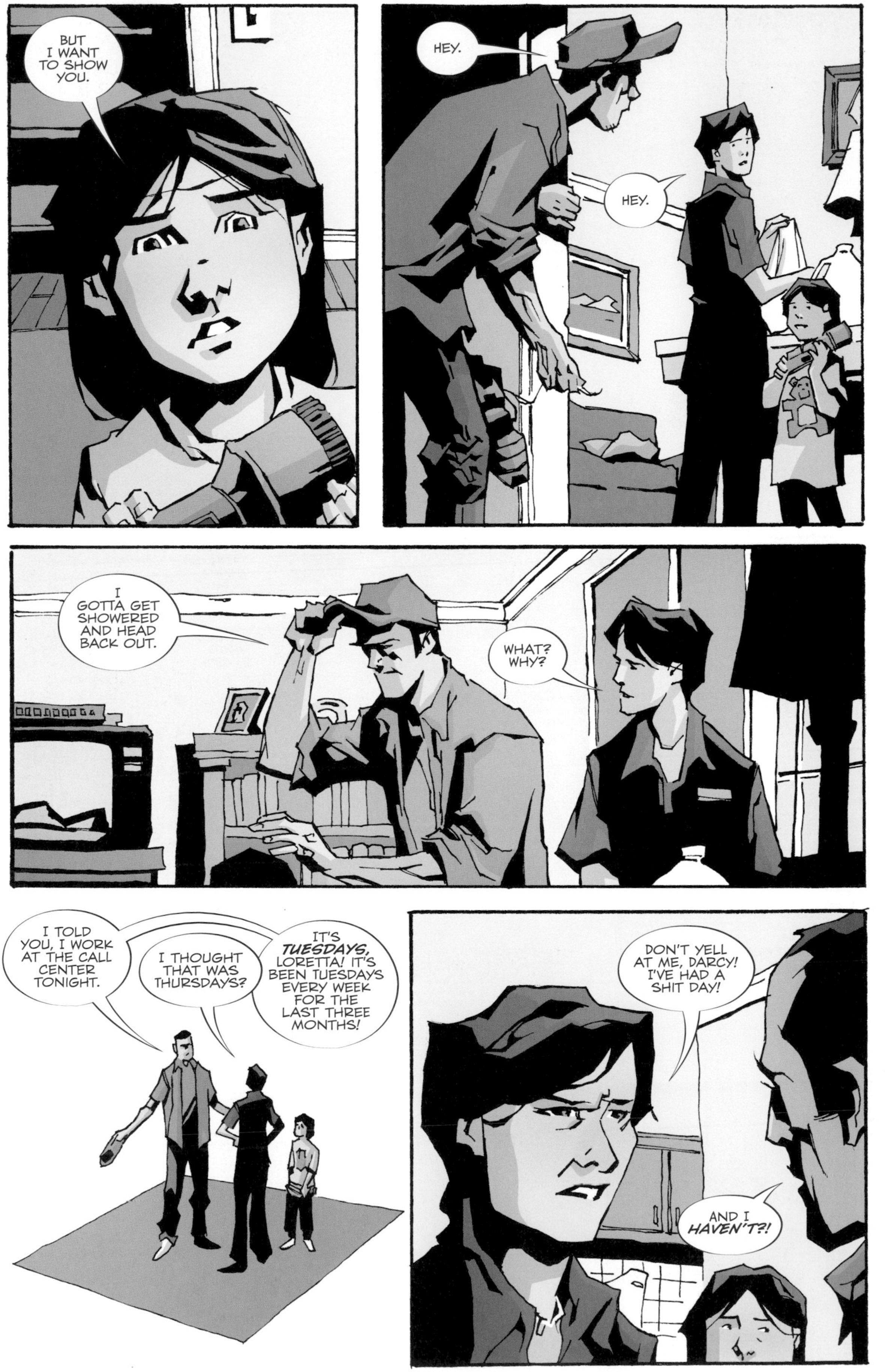
BUT I WANT TO SHOW YOU.
HEY.
HEY.
I GOTTA GET SHOWERED AND HEAD BACK OUT.
WHAT? WHY?
I TOLD YOU, I WORK AT THE CALL CENTER TONIGHT.
I THOUGHT THAT WAS THURSDAYS?
IT'S *TUESDAYS,* LORETTA! IT'S BEEN TUESDAYS EVERY WEEK FOR THE LAST THREE MONTHS!
DON'T YELL AT ME, DARCY! I'VE HAD A SHIT DAY!
AND I *HAVEN'T?!*

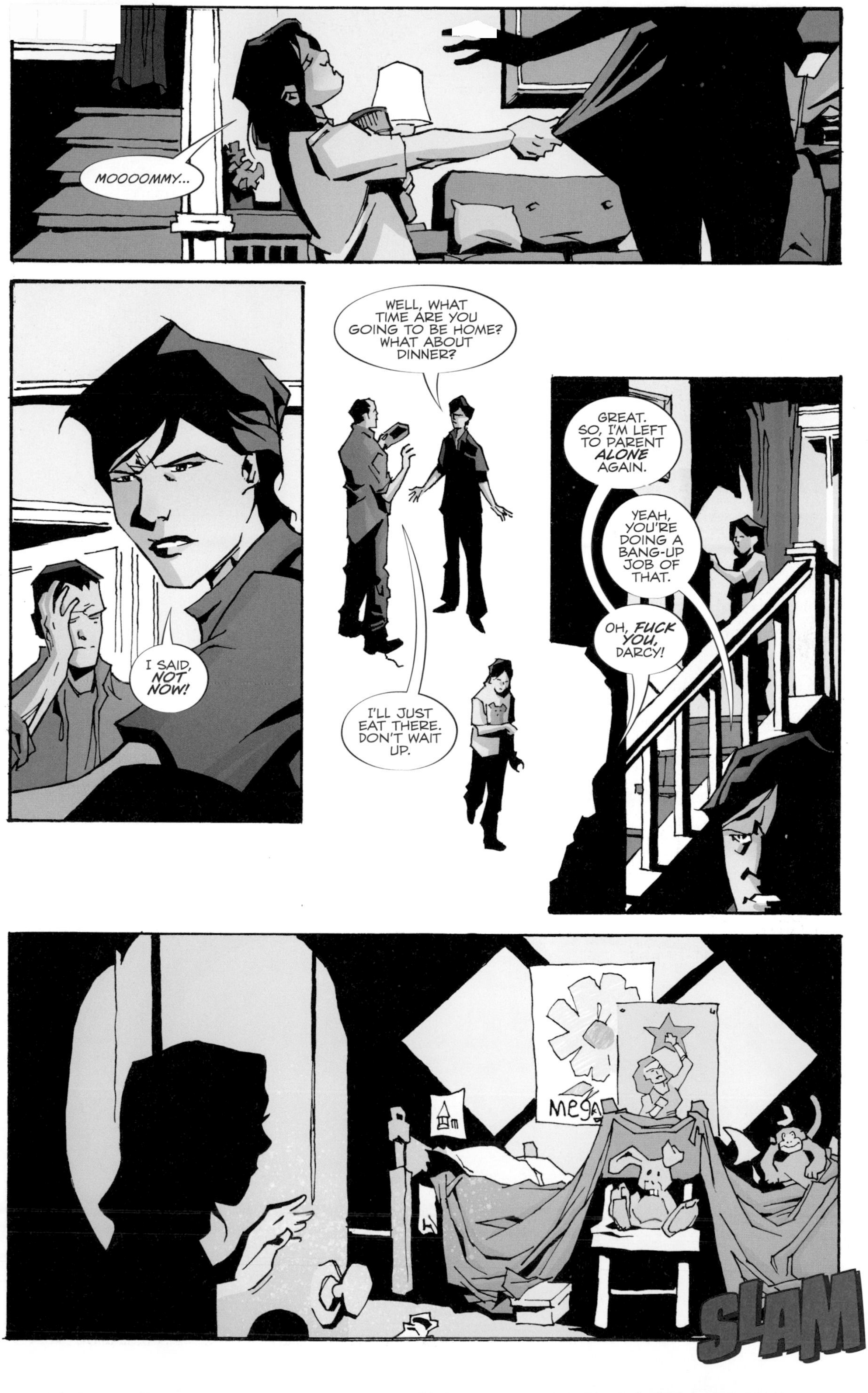
MOOOOMMY...
I SAID, NOT NOW!
WELL, WHAT TIME ARE YOU GOING TO BE HOME? WHAT ABOUT DINNER?
I'LL JUST EAT THERE. DON'T WAIT UP.
GREAT. SO, I'M LEFT TO PARENT ALONE AGAIN.
YEAH, YOU'RE DOING A BANG-UP JOB OF THAT.
OH, FUCK YOU, DARCY!
MEGA
SLAM

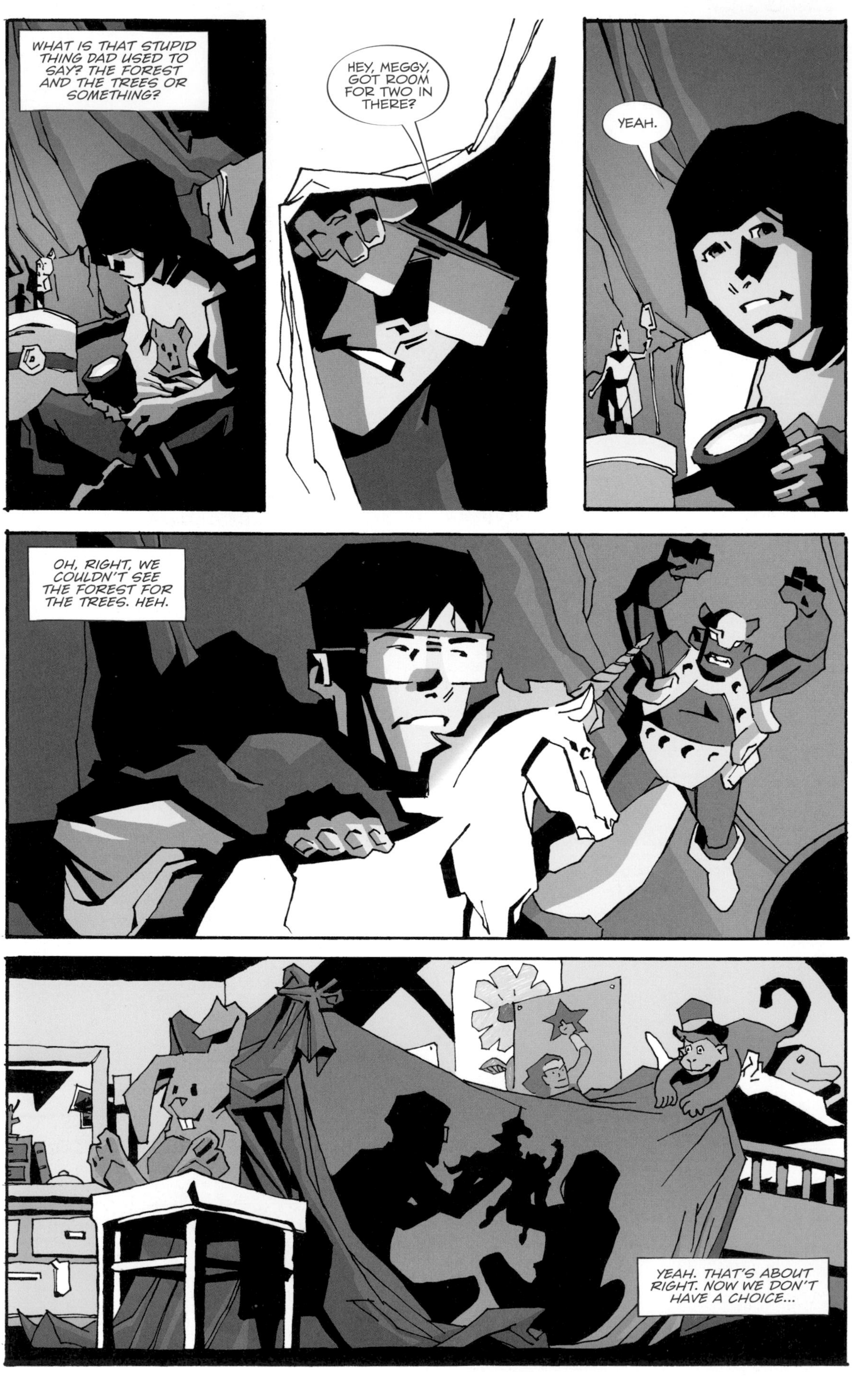
WHAT IS THAT STUPID THING DAD USED TO SAY? THE FOREST AND THE TREES OR SOMETHING?
HEY, MEGGY, GOT ROOM FOR TWO IN THERE?
YEAH.
OH, RIGHT, WE COULDN'T SEE THE FOREST FOR THE TREES. HEH.
YEAH. THAT'S ABOUT RIGHT. NOW WE DON'T HAVE A CHOICE...

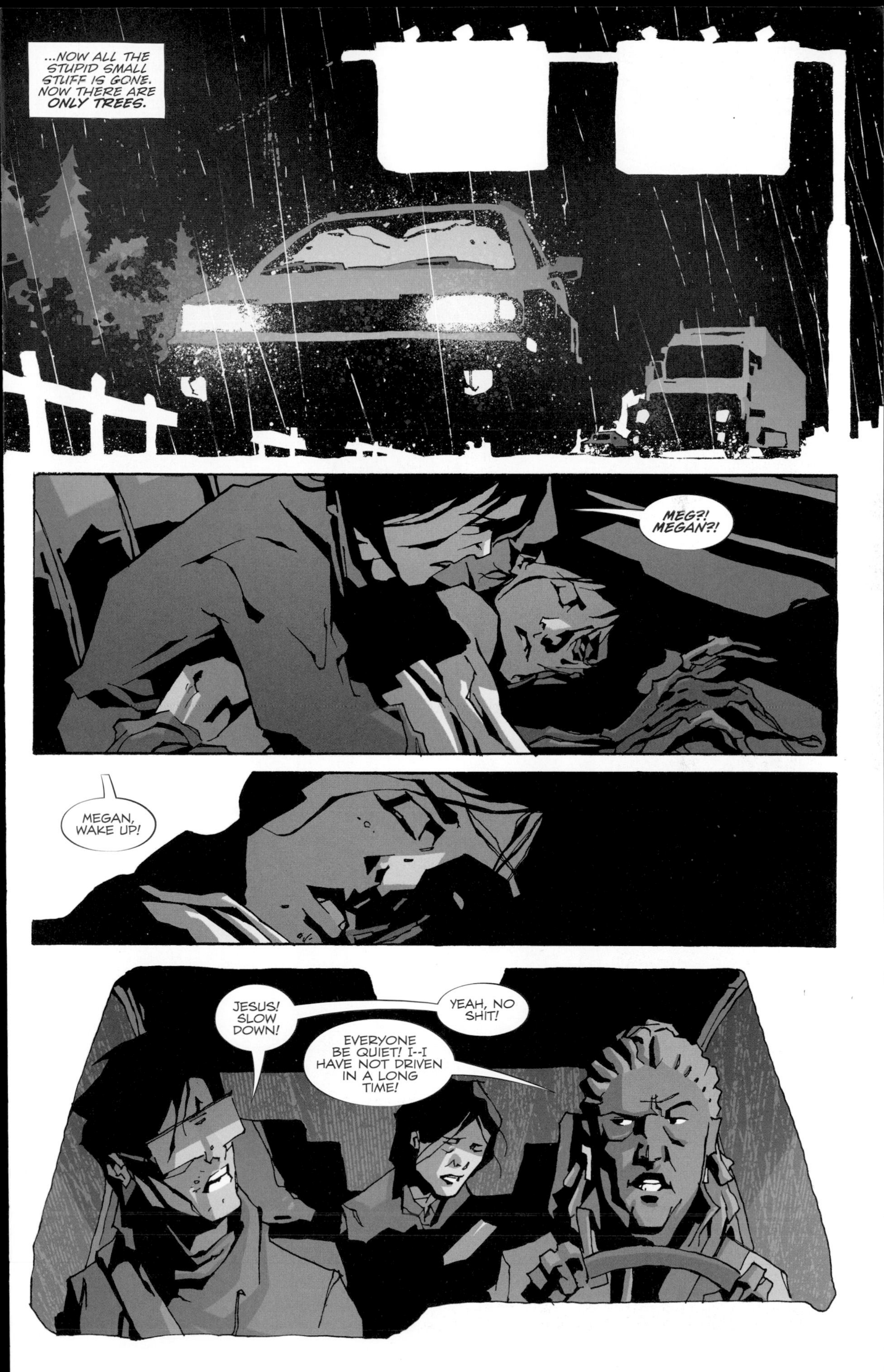
...NOW ALL THE STUPID SMALL STUFF IS GONE. NOW THERE ARE ONLY TREES.
MEG?! MEGAN?!
MEGAN, WAKE UP!
JESUS! SLOW DOWN!
YEAH, NO SHIT!
EVERYONE BE QUIET! I--I HAVE NOT DRIVEN IN A LONG TIME!

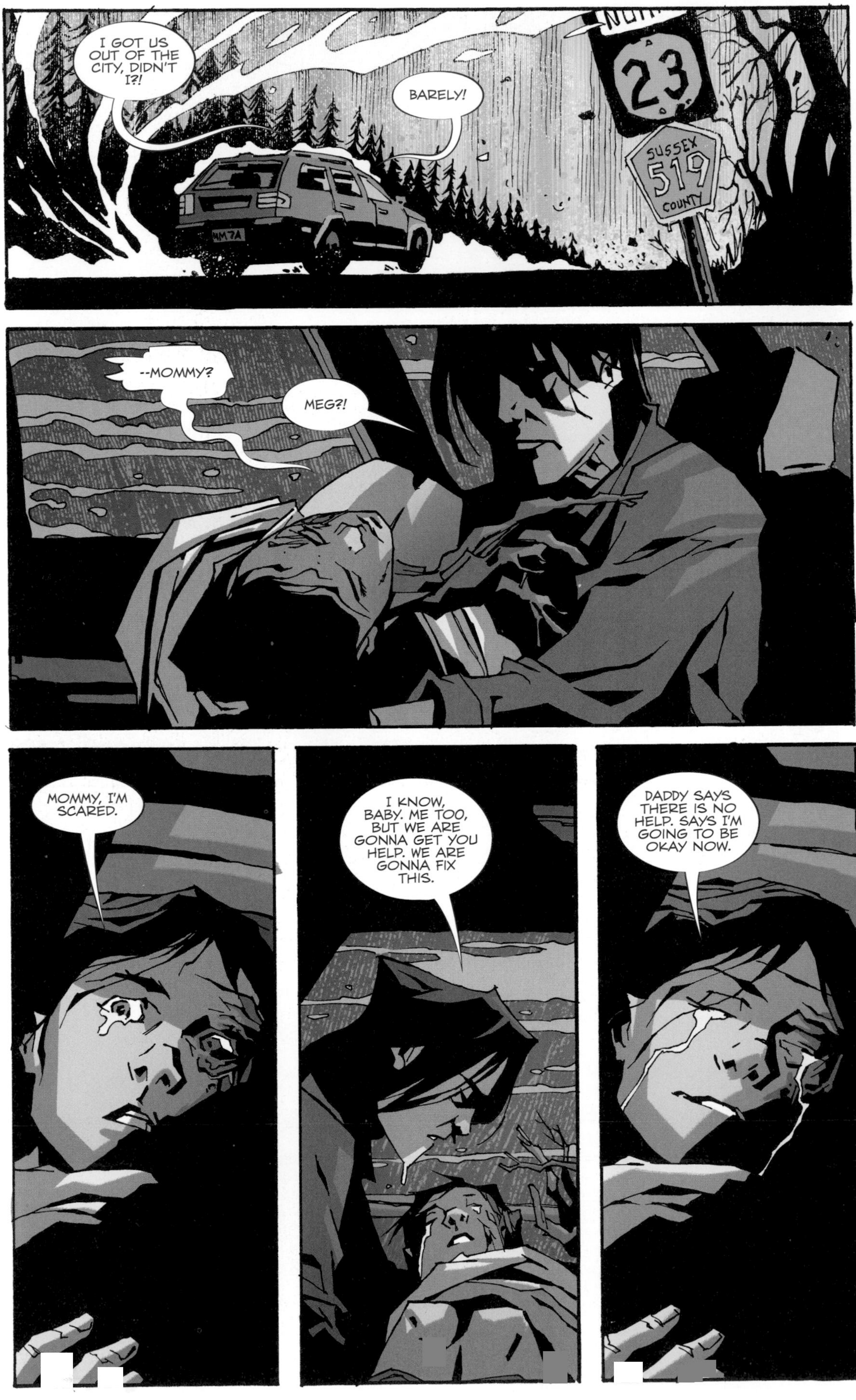
I GOT US OUT OF THE CITY, DIDN'T I?!
BARELY!
23
SUSSEX
519
COUNTY
--MOMMY?
MEG?!
MOMMY, I'M SCARED.
I KNOW, BABY. ME TOO, BUT WE ARE GONNA GET YOU HELP. WE ARE GONNA FIX THIS.
DADDY SAYS THERE IS NO HELP. SAYS I'M GOING TO BE OKAY NOW.

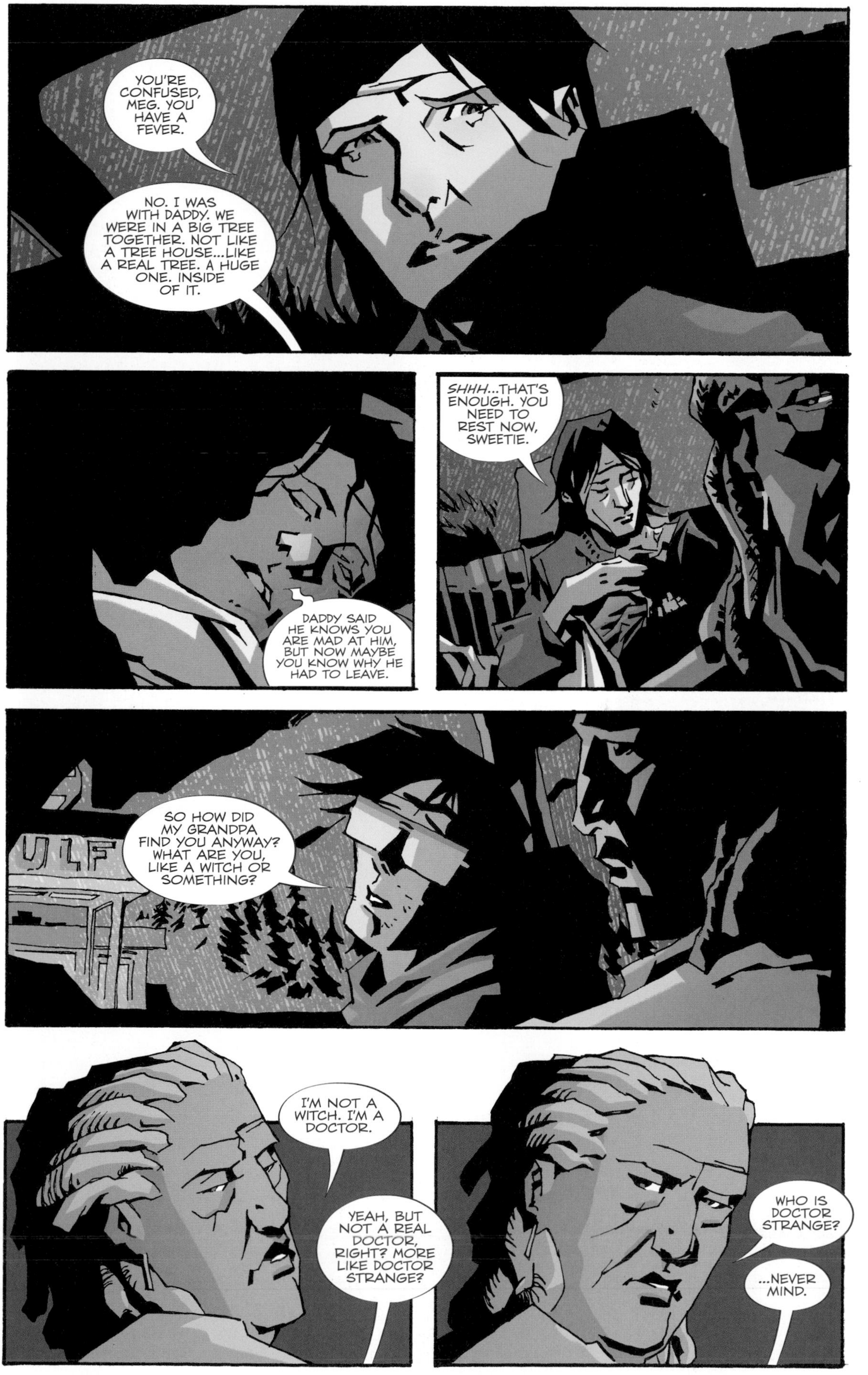
YOU'RE CONFUSED, MEG. YOU HAVE A FEVER.
NO. I WAS WITH DADDY. WE WERE IN A BIG TREE TOGETHER. NOT LIKE A TREE HOUSE...LIKE A REAL TREE. A HUGE ONE. INSIDE OF IT.
DADDY SAID HE KNOWS YOU ARE MAD AT HIM, BUT NOW MAYBE YOU KNOW WHY HE HAD TO LEAVE.
SHHH...THAT'S ENOUGH. YOU NEED TO REST NOW, SWEETIE.
ULF
SO HOW DID MY GRANDPA FIND YOU ANYWAY? WHAT ARE YOU, LIKE A WITCH OR SOMETHING?
I'M NOT A WITCH. I'M A DOCTOR.
YEAH, BUT NOT A REAL DOCTOR, RIGHT? MORE LIKE DOCTOR STRANGE?
WHO IS DOCTOR STRANGE?
...NEVER MIND.

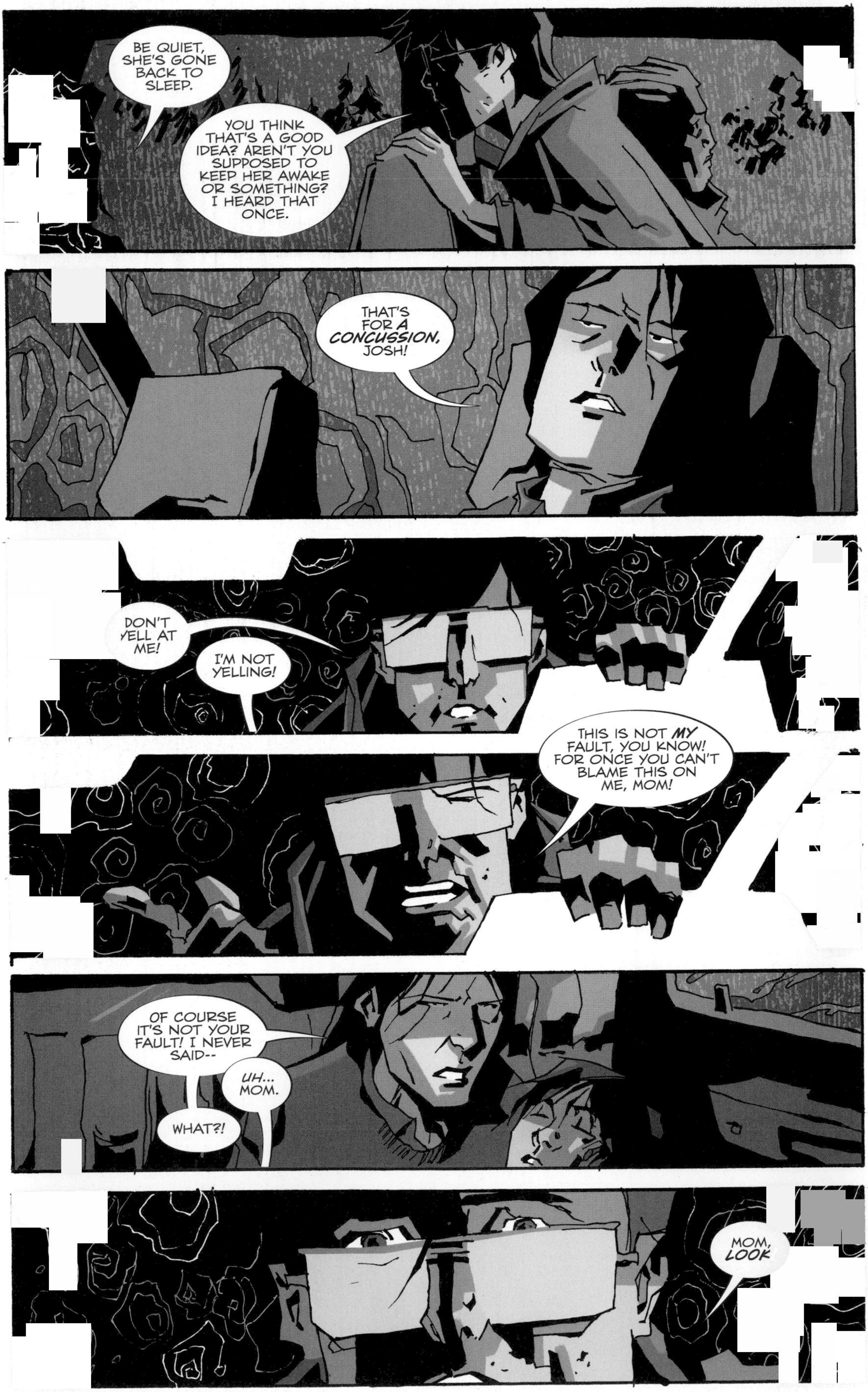
BE QUIET, SHE'S GONE BACK TO SLEEP.
YOU THINK THAT'S A GOOD IDEA? AREN'T YOU SUPPOSED TO KEEP HER AWAKE OR SOMETHING? I HEARD THAT ONCE.
THAT'S FOR A CONCUSSION, JOSH!
DON'T YELL AT ME!
I'M NOT YELLING!
THIS IS NOT MY FAULT, YOU KNOW! FOR ONCE YOU CAN'T BLAME THIS ON ME, MOM!
OF COURSE IT'S NOT YOUR FAULT! I NEVER SAID--
UH... MOM.
WHAT?!
MOM, LOOK

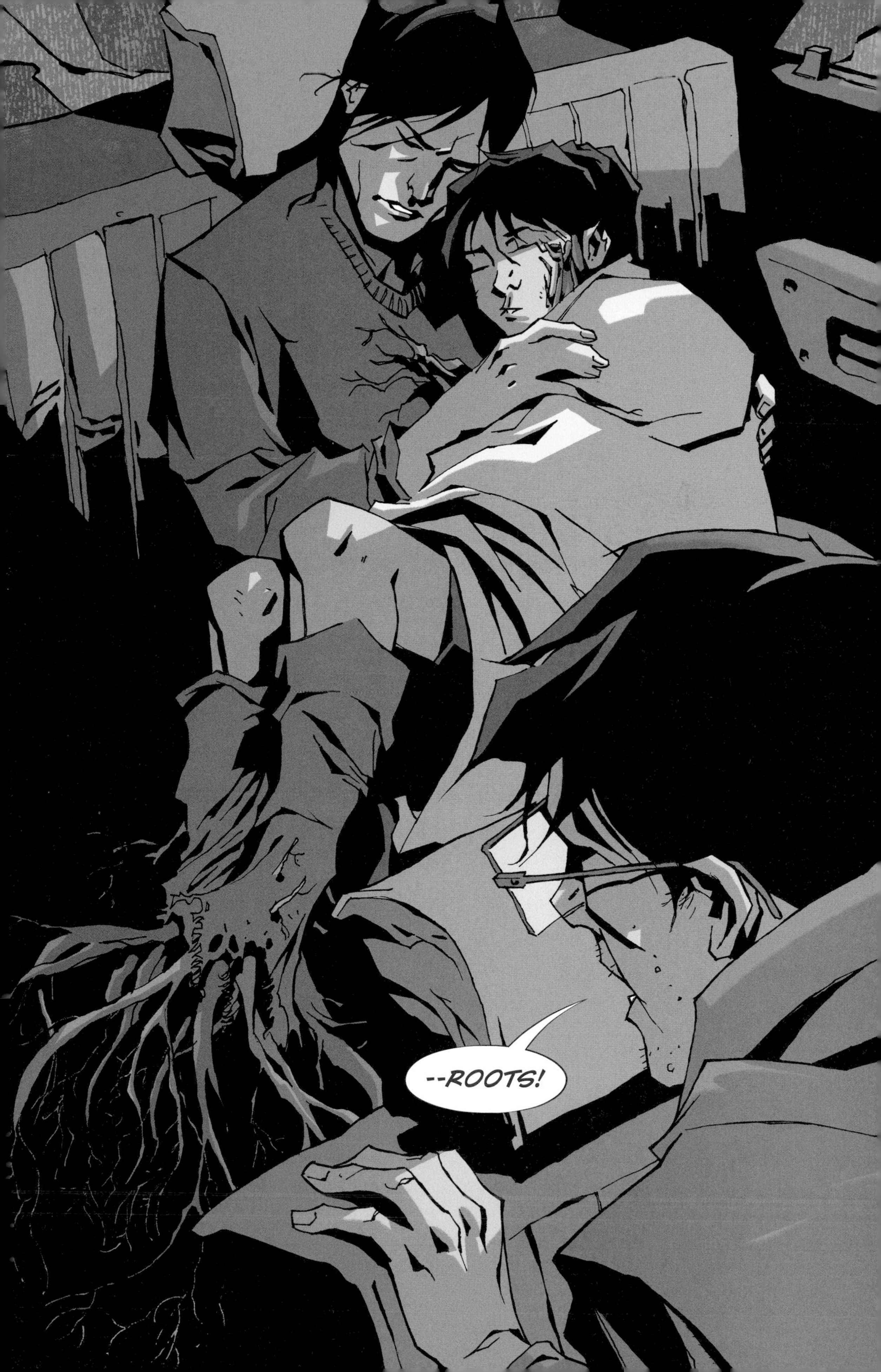
--ROOTS!

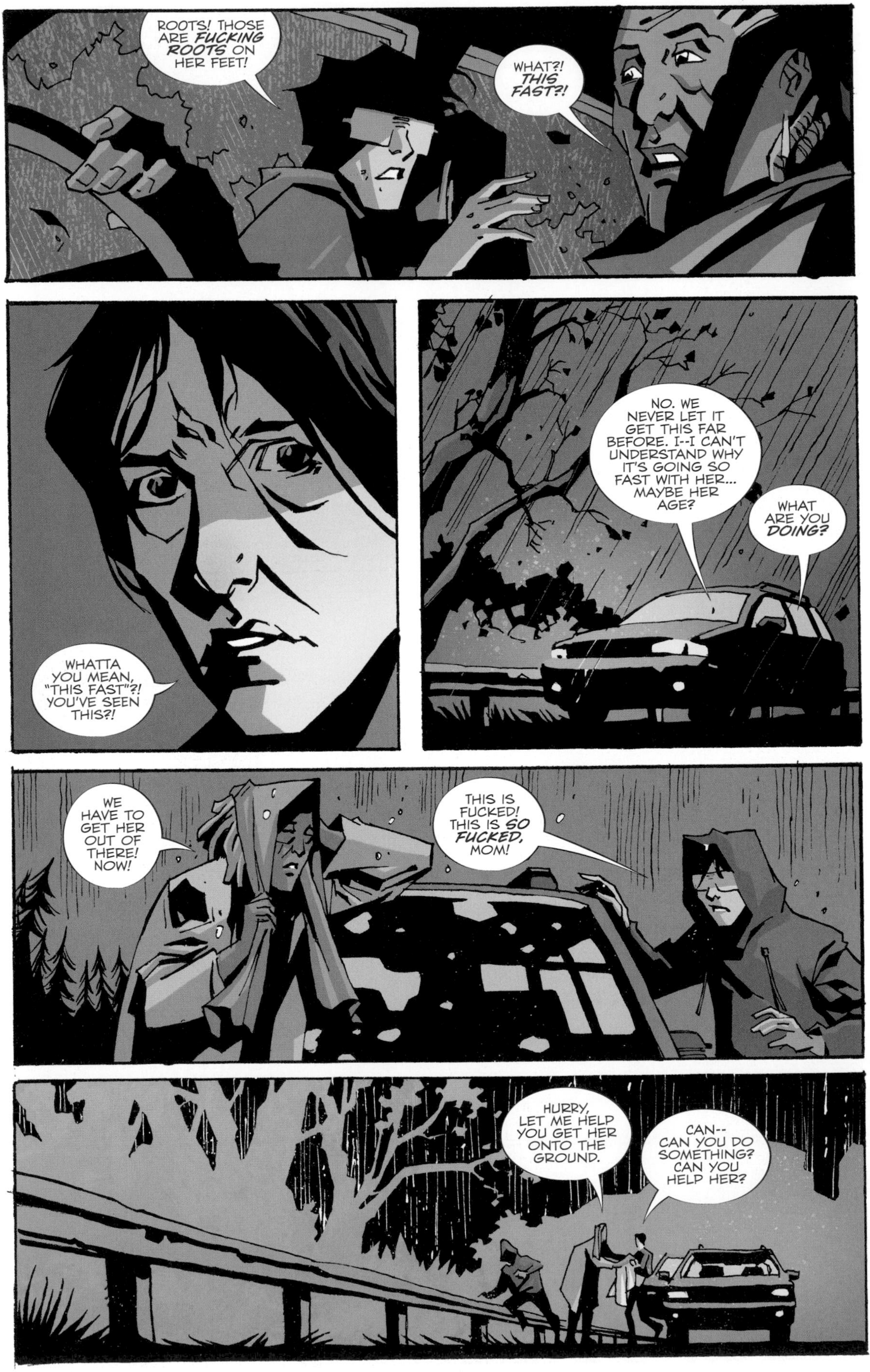
ROOTS! THOSE ARE *FUCKING ROOTS* ON HER FEET!
WHAT?! *THIS FAST?!*
WHATTA YOU MEAN, "THIS FAST"?! YOU'VE SEEN THIS?!
NO. WE NEVER LET IT GET THIS FAR BEFORE. I--I CAN'T UNDERSTAND WHY IT'S GOING SO FAST WITH HER... MAYBE HER AGE?
WHAT ARE YOU *DOING?*
WE HAVE TO GET HER OUT OF THERE! NOW!
THIS IS FUCKED! THIS IS *SO FUCKED,* MOM!
HURRY, LET ME HELP YOU GET HER ONTO THE GROUND.
CAN-- CAN YOU DO SOMETHING? CAN YOU HELP HER?

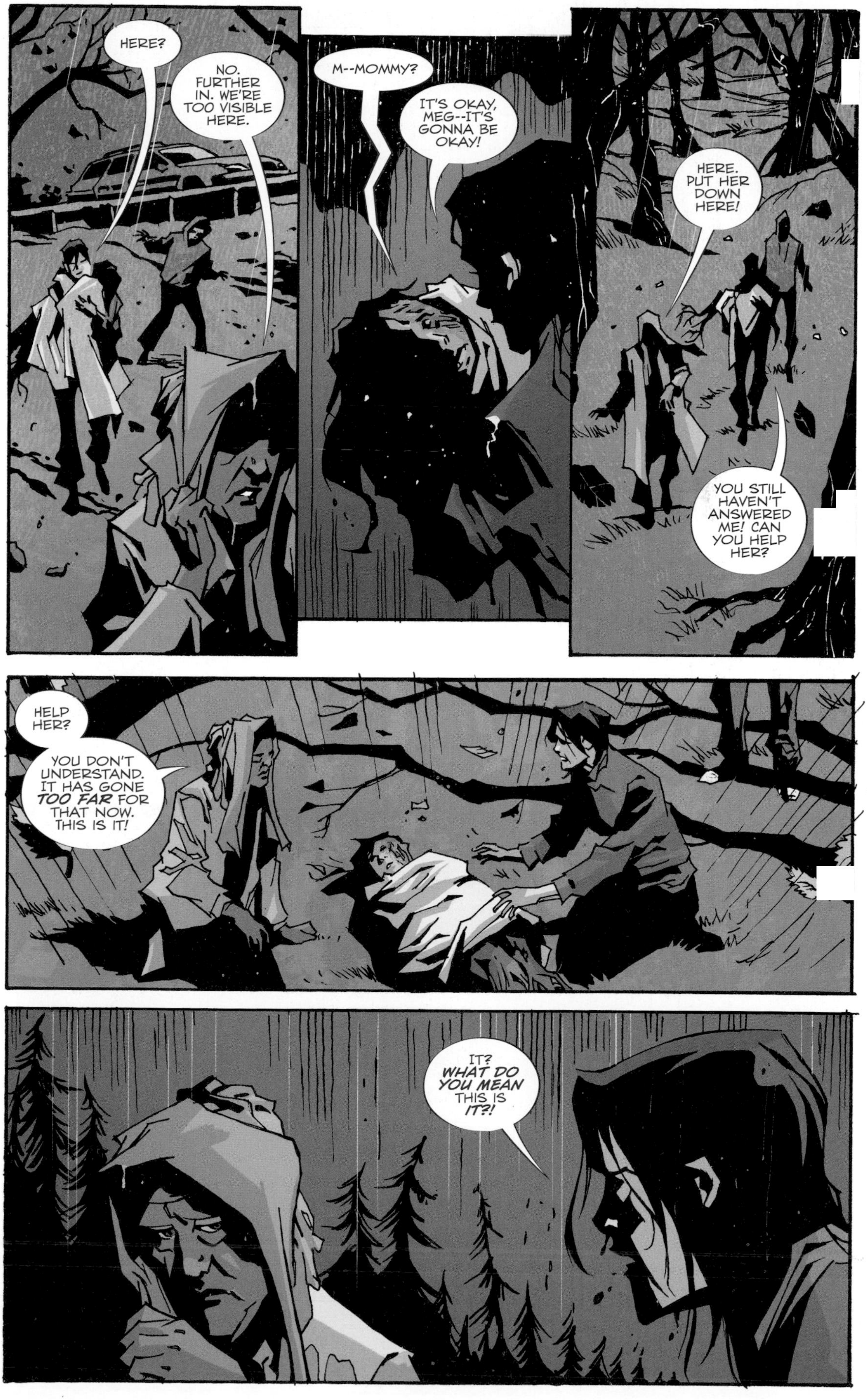
HERE?
NO. FURTHER IN. WE'RE TOO VISIBLE HERE.
M--MOMMY?
IT'S OKAY, MEG--IT'S GONNA BE OKAY!
HERE. PUT HER DOWN HERE!
YOU STILL HAVEN'T ANSWERED ME! CAN YOU HELP HER?
HELP HER?
YOU DON'T UNDERSTAND. IT HAS GONE TOO FAR FOR THAT NOW. THIS IS IT!
IT? WHAT DO YOU MEAN THIS IS IT?!

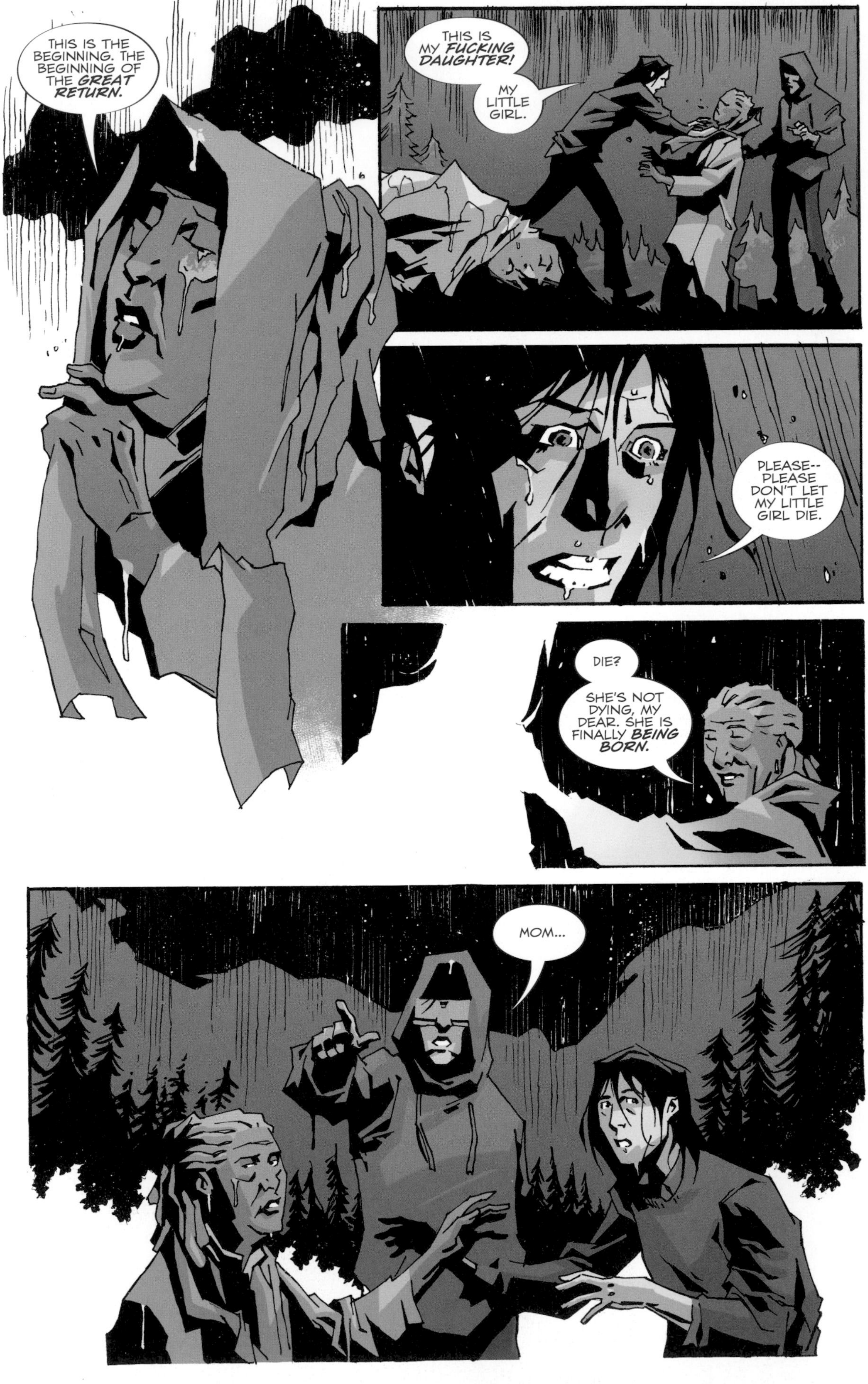
THIS IS THE BEGINNING. THE BEGINNING OF THE GREAT RETURN.
THIS IS MY FUCKING DAUGHTER!
MY LITTLE GIRL.
PLEASE-- PLEASE DON'T LET MY LITTLE GIRL DIE.
DIE?
SHE'S NOT DYING, MY DEAR. SHE IS FINALLY BEING BORN.
MOM...

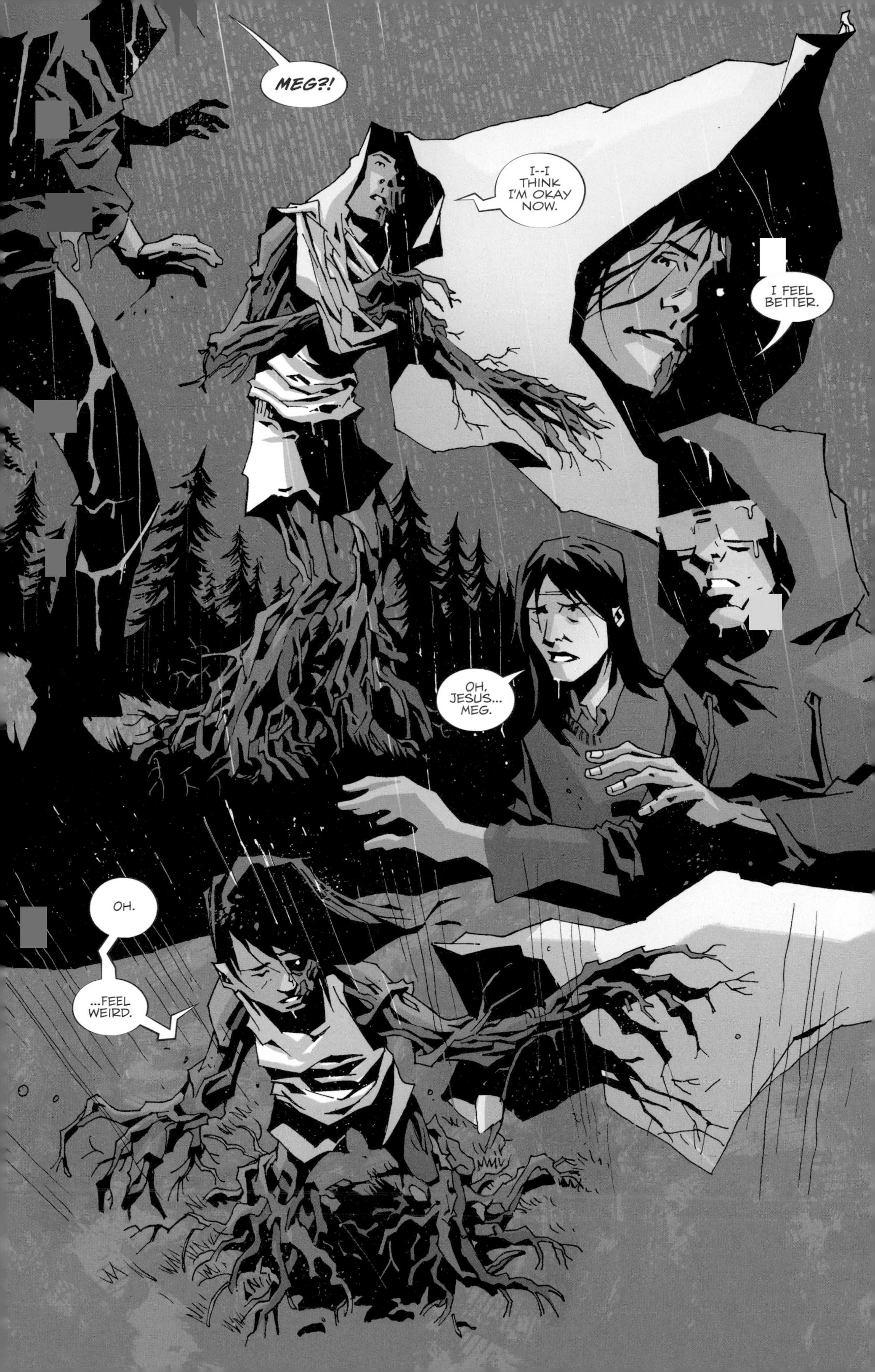
MEG?!
I--I THINK I'M OKAY NOW.
I FEEL BETTER.
OH, JESUS... MEG.
OH.
...FEEL WEIRD.

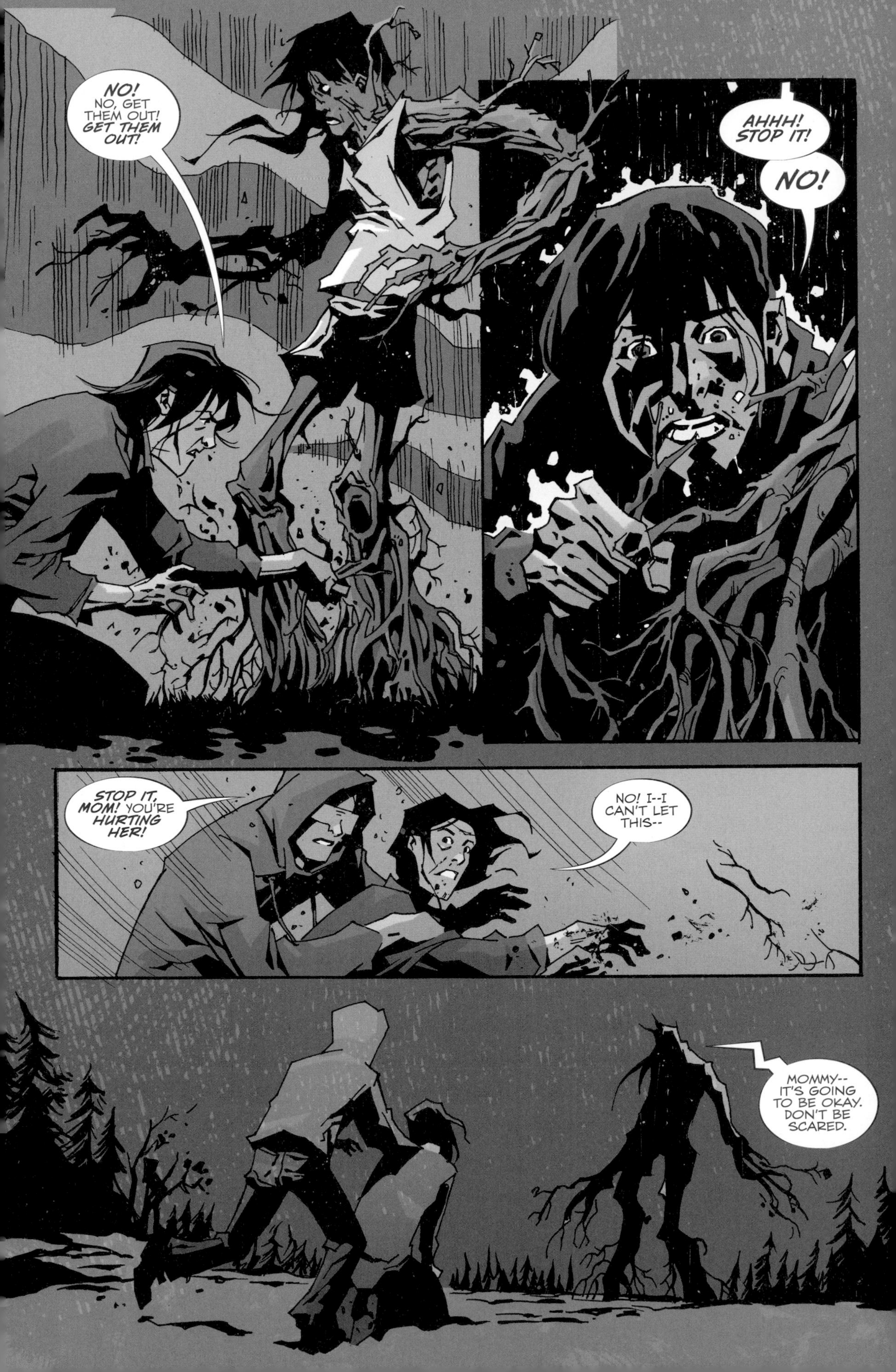
NO! NO, GET THEM OUT! GET THEM OUT!
AHHH! STOP IT!
NO!
STOP IT, MOM! YOU'RE HURTING HER!
NO! I--I CAN'T LET THIS--
MOMMY-- IT'S GOING TO BE OKAY. DON'T BE SCARED.

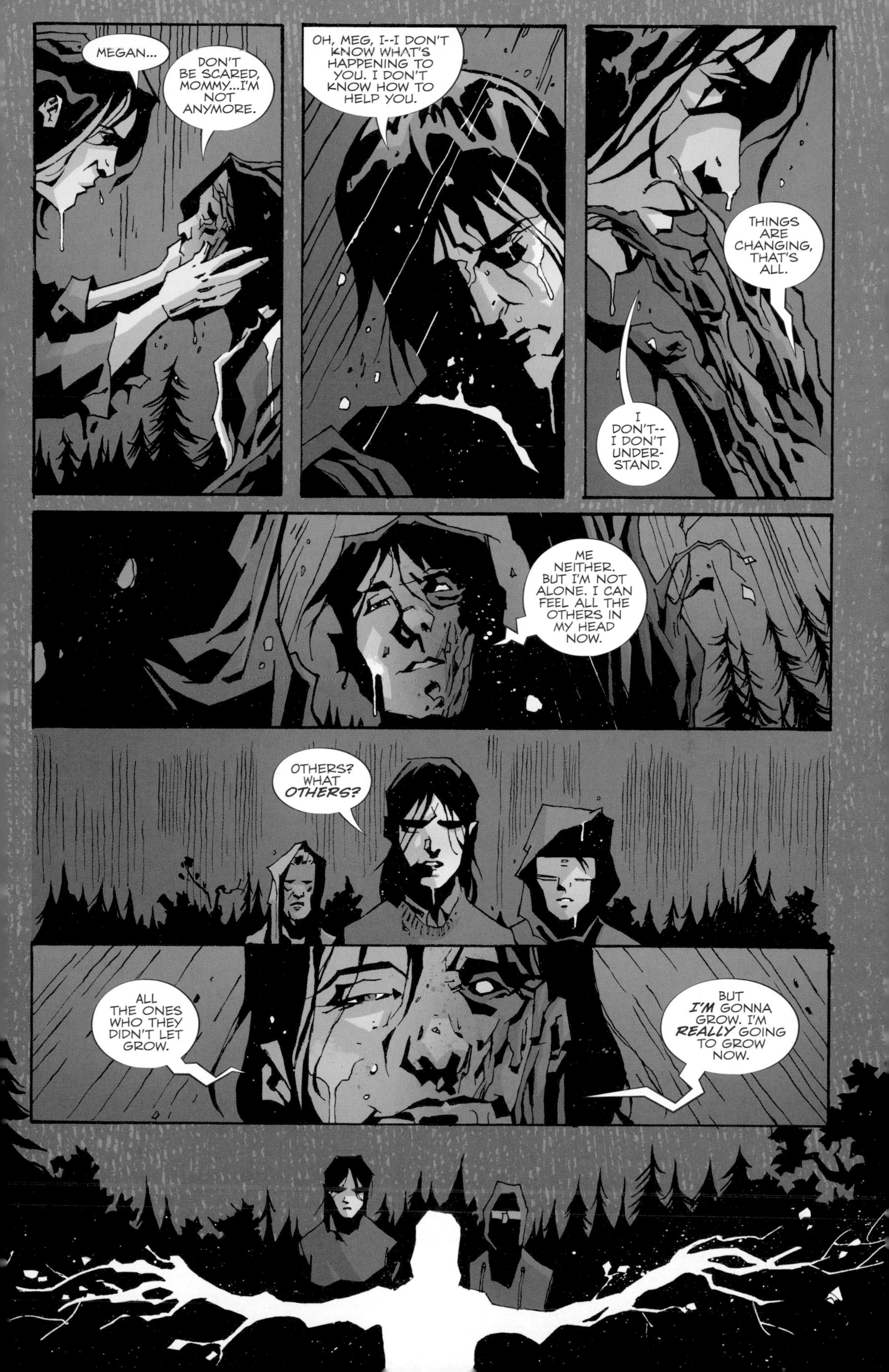
MEGAN...
DON'T BE SCARED, MOMMY...I'M NOT ANYMORE.
OH, MEG, I--I DON'T KNOW WHAT'S HAPPENING TO YOU. I DON'T KNOW HOW TO HELP YOU.
THINGS ARE CHANGING, THAT'S ALL.
I DON'T-- I DON'T UNDER-STAND.
ME NEITHER. BUT I'M NOT ALONE. I CAN FEEL ALL THE OTHERS IN MY HEAD NOW.
OTHERS? WHAT *OTHERS?*
ALL THE ONES WHO THEY DIDN'T LET GROW.
BUT *I'M* GONNA GROW. I'M *REALLY* GOING TO GROW NOW.

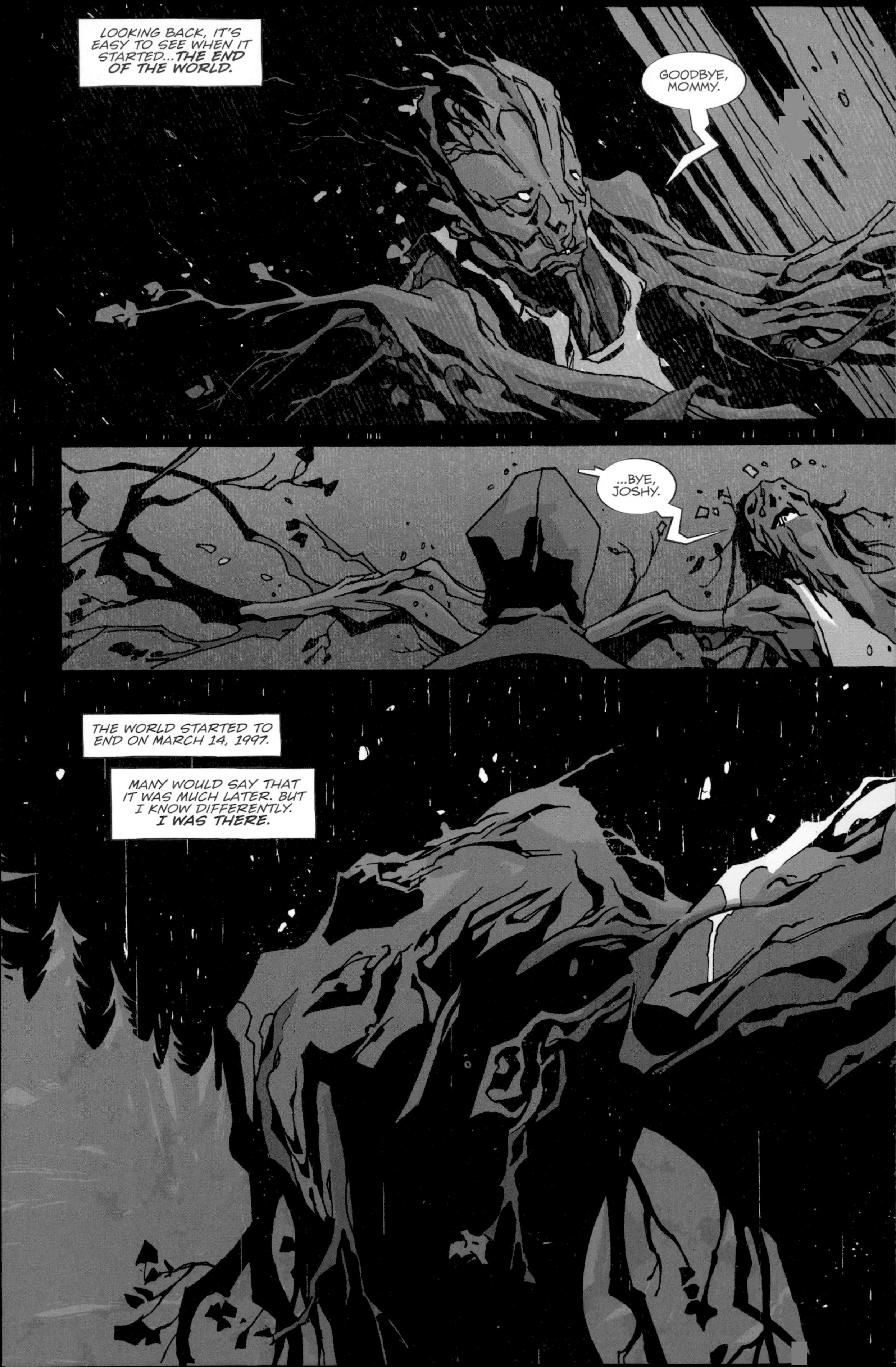
LOOKING BACK, IT'S EASY TO SEE WHEN IT STARTED...THE END OF THE WORLD.
GOODBYE, MOMMY.
...BYE, JOSHY.
THE WORLD STARTED TO END ON MARCH 14, 1997.
MANY WOULD SAY THAT IT WAS MUCH LATER. BUT I KNOW DIFFERENTLY. I WAS THERE.

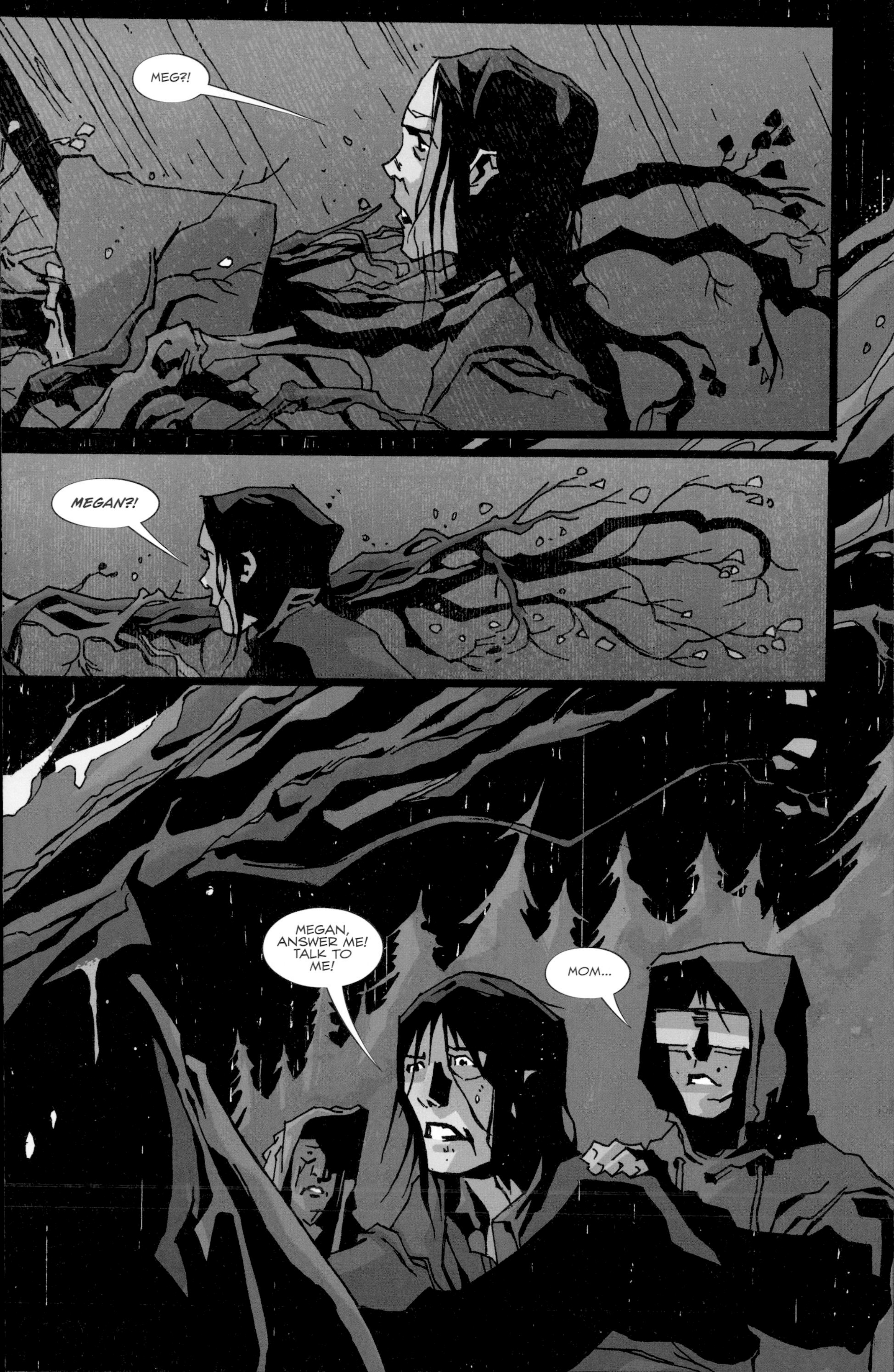
MEG?!
MEGAN?!
MEGAN, ANSWER ME! TALK TO ME!
MOM...

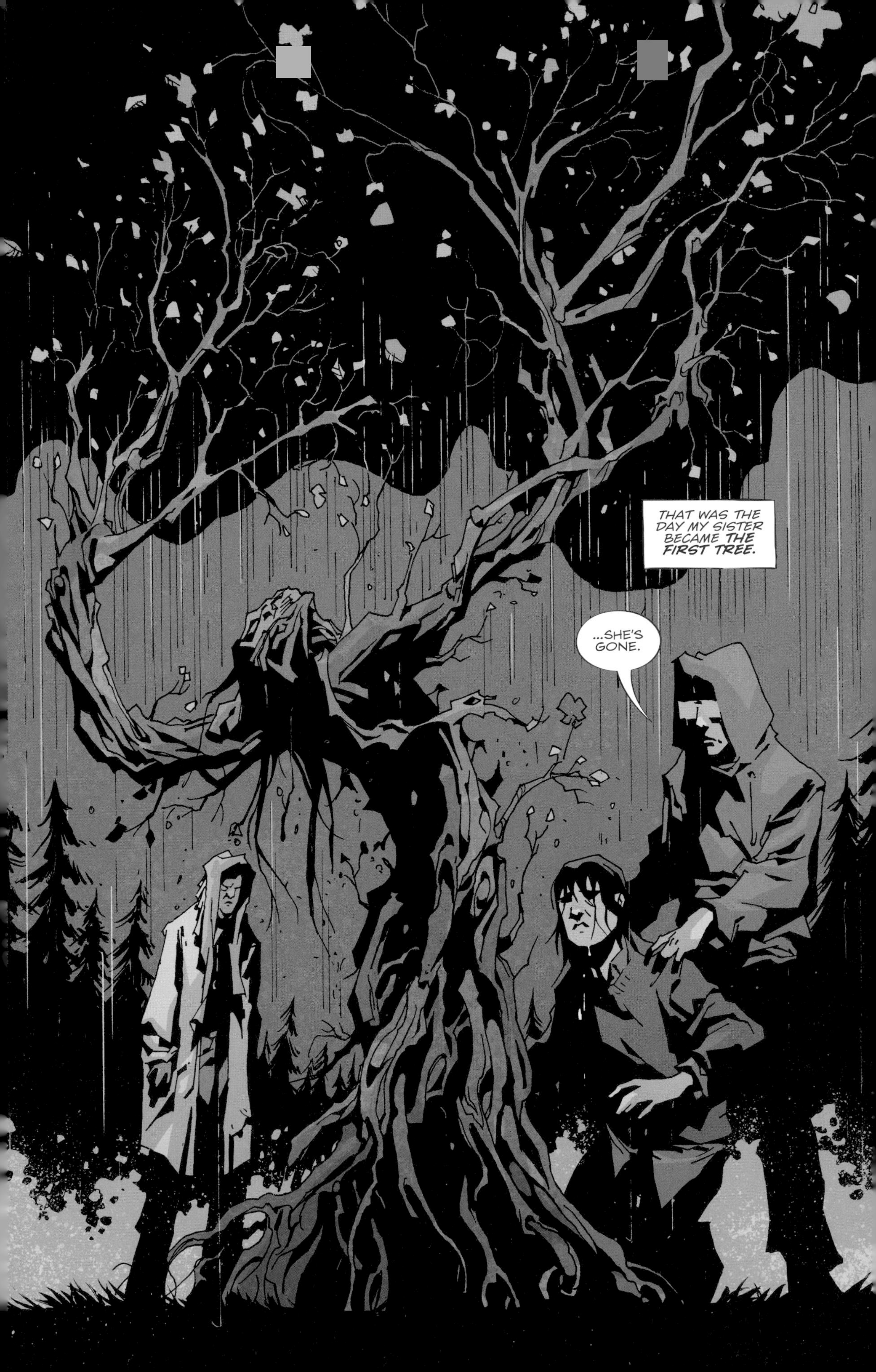
THAT WAS THE DAY MY SISTER BECAME THE FIRST TREE.
...SHE'S GONE.

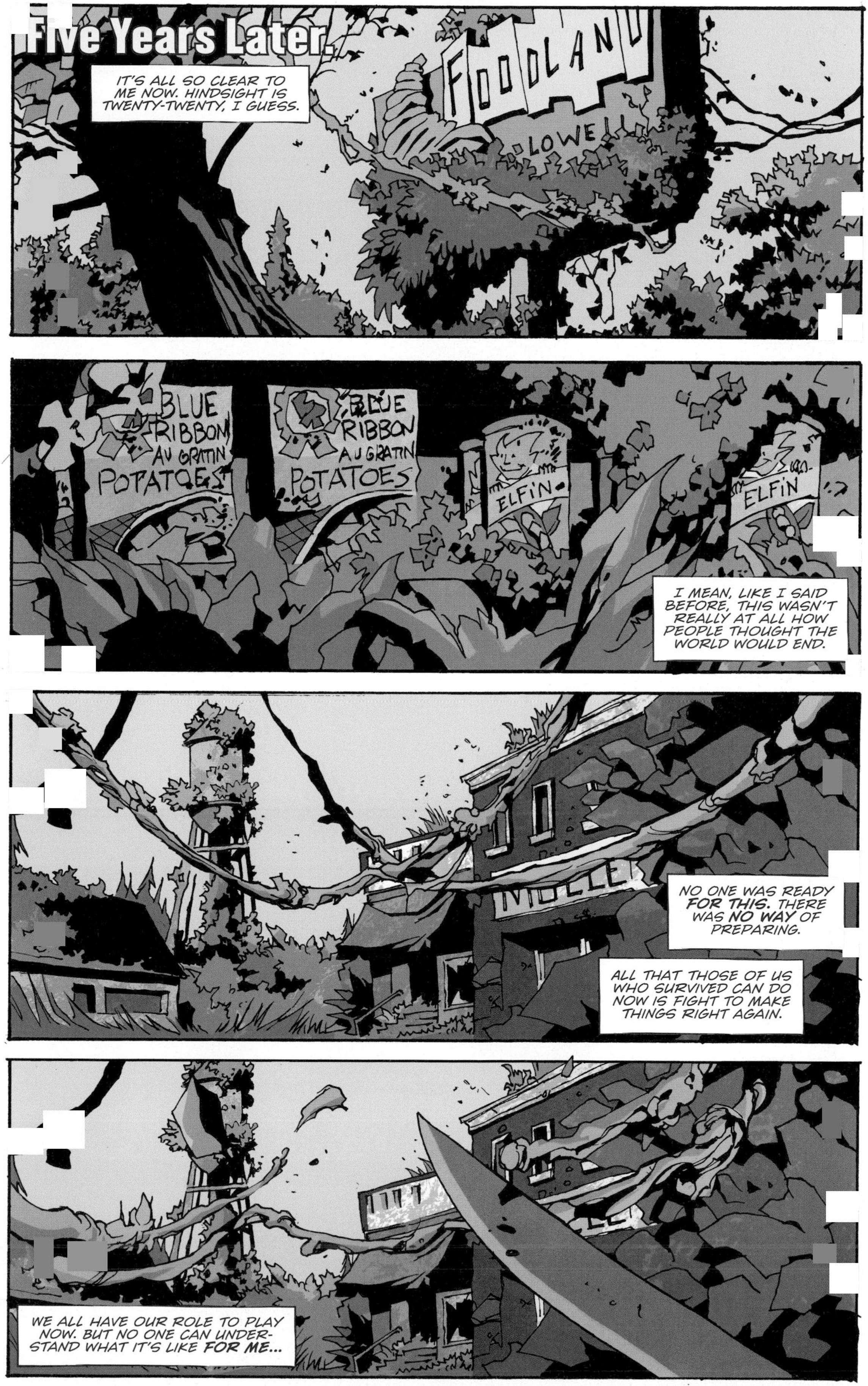

Five Years Later.
IT'S ALL SO CLEAR TO ME NOW. HINDSIGHT IS TWENTY-TWENTY, I GUESS.
FOODLAND
LOWE
BLUE RIBBON AU GRATIN POTATOES
BLUE RIBBON AU GRATIN POTATOES
ELFIN
ELFIN
I MEAN, LIKE I SAID BEFORE, THIS WASN'T REALLY AT ALL HOW PEOPLE THOUGHT THE WORLD WOULD END.
NO ONE WAS READY **FOR THIS.** THERE WAS **NO WAY** OF PREPARING.
ALL THAT THOSE OF US WHO SURVIVED CAN DO NOW IS FIGHT TO MAKE THINGS RIGHT AGAIN.
WE ALL HAVE OUR ROLE TO PLAY NOW. BUT NO ONE CAN UNDERSTAND WHAT IT'S LIKE **FOR ME...**

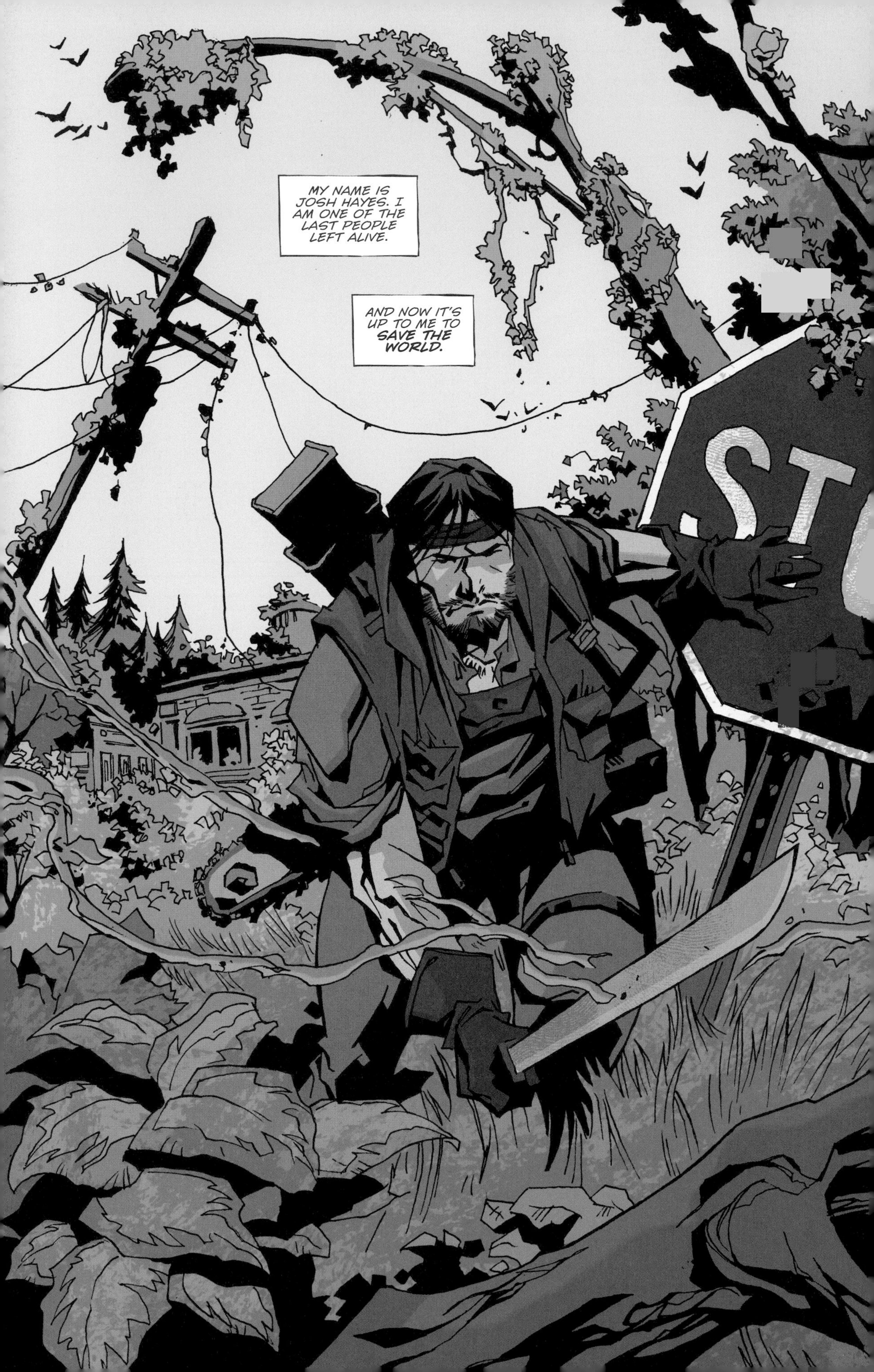
MY NAME IS JOSH HAYES. I AM ONE OF THE LAST PEOPLE LEFT ALIVE.
AND NOW IT'S UP TO ME TO SAVE THE WORLD.
STO

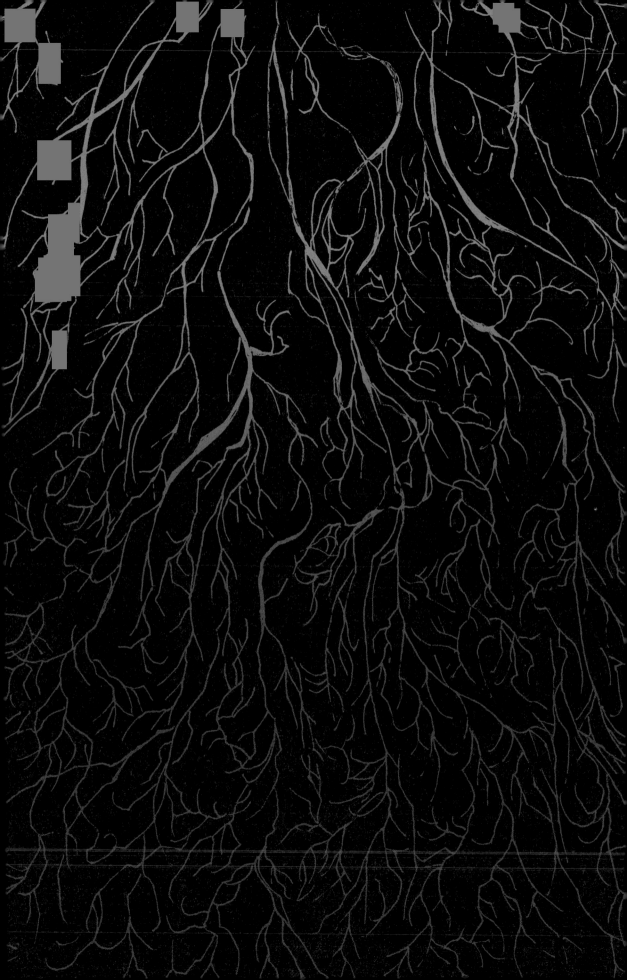

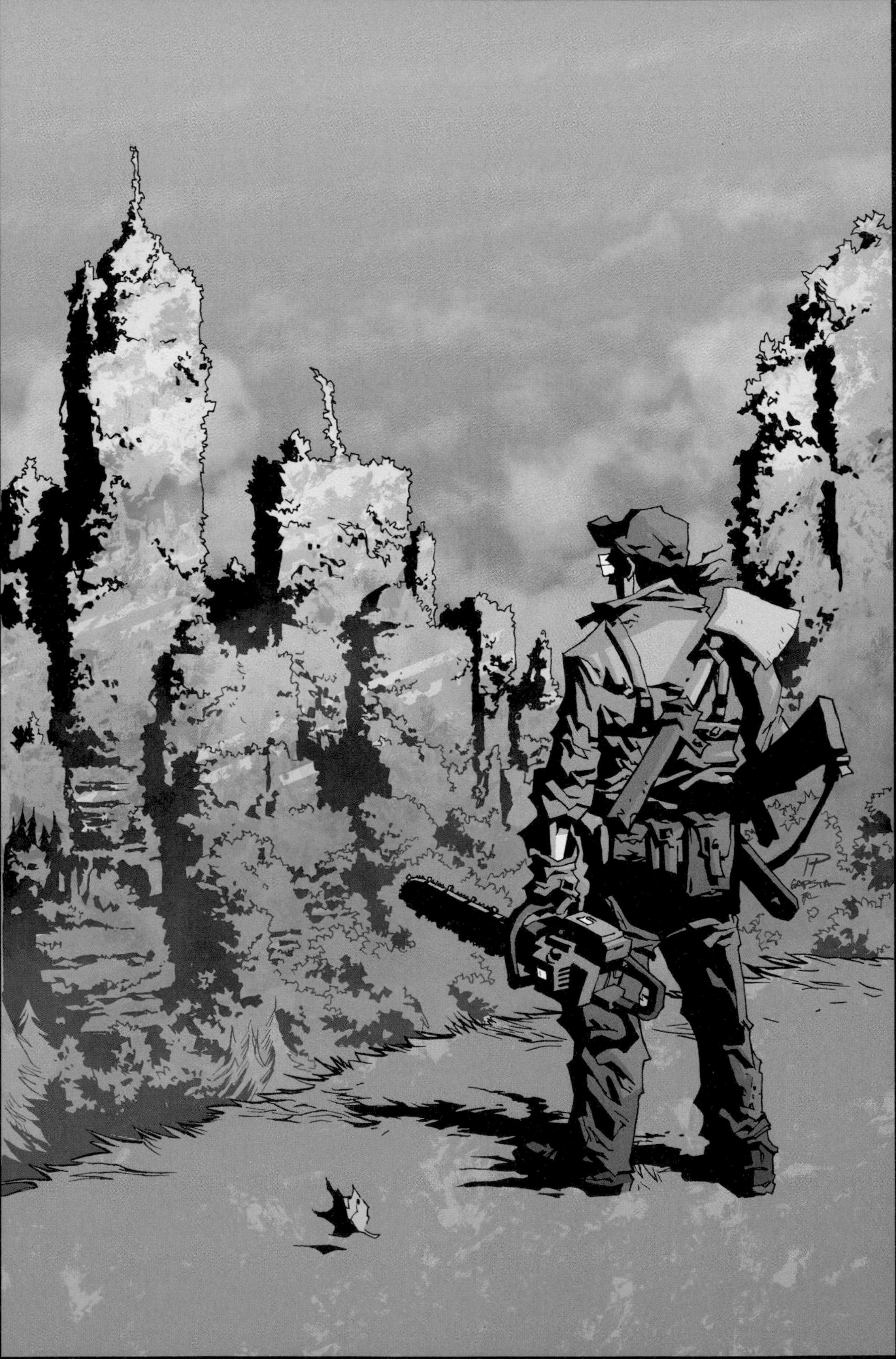

CHAPTER

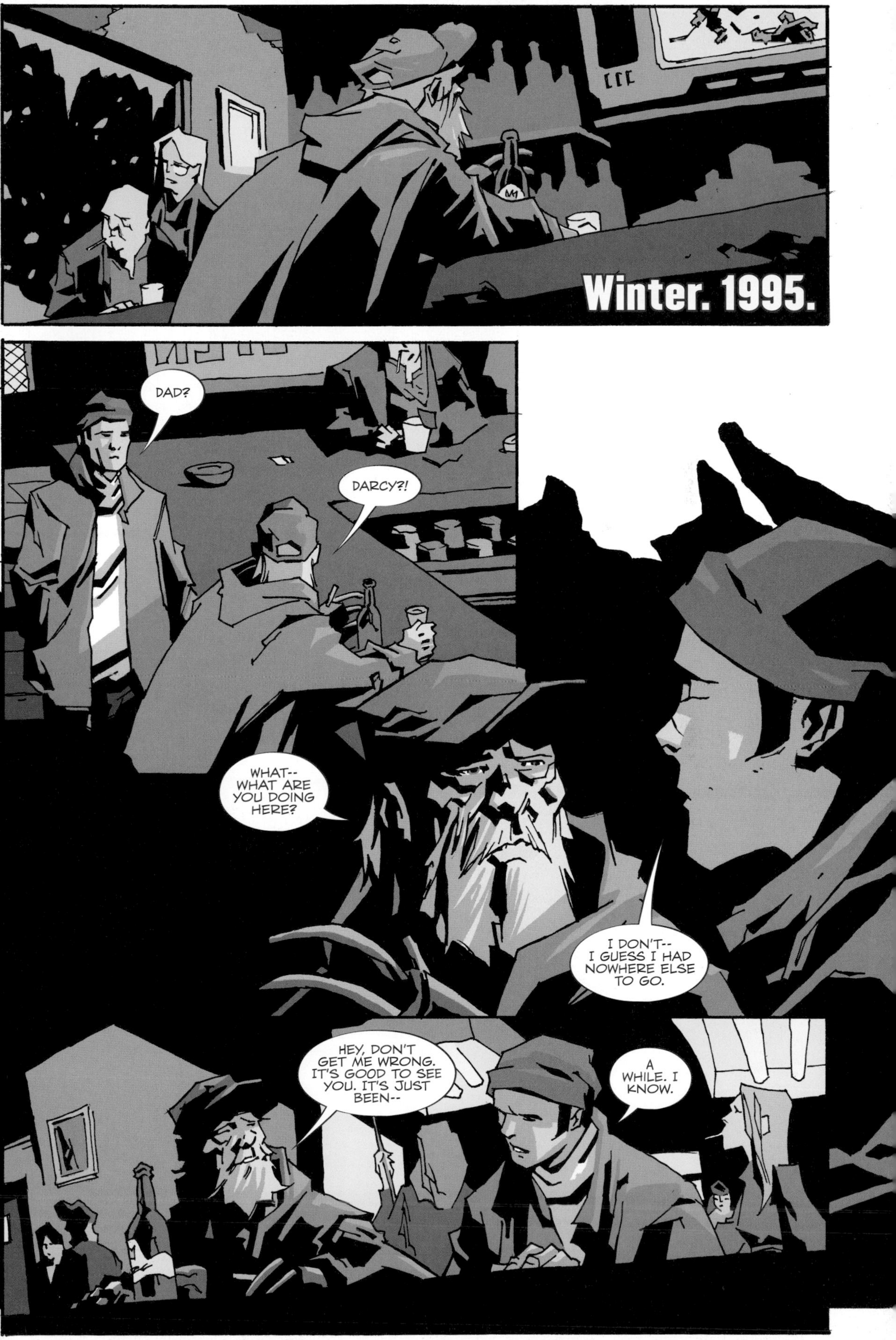
Winter. 1995.
DAD?
DARCY?!
WHAT-- WHAT ARE YOU DOING HERE?
I DON'T-- I GUESS I HAD NOWHERE ELSE TO GO.
HEY, DON'T GET ME WRONG. IT'S GOOD TO SEE YOU. IT'S JUST BEEN--
A WHILE. I KNOW.

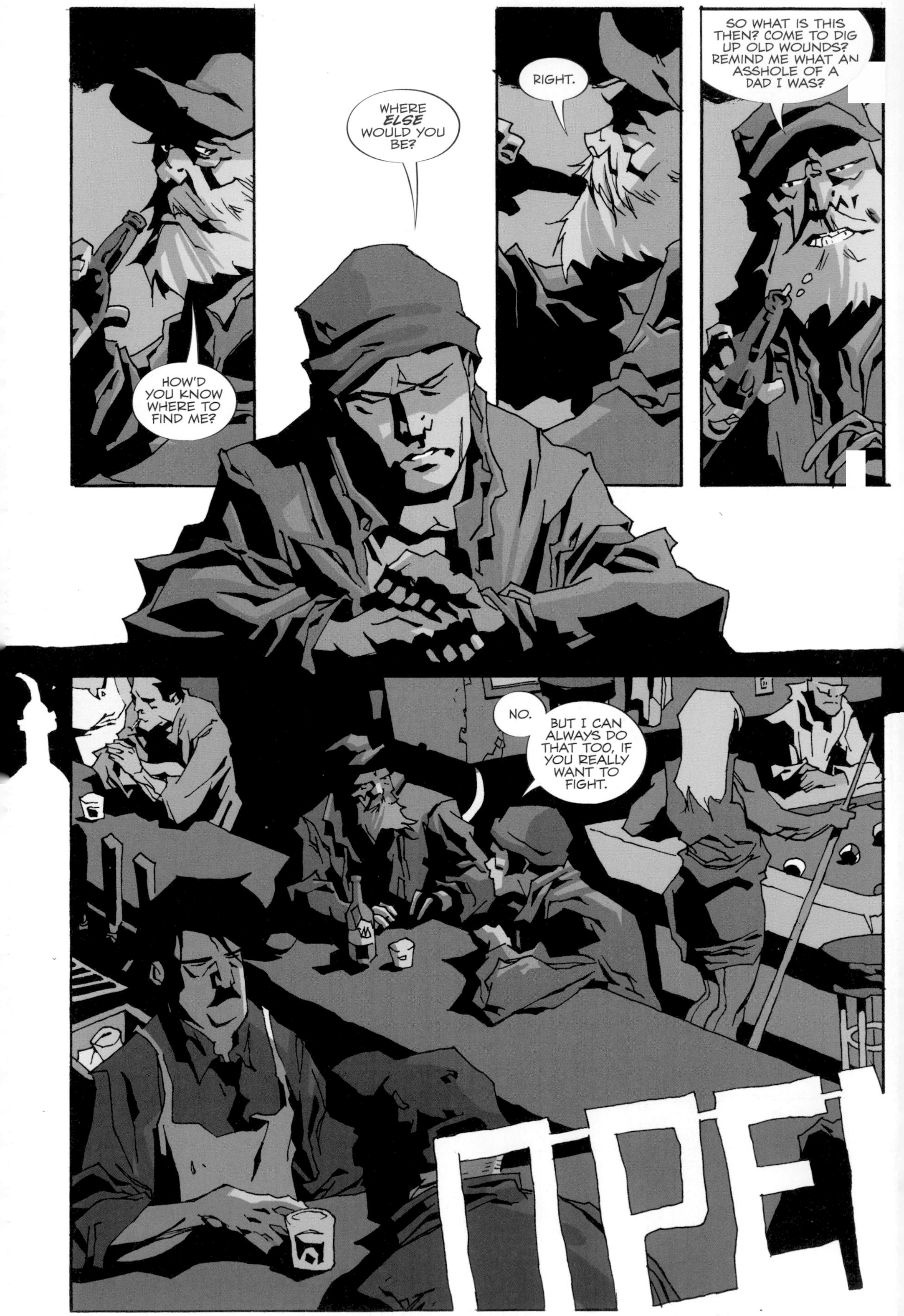

HOW'D YOU KNOW WHERE TO FIND ME?
WHERE *ELSE* WOULD YOU BE?
RIGHT.
SO WHAT IS THIS THEN? COME TO DIG UP OLD WOUNDS? REMIND ME WHAT AN ASSHOLE OF A DAD I WAS?
NO.
BUT I CAN ALWAYS DO THAT TOO, IF YOU REALLY WANT TO FIGHT.
OPE

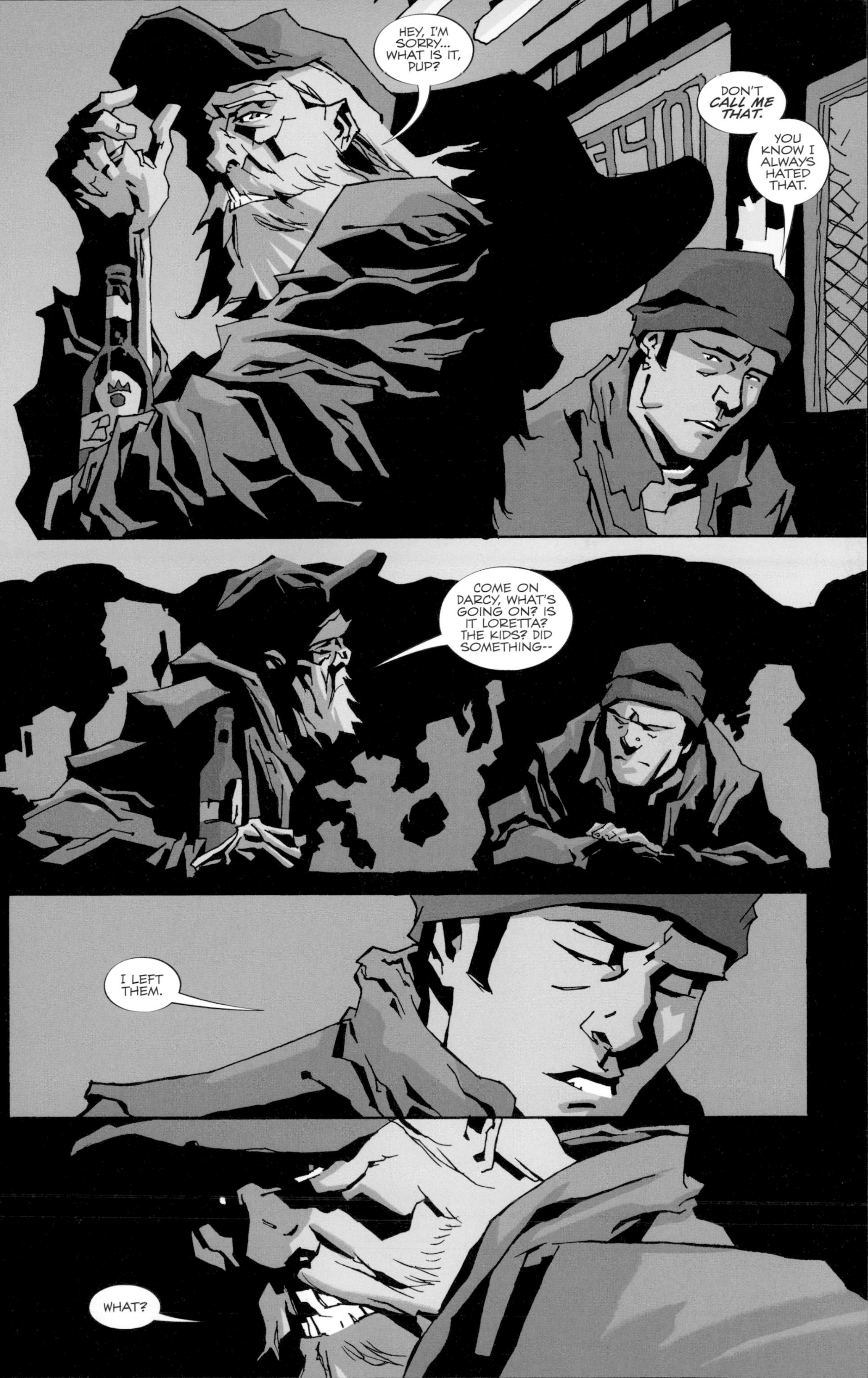
HEY, I'M SORRY... WHAT IS IT, PUP?
DON'T CALL ME THAT.
YOU KNOW I ALWAYS HATED THAT.
COME ON DARCY, WHAT'S GOING ON? IS IT LORETTA? THE KIDS? DID SOMETHING--
I LEFT THEM.
WHAT?

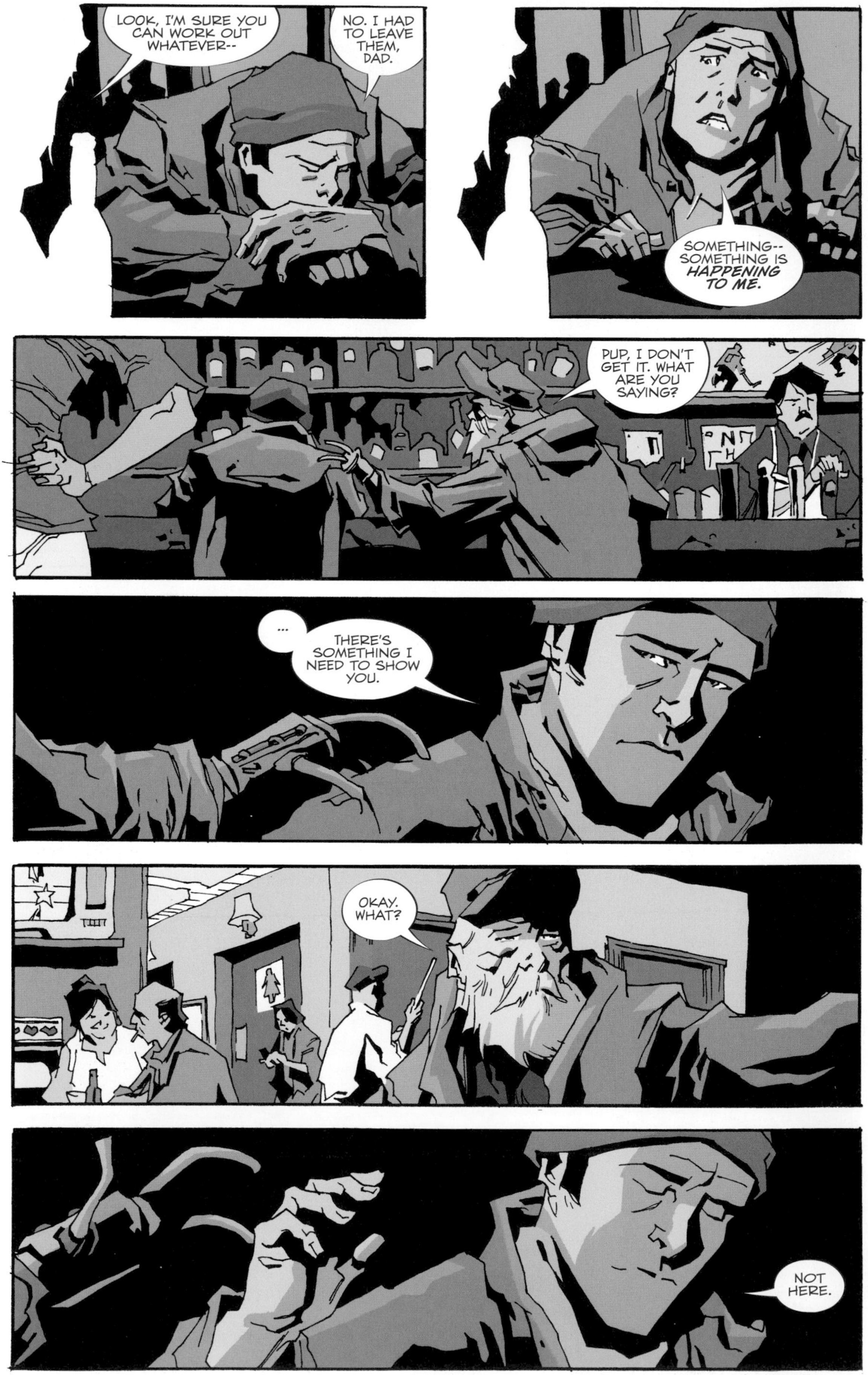
LOOK, I'M SURE YOU CAN WORK OUT WHATEVER--
NO. I HAD TO LEAVE THEM, DAD.
SOMETHING-- SOMETHING IS HAPPENING TO ME.
PUP, I DON'T GET IT. WHAT ARE YOU SAYING?
...
THERE'S SOMETHING I NEED TO SHOW YOU.
OKAY. WHAT?
NOT HERE.

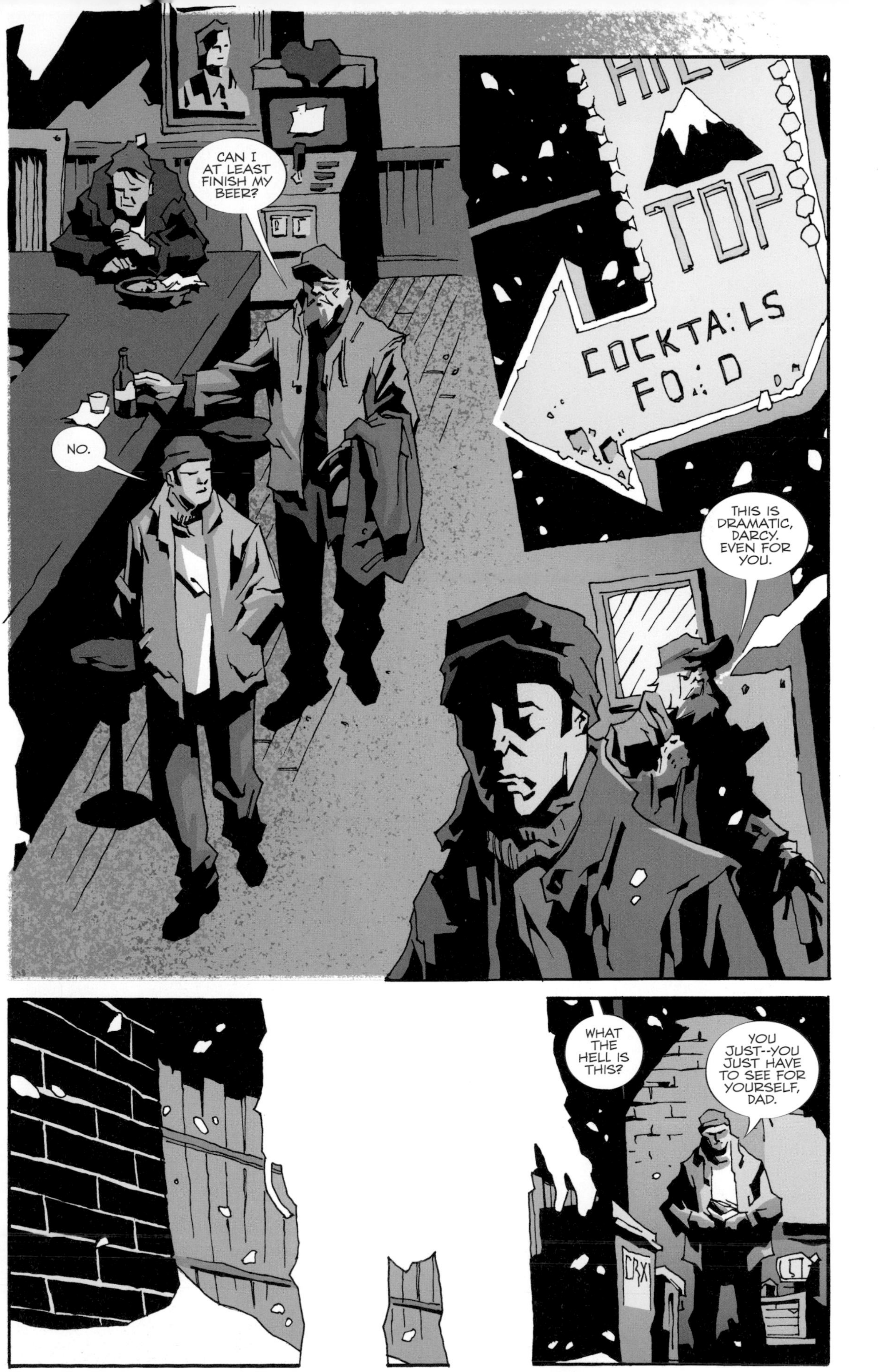
CAN I AT LEAST FINISH MY BEER?
NO.
TOP
THIS IS DRAMATIC, DARCY. EVEN FOR YOU.
WHAT THE HELL IS THIS?
YOU JUST--YOU JUST HAVE TO SEE FOR YOURSELF, DAD.

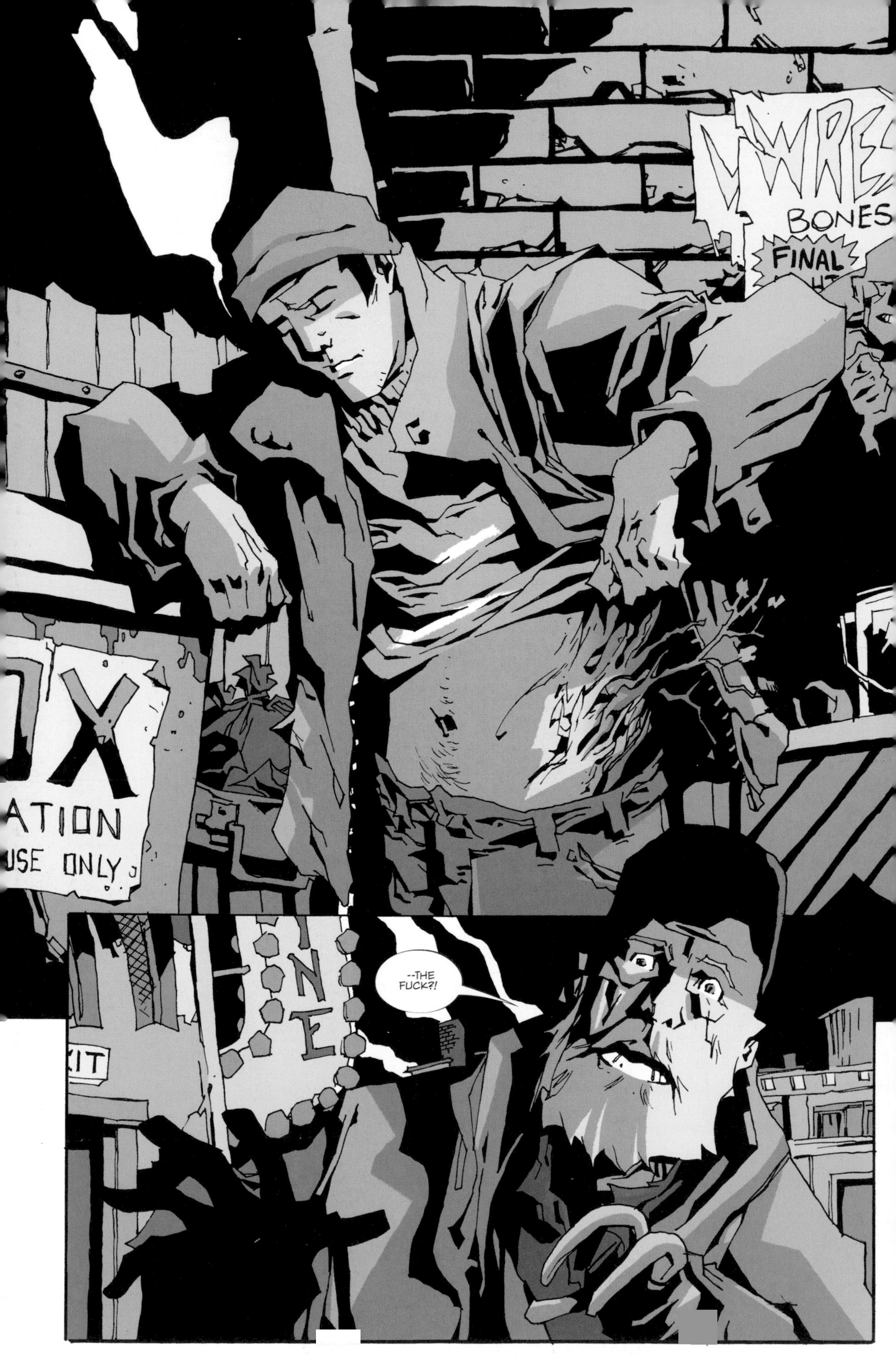
BONES
FINAL
ATION
USE ONLY
--THE FUCK?!

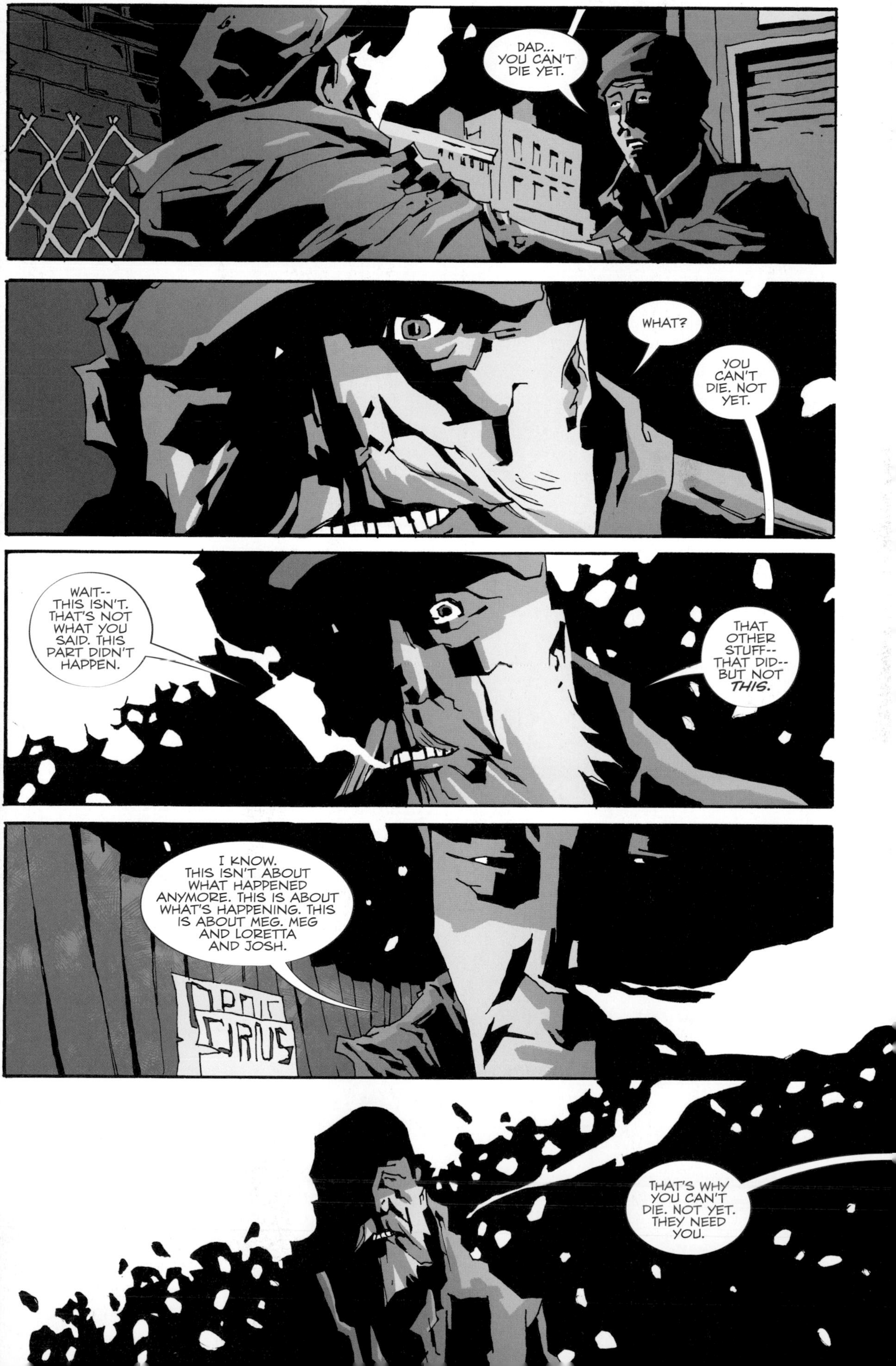
DAD... YOU CAN'T DIE YET.
WHAT?
YOU CAN'T DIE. NOT YET.
WAIT-- THIS ISN'T. THAT'S NOT WHAT YOU SAID. THIS PART DIDN'T HAPPEN.
THAT OTHER STUFF-- THAT DID-- BUT NOT *THIS.*
I KNOW. THIS ISN'T ABOUT WHAT HAPPENED ANYMORE. THIS IS ABOUT WHAT'S HAPPENING. THIS IS ABOUT MEG. MEG AND LORETTA AND JOSH.
THAT'S WHY YOU CAN'T DIE. NOT YET. THEY NEED YOU.

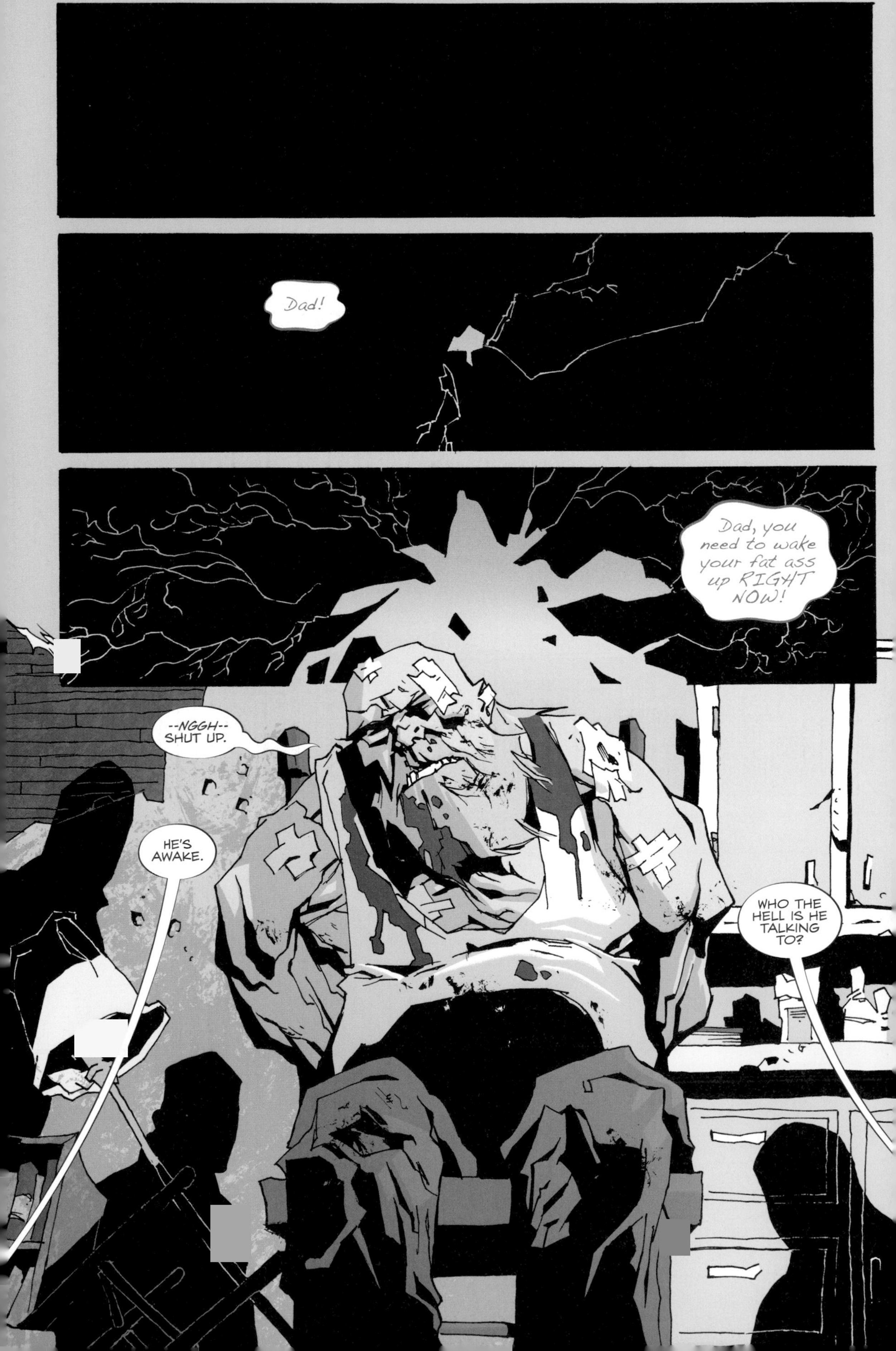

Dad!
Dad, you need to wake your fat ass up RIGHT NOW!
--NGGH-- SHUT UP.
HE'S AWAKE.
WHO THE HELL IS HE TALKING TO?

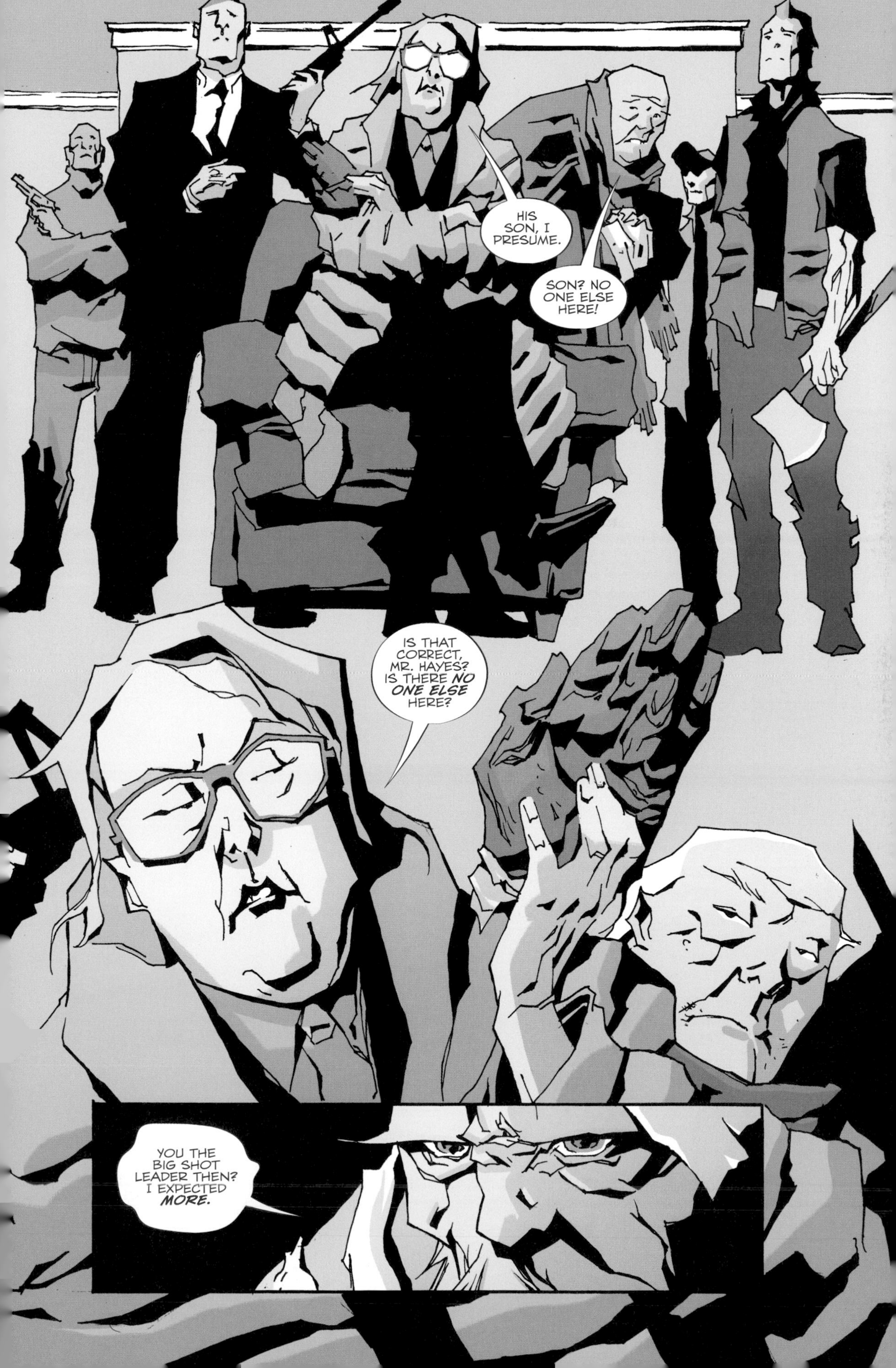
HIS SON, I PRESUME.
SON? NO ONE ELSE HERE!
IS THAT CORRECT, MR. HAYES? IS THERE *NO ONE ELSE* HERE?
YOU THE BIG SHOT LEADER THEN? I EXPECTED *MORE.*

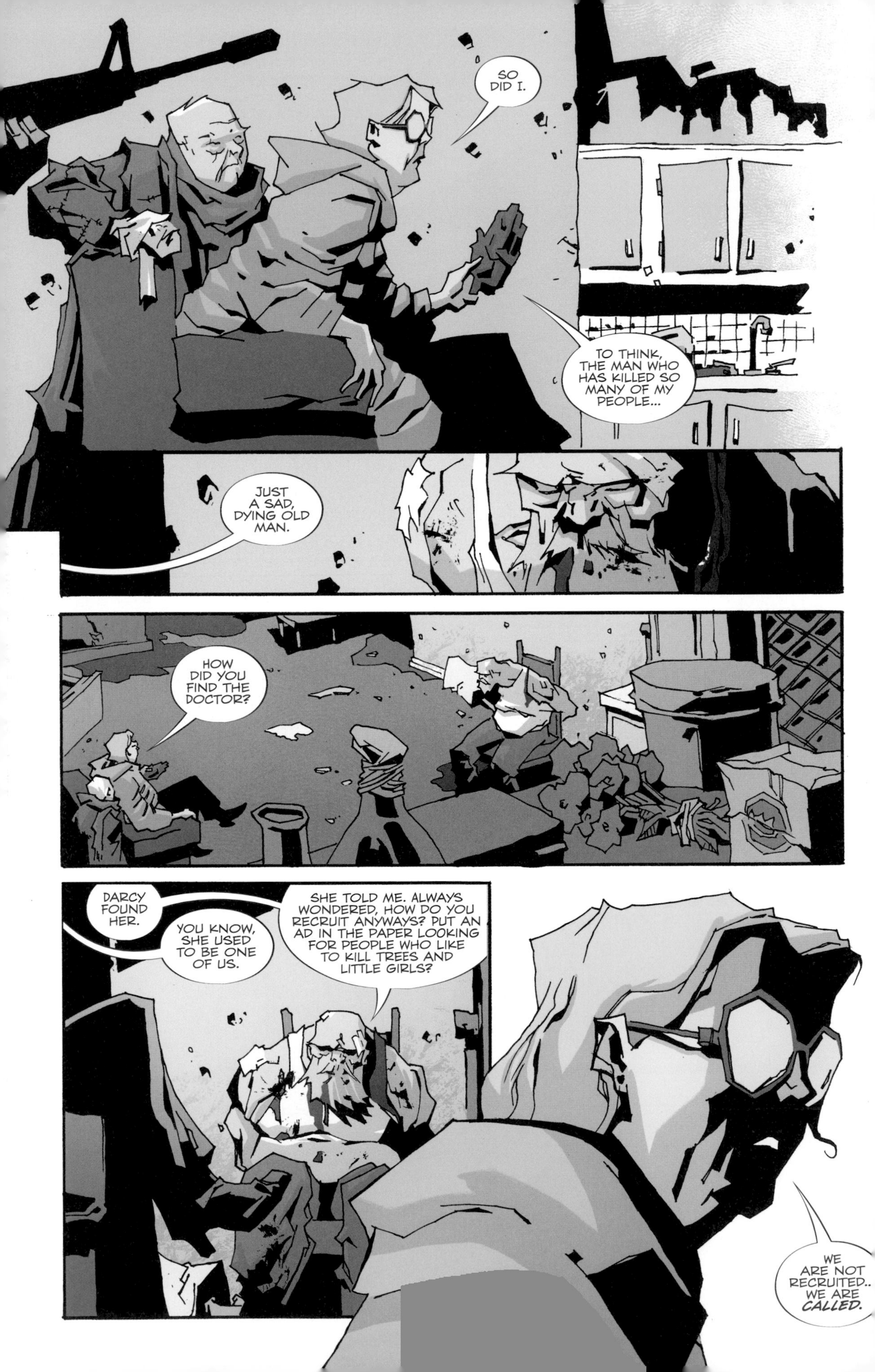
SO DID I.
TO THINK, THE MAN WHO HAS KILLED SO MANY OF MY PEOPLE...
JUST A SAD, DYING OLD MAN.
HOW DID YOU FIND THE DOCTOR?
DARCY FOUND HER.
YOU KNOW, SHE USED TO BE ONE OF US.
SHE TOLD ME. ALWAYS WONDERED, HOW DO YOU RECRUIT ANYWAYS? PUT AN AD IN THE PAPER LOOKING FOR PEOPLE WHO LIKE TO KILL TREES AND LITTLE GIRLS?
WE ARE NOT RECRUITED.. WE ARE *CALLED*.

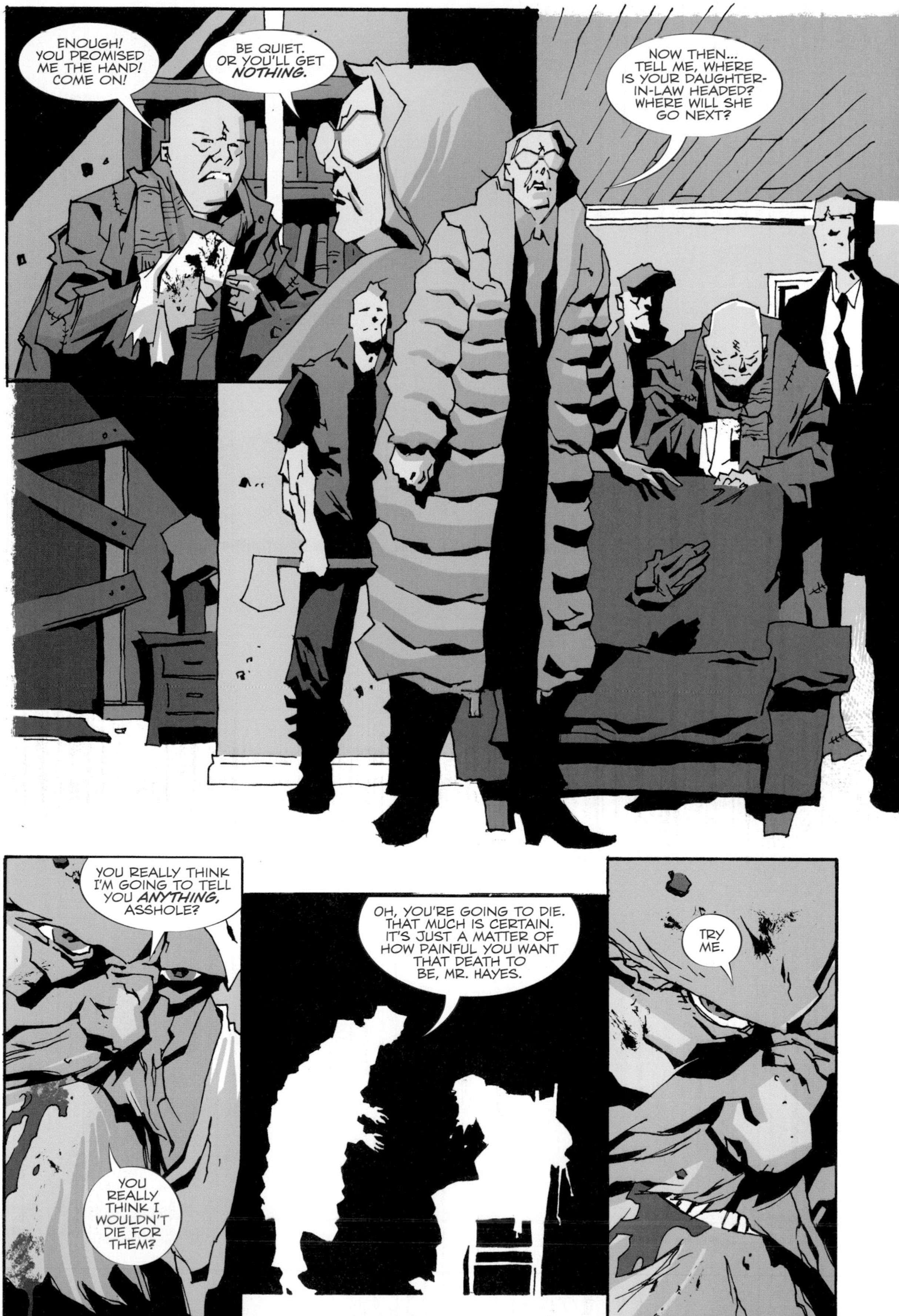
ENOUGH! YOU PROMISED ME THE HAND! COME ON!
BE QUIET. OR YOU'LL GET *NOTHING.*
NOW THEN... TELL ME, WHERE IS YOUR DAUGHTER-IN-LAW HEADED? WHERE WILL SHE GO NEXT?
YOU REALLY THINK I'M GOING TO TELL YOU *ANYTHING,* ASSHOLE?
YOU REALLY THINK I WOULDN'T DIE FOR THEM?
OH, YOU'RE GOING TO DIE. THAT MUCH IS CERTAIN. IT'S JUST A MATTER OF HOW PAINFUL YOU WANT THAT DEATH TO BE, MR. HAYES.
TRY ME.

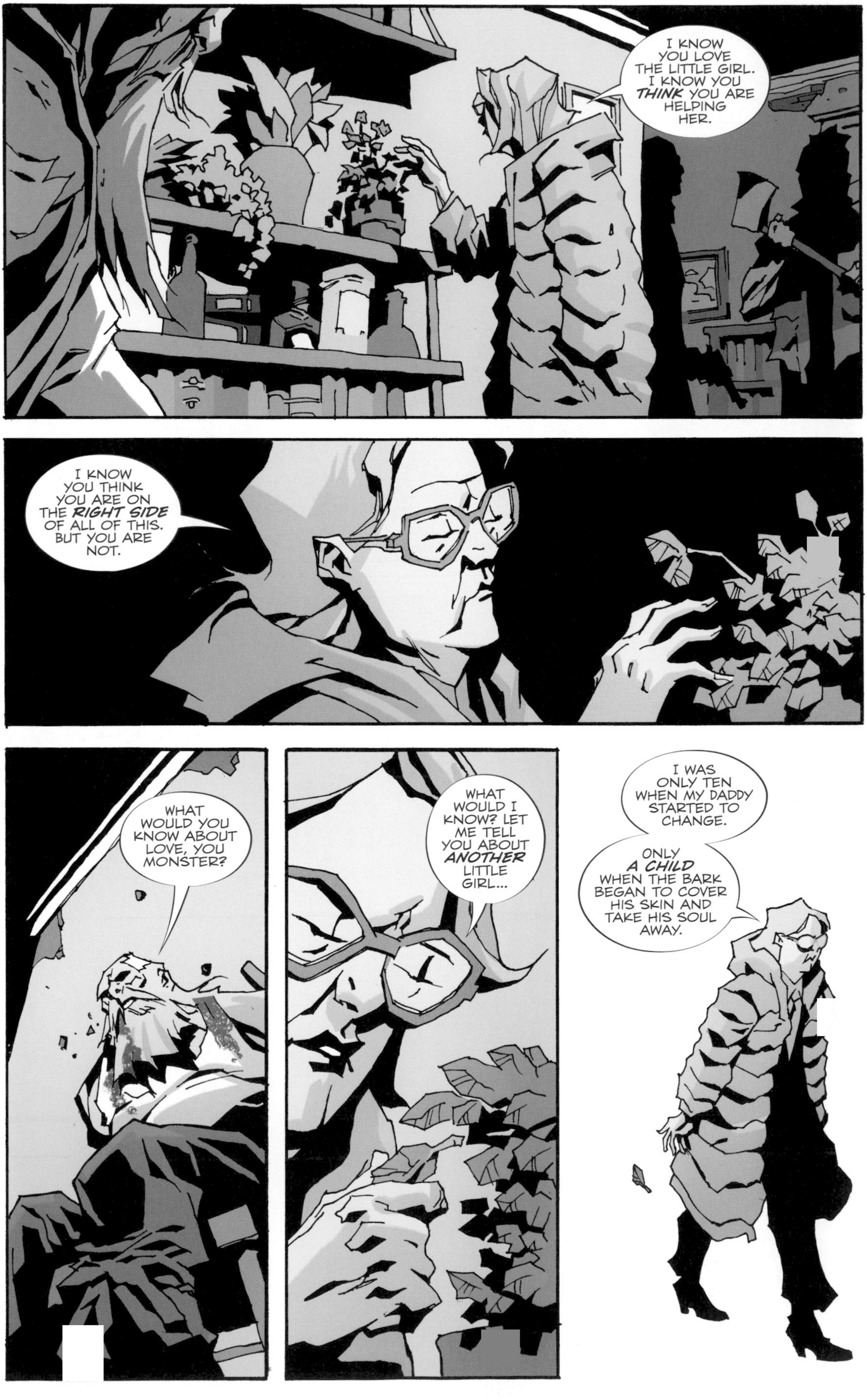
I KNOW YOU LOVE THE LITTLE GIRL. I KNOW YOU *THINK* YOU ARE HELPING HER.
I KNOW YOU THINK YOU ARE ON THE *RIGHT SIDE* OF ALL OF THIS. BUT YOU ARE NOT.
WHAT WOULD YOU KNOW ABOUT LOVE, YOU MONSTER?
WHAT WOULD I KNOW? LET ME TELL YOU ABOUT *ANOTHER* LITTLE GIRL...
I WAS ONLY TEN WHEN MY DADDY STARTED TO CHANGE.
ONLY *A CHILD* WHEN THE BARK BEGAN TO COVER HIS SKIN AND TAKE HIS SOUL AWAY.

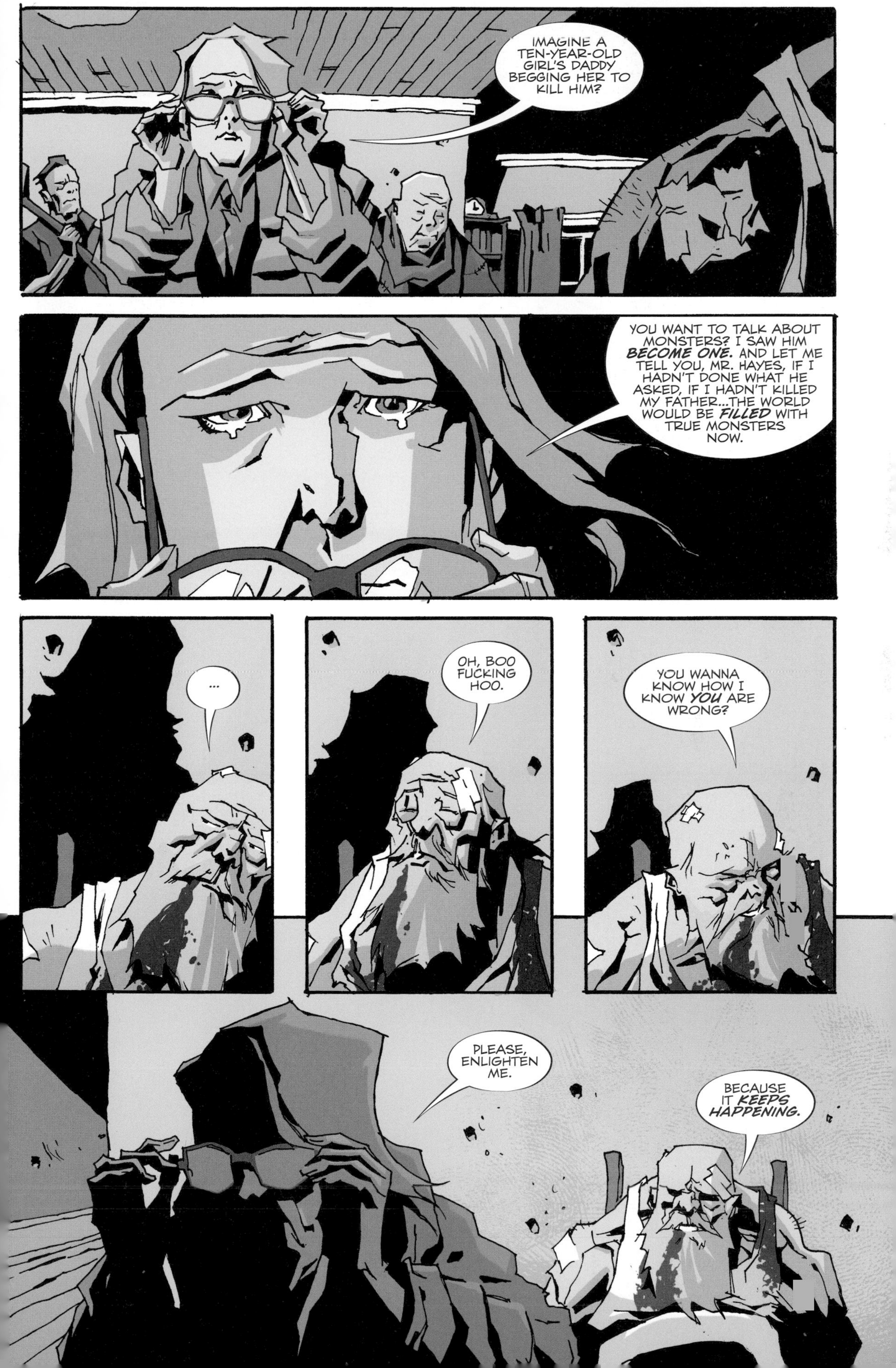
IMAGINE A TEN-YEAR-OLD GIRL'S DADDY BEGGING HER TO KILL HIM?
YOU WANT TO TALK ABOUT MONSTERS? I SAW HIM BECOME ONE. AND LET ME TELL YOU, MR. HAYES, IF I HADN'T DONE WHAT HE ASKED, IF I HADN'T KILLED MY FATHER...THE WORLD WOULD BE FILLED WITH TRUE MONSTERS NOW.
...
OH, BOO FUCKING HOO.
YOU WANNA KNOW HOW I KNOW YOU ARE WRONG?
PLEASE, ENLIGHTEN ME.
BECAUSE IT KEEPS HAPPENING.

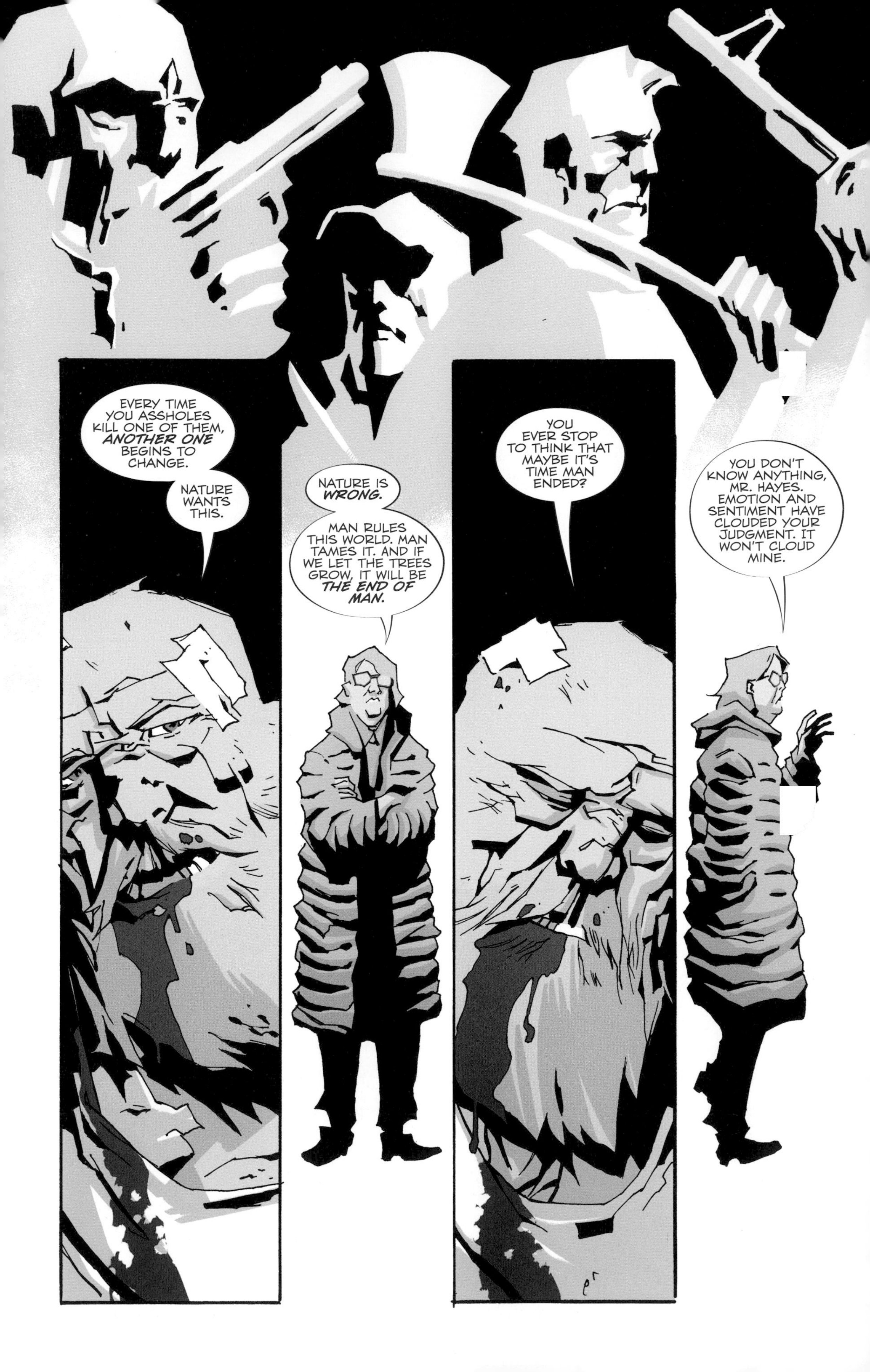
EVERY TIME YOU ASSHOLES KILL ONE OF THEM, ANOTHER ONE BEGINS TO CHANGE.
NATURE WANTS THIS.
NATURE IS WRONG.
MAN RULES THIS WORLD. MAN TAMES IT. AND IF WE LET THE TREES GROW, IT WILL BE THE END OF MAN.
YOU EVER STOP TO THINK THAT MAYBE IT'S TIME MAN ENDED?
YOU DON'T KNOW ANYTHING, MR. HAYES. EMOTION AND SENTIMENT HAVE CLOUDED YOUR JUDGMENT. IT WON'T CLOUD MINE.

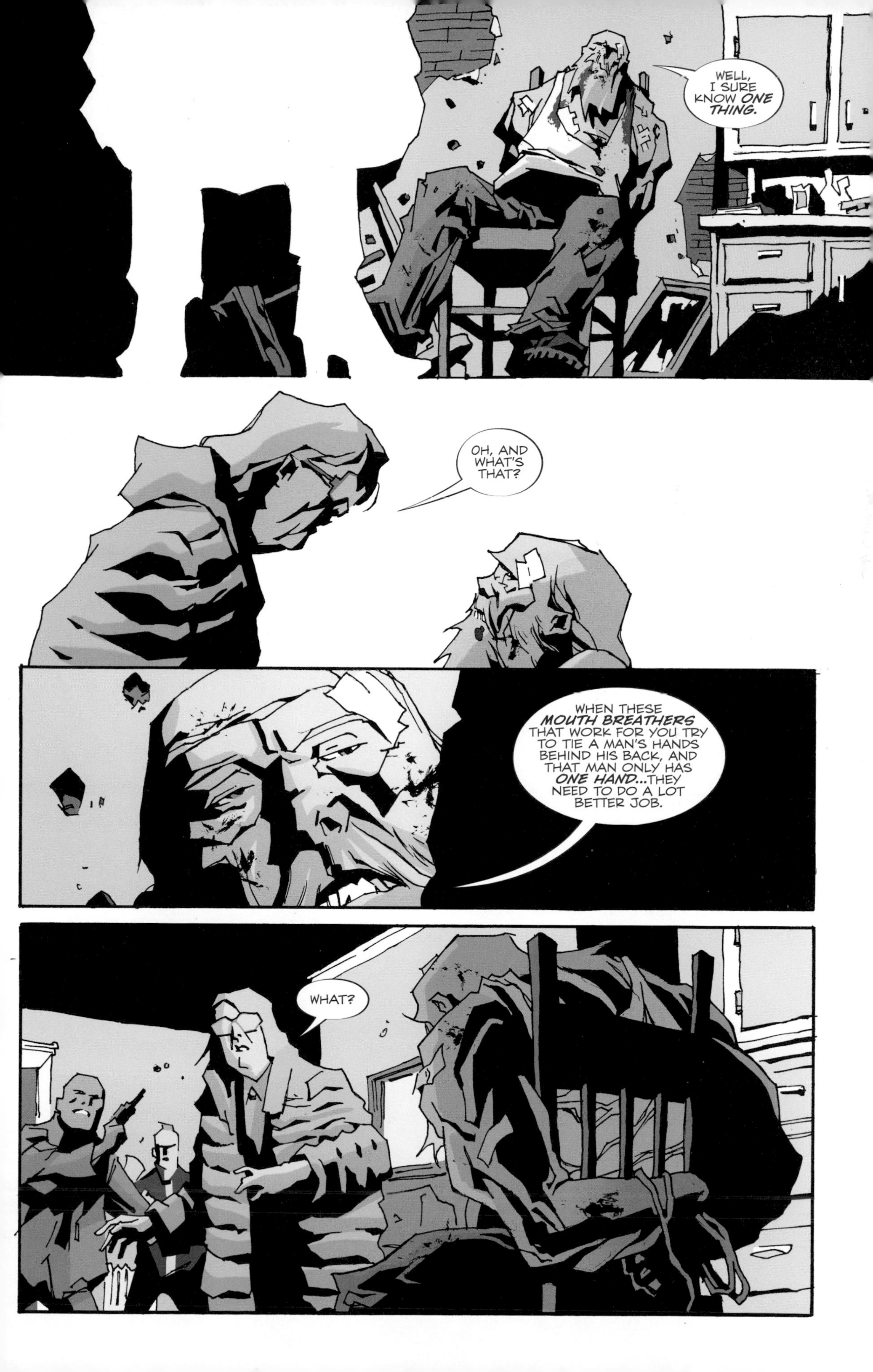
WELL, I SURE KNOW ONE THING.
OH, AND WHAT'S THAT?
WHEN THESE MOUTH BREATHERS THAT WORK FOR YOU TRY TO TIE A MAN'S HANDS BEHIND HIS BACK, AND THAT MAN ONLY HAS ONE HAND...THEY NEED TO DO A LOT BETTER JOB.
WHAT?

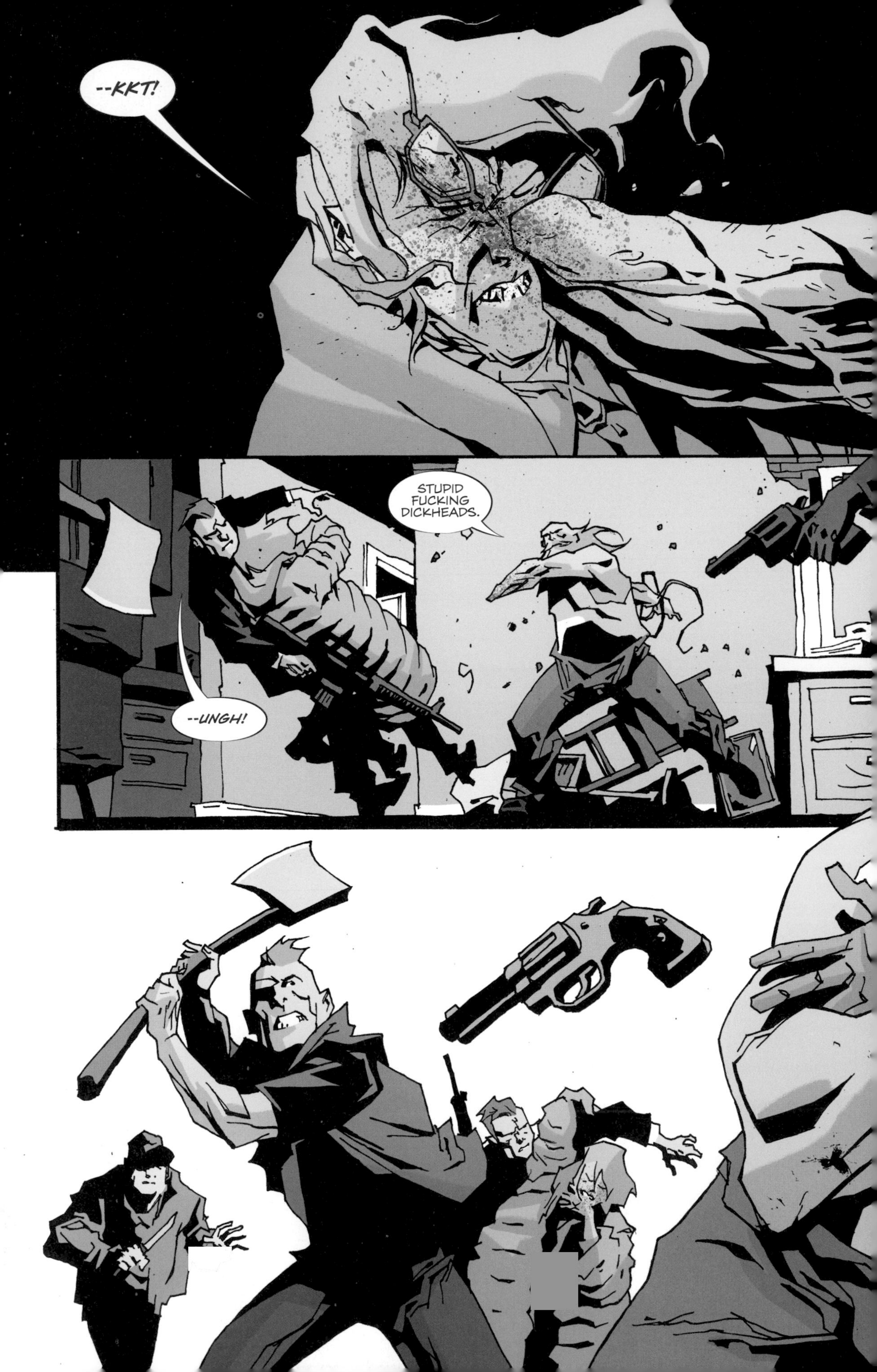
--KKT!
STUPID FUCKING DICKHEADS.
--UNGH!

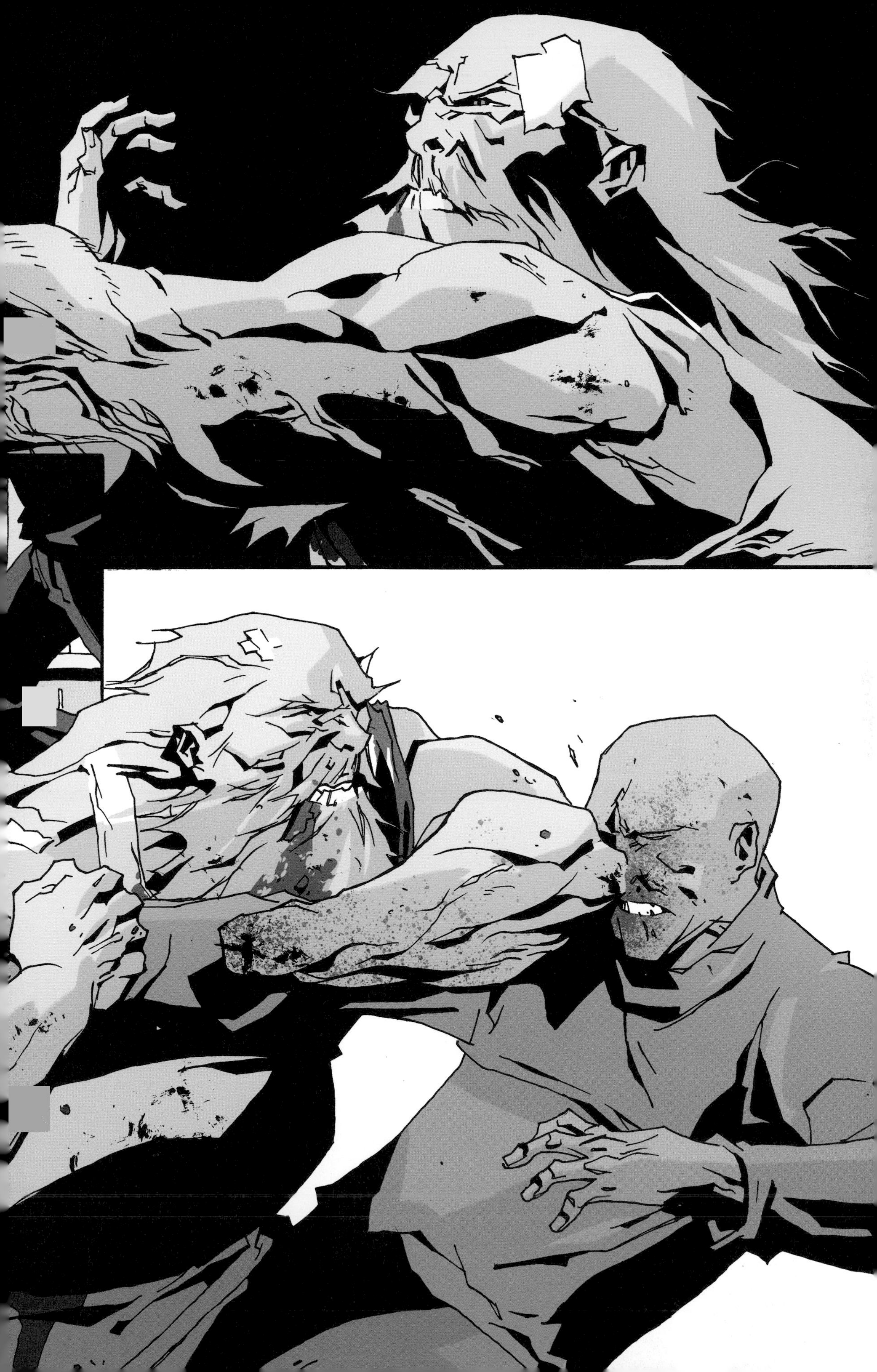

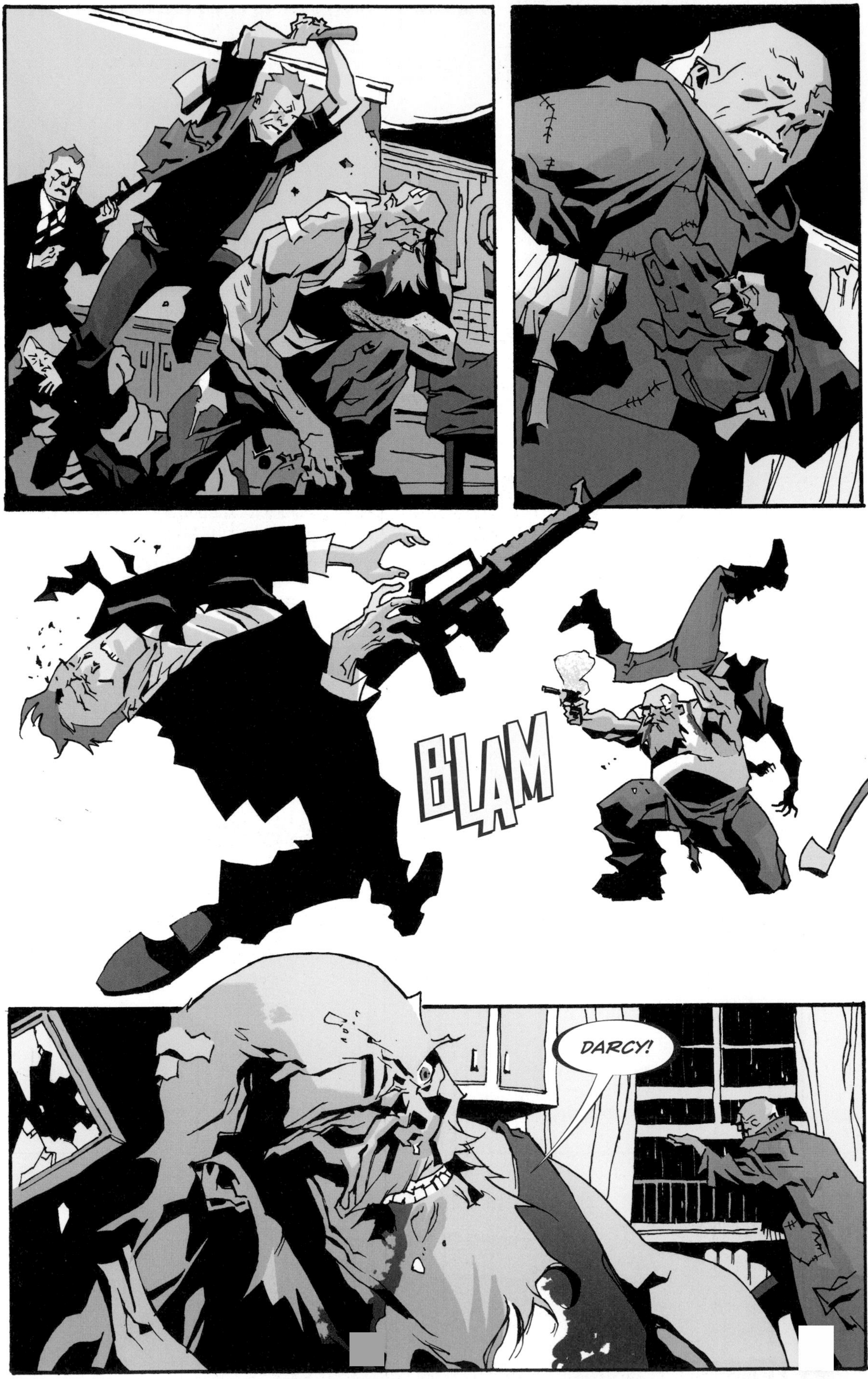
BLAM
DARCY!

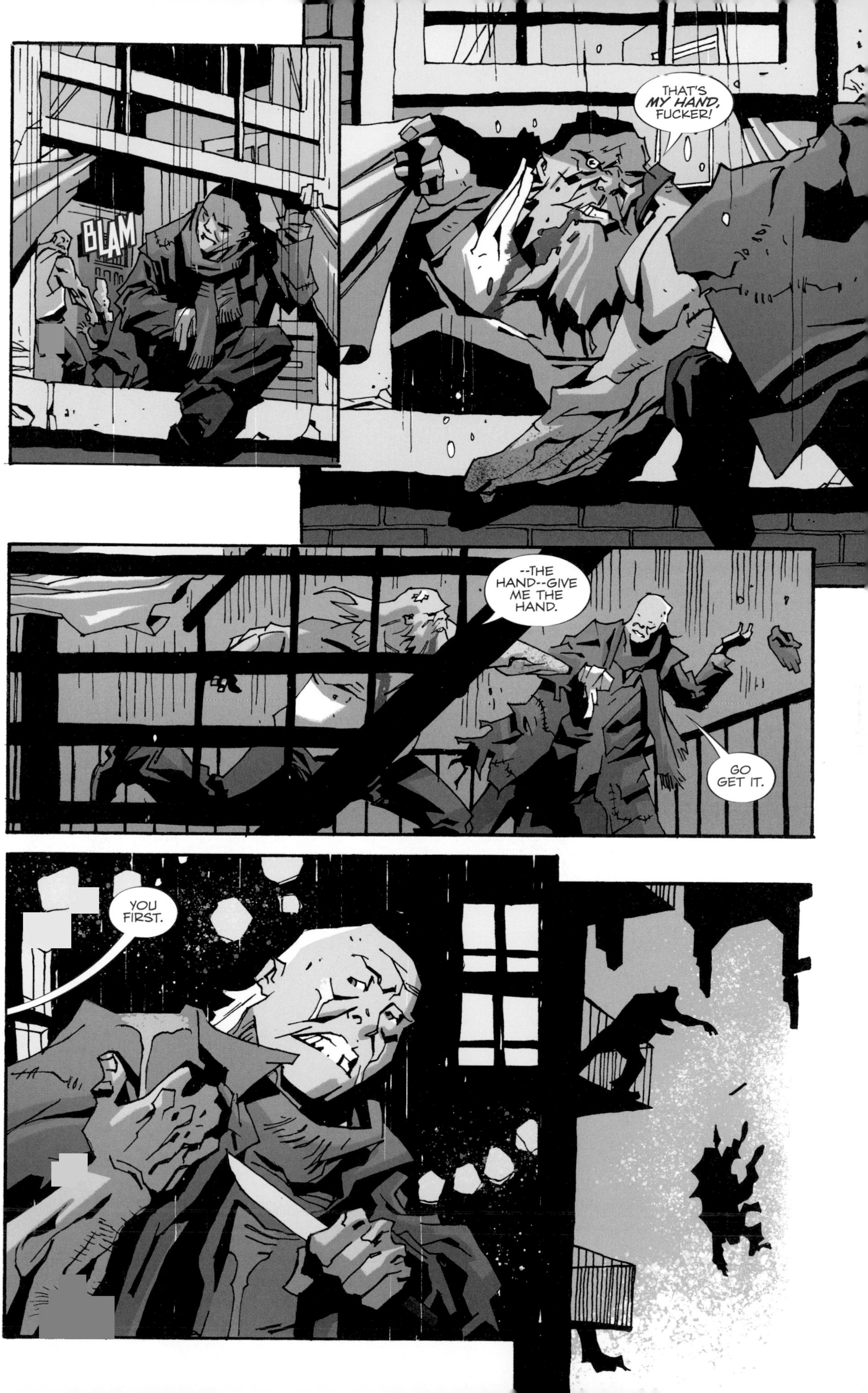
BLAM
THAT'S MY HAND, FUCKER!
--THE HAND--GIVE ME THE HAND.
GO GET IT.
YOU FIRST.

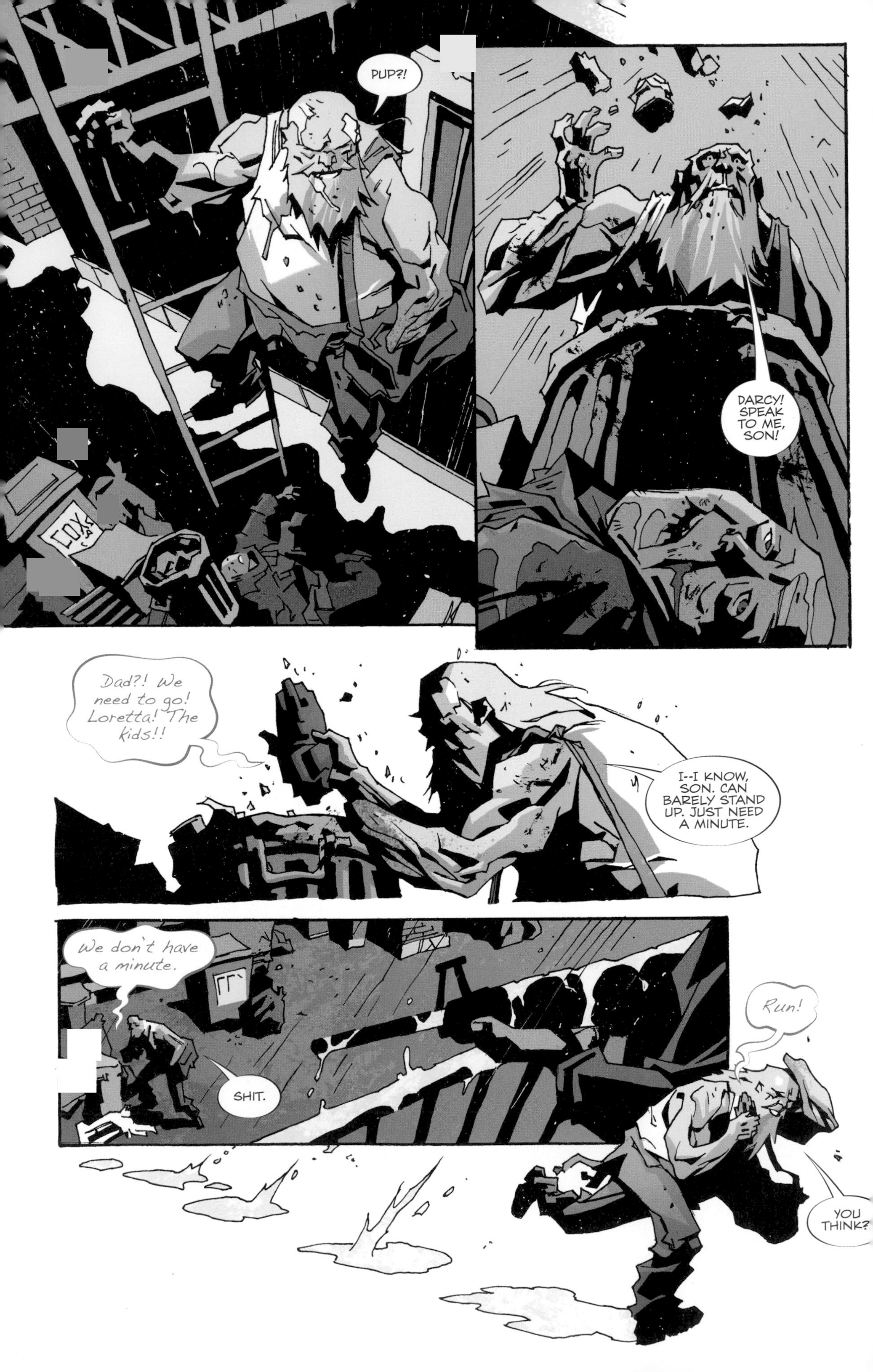
PUP?!
DARCY! SPEAK TO ME, SON!
Dad?! We need to go! Loretta! The kids!!
I--I KNOW, SON. CAN BARELY STAND UP. JUST NEED A MINUTE.
We don't have a minute.
SHIT.
Run!
YOU THINK?

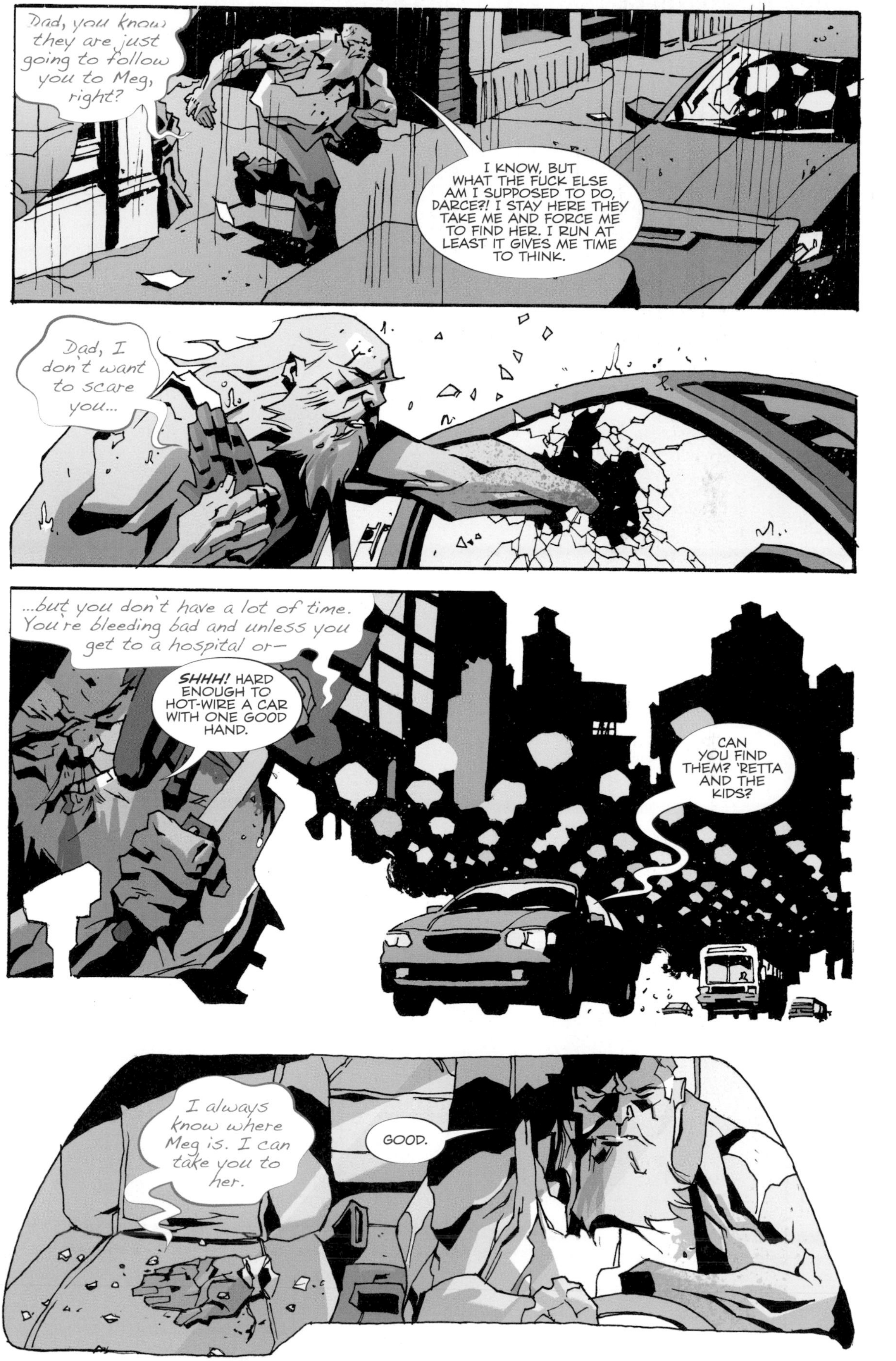
Dad, you know they are just going to follow you to Meg, right?
I KNOW, BUT WHAT THE FUCK ELSE AM I SUPPOSED TO DO, DARCE?! I STAY HERE THEY TAKE ME AND FORCE ME TO FIND HER. I RUN AT LEAST IT GIVES ME TIME TO THINK.
Dad, I don't want to scare you...
...but you don't have a lot of time. You're bleeding bad and unless you get to a hospital or—
SHHH! HARD ENOUGH TO HOT-WIRE A CAR WITH ONE GOOD HAND.
CAN YOU FIND THEM? 'RETTA AND THE KIDS?
I always know where Meg is. I can take you to her.
GOOD.

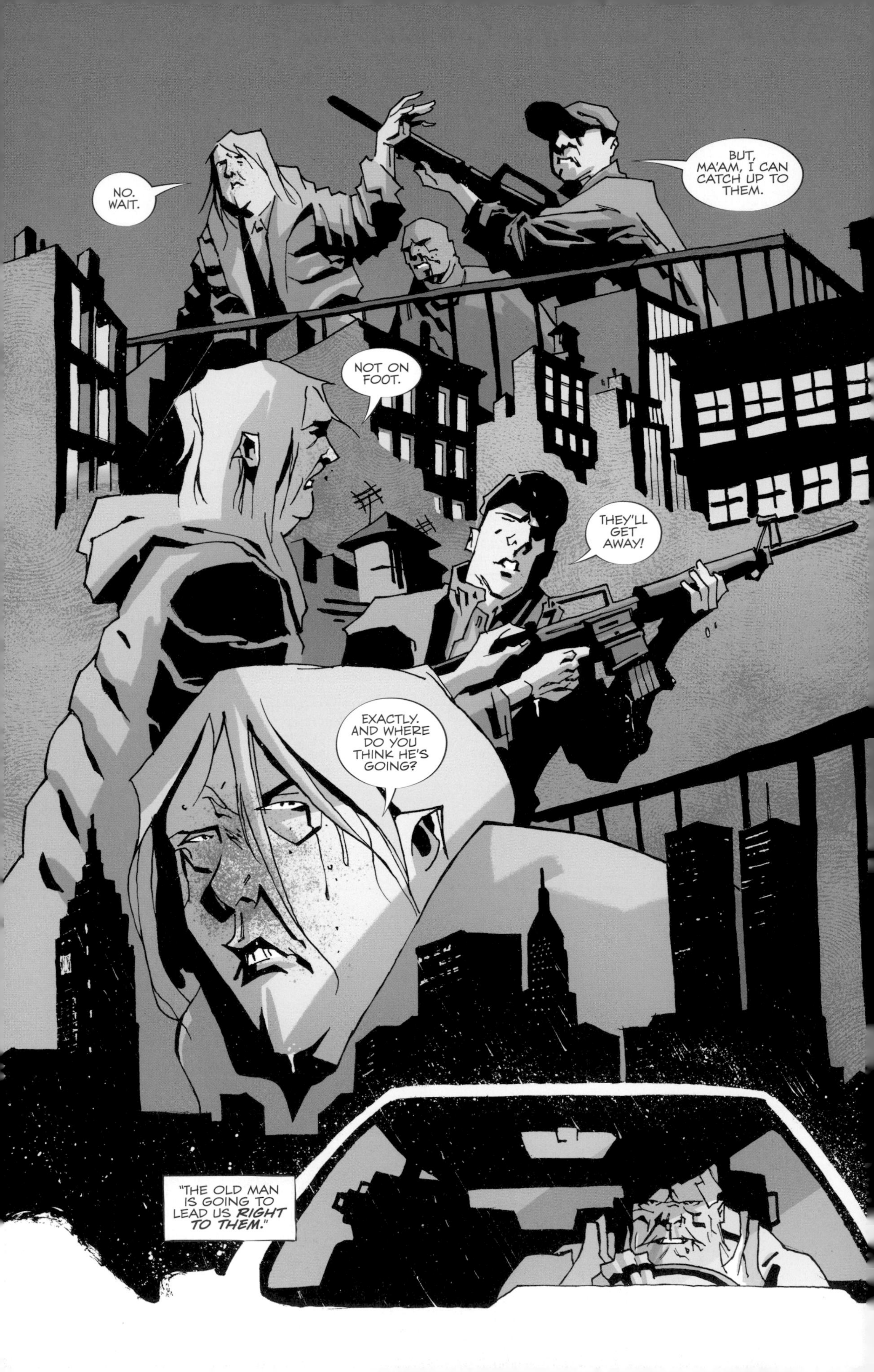
NO. WAIT.
BUT, MA'AM, I CAN CATCH UP TO THEM.
NOT ON FOOT.
THEY'LL GET AWAY!
EXACTLY. AND WHERE DO YOU THINK HE'S GOING?
"THE OLD MAN IS GOING TO LEAD US *RIGHT TO THEM.*"

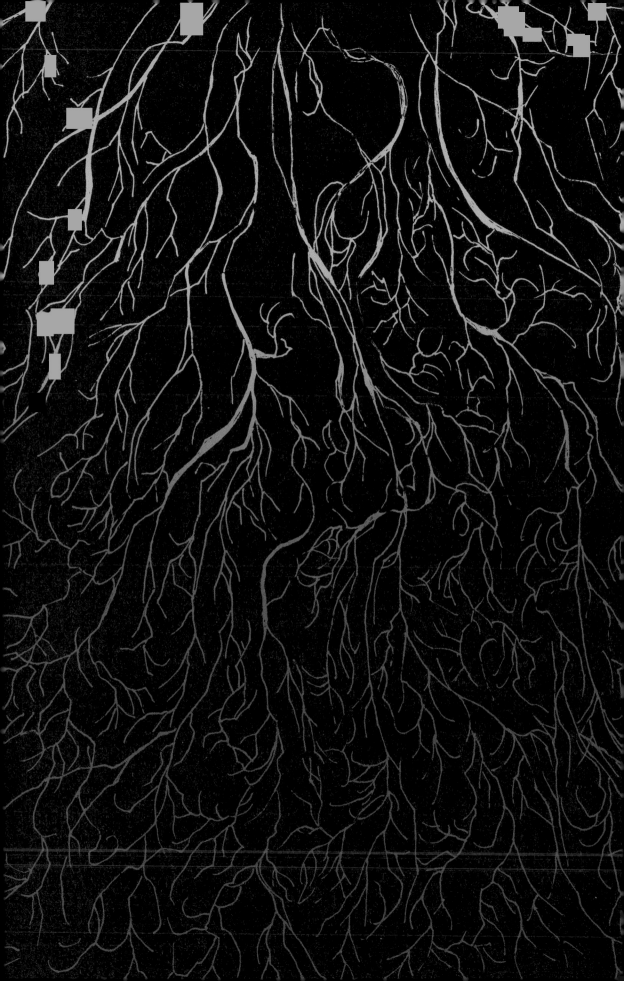

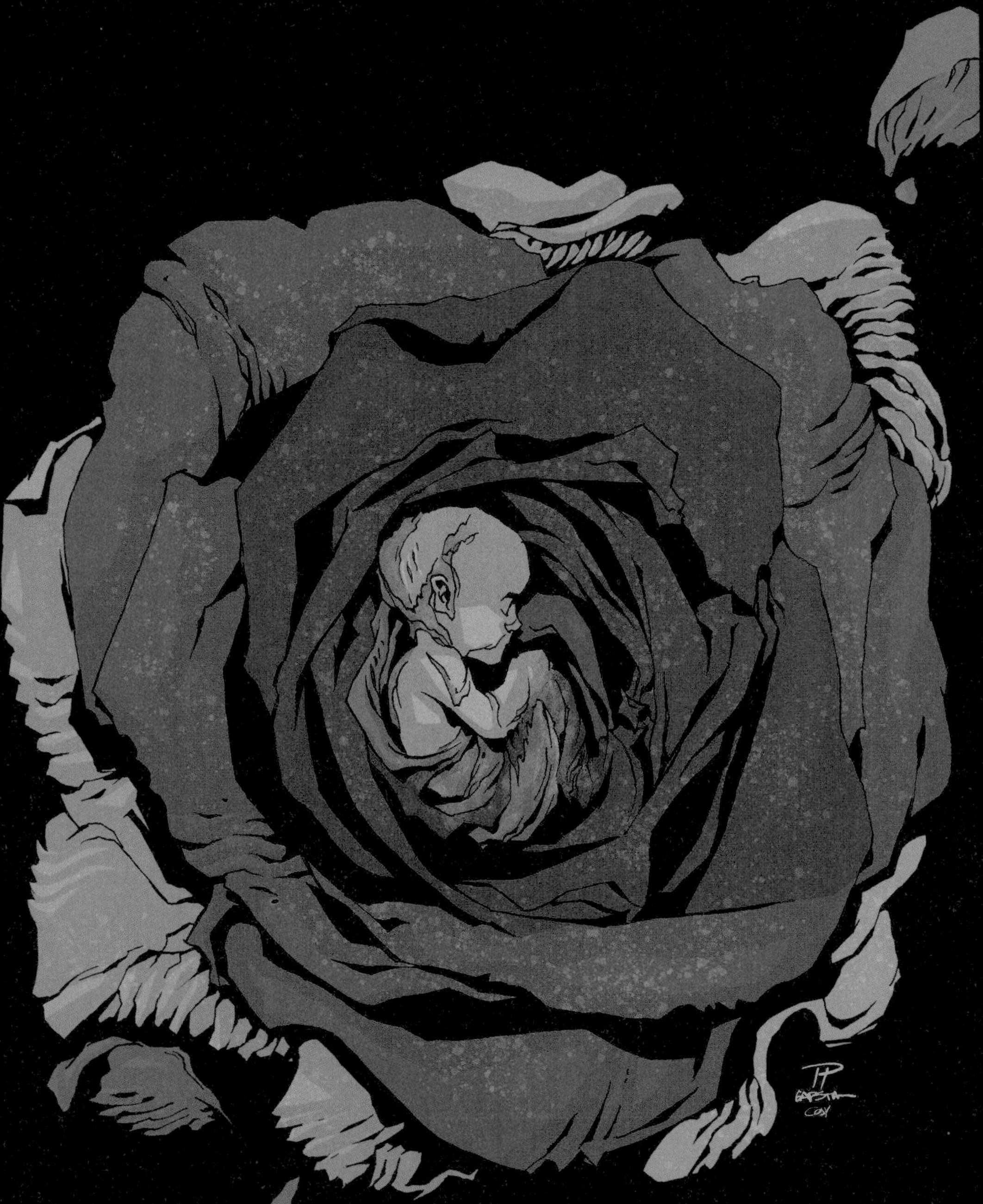

CHAPTER
SEVEN

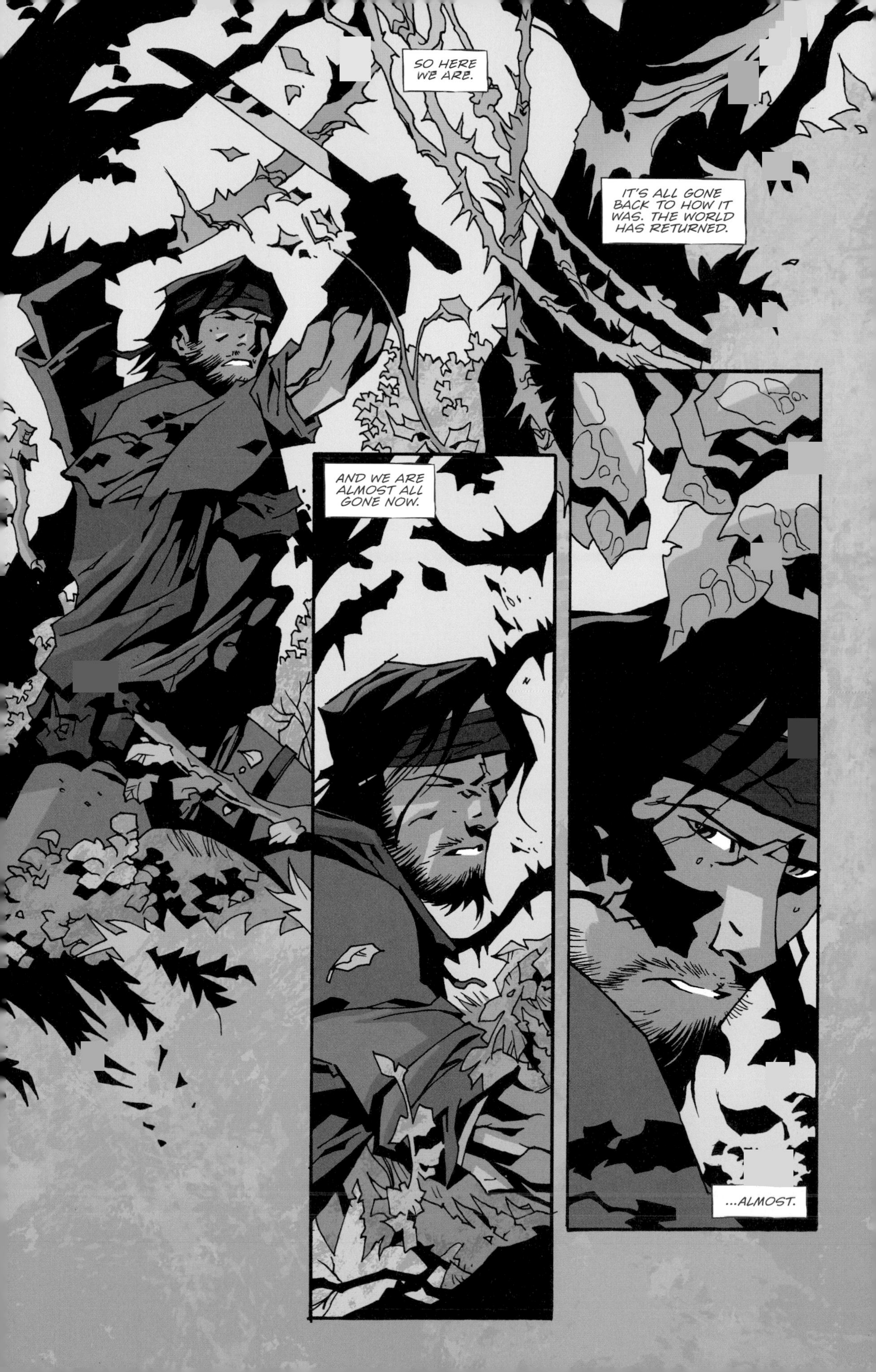
SO HERE WE ARE.
IT'S ALL GONE BACK TO HOW IT WAS. THE WORLD HAS RETURNED.
AND WE ARE ALMOST ALL GONE NOW.
...ALMOST.

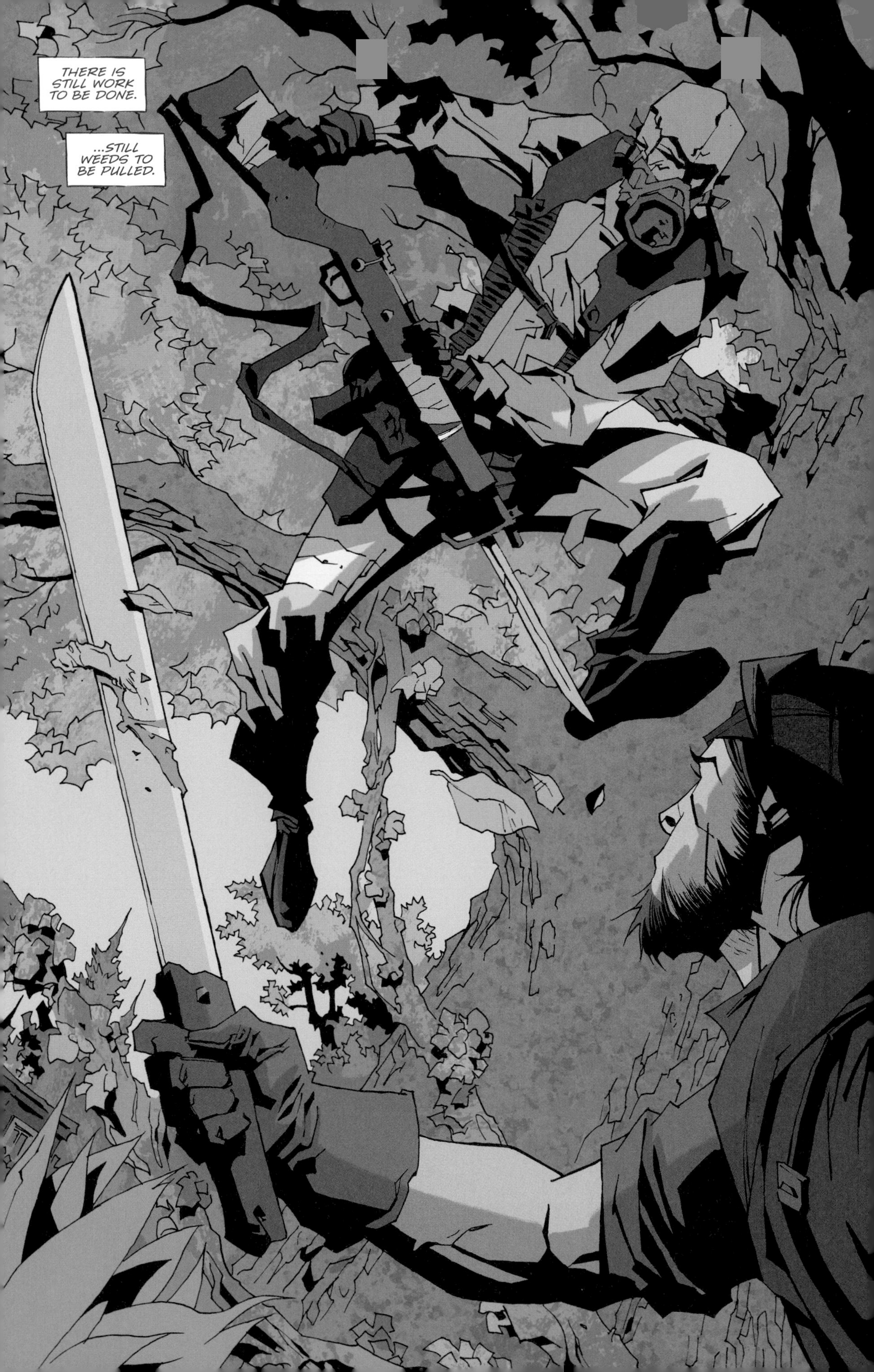
THERE IS STILL WORK TO BE DONE.
...STILL WEEDS TO BE PULLED.

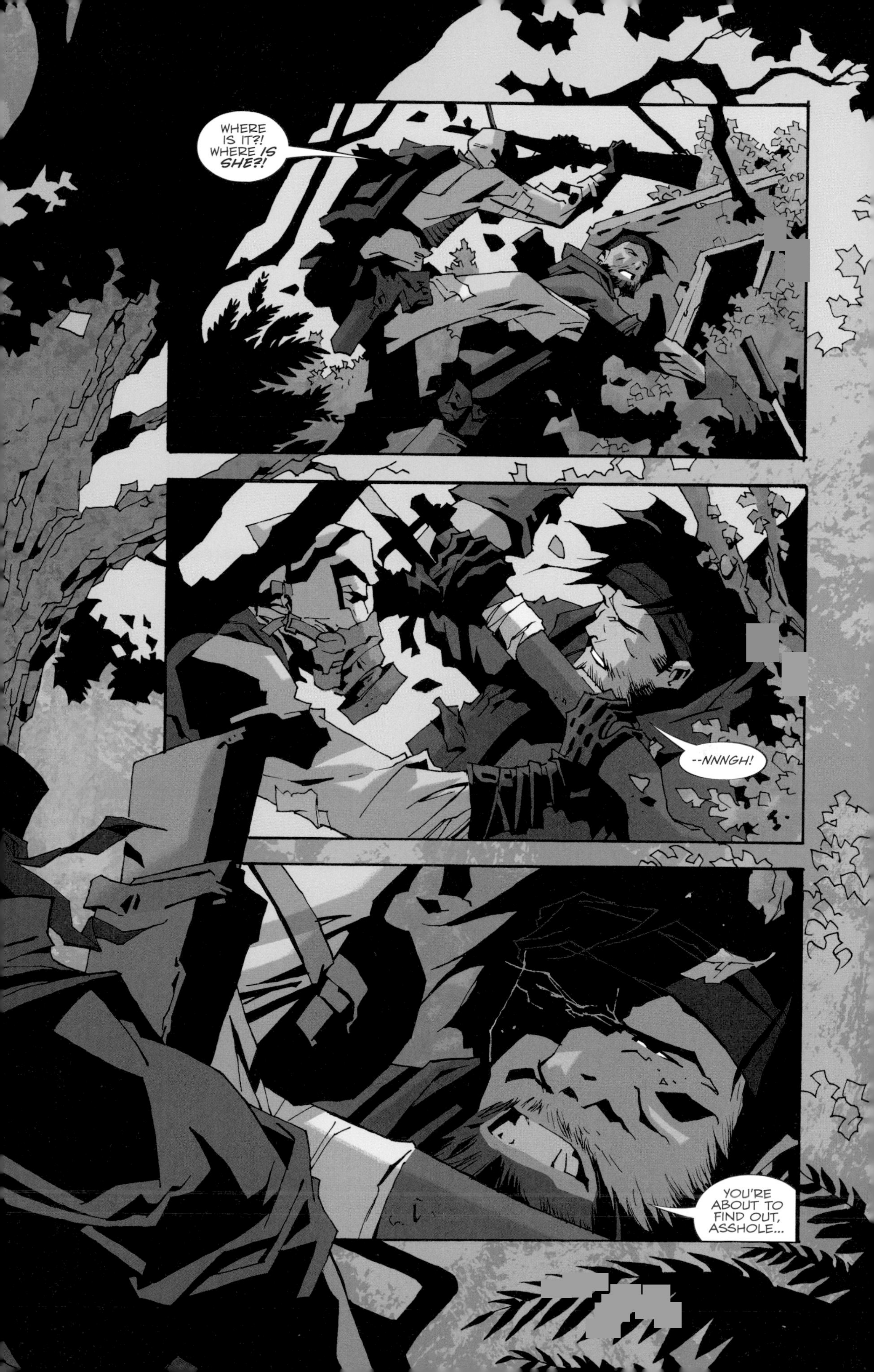
WHERE IS IT?! WHERE IS SHE?!
--NNNGH!
YOU'RE ABOUT TO FIND OUT, ASSHOLE...

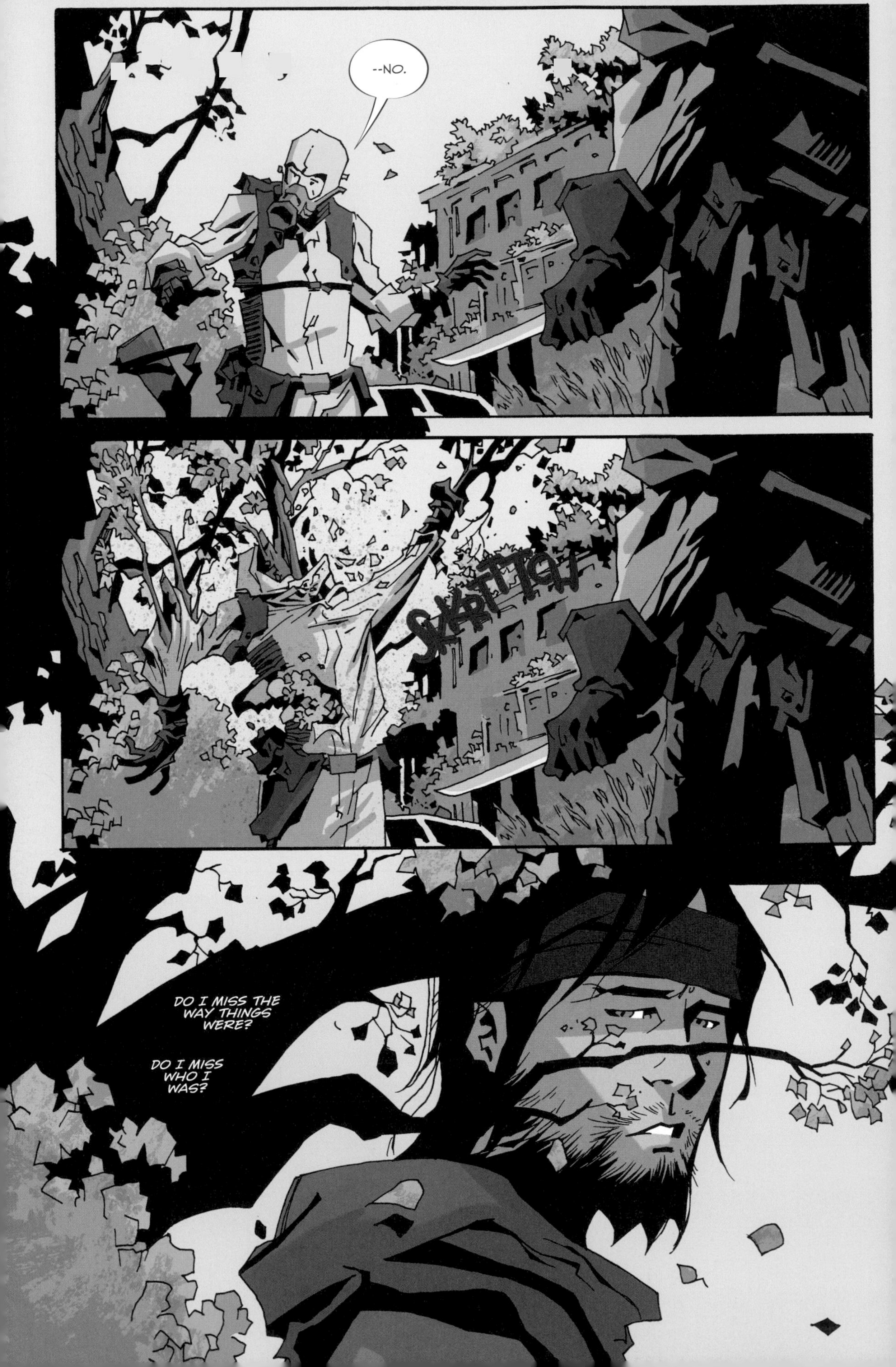
--NO.
SKRITTCH
DO I MISS THE WAY THINGS WERE?
DO I MISS WHO I WAS?

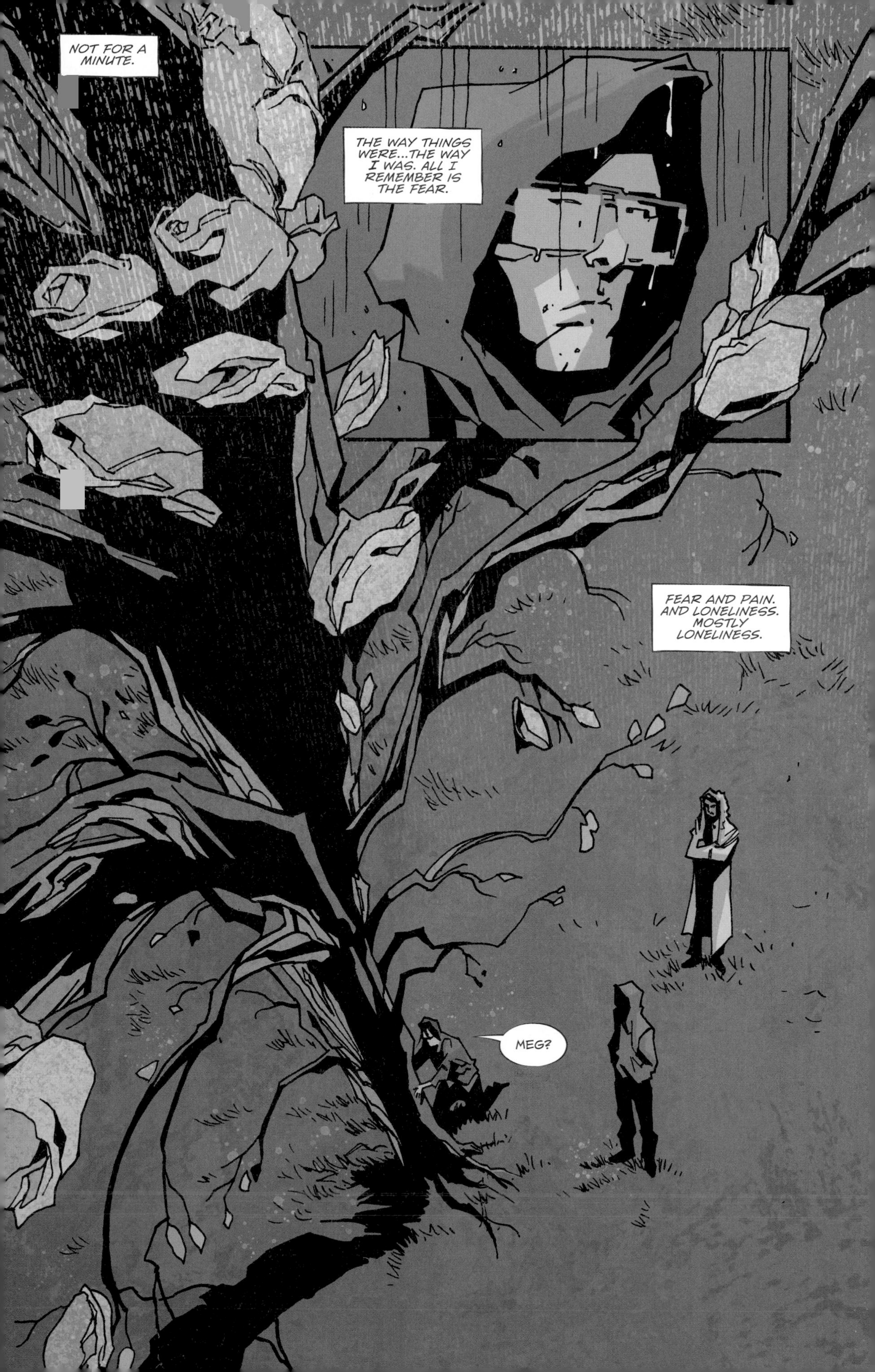
NOT FOR A MINUTE.
THE WAY THINGS WERE...THE WAY I WAS. ALL I REMEMBER IS THE FEAR.
FEAR AND PAIN. AND LONELINESS. MOSTLY LONELINESS.
MEG?

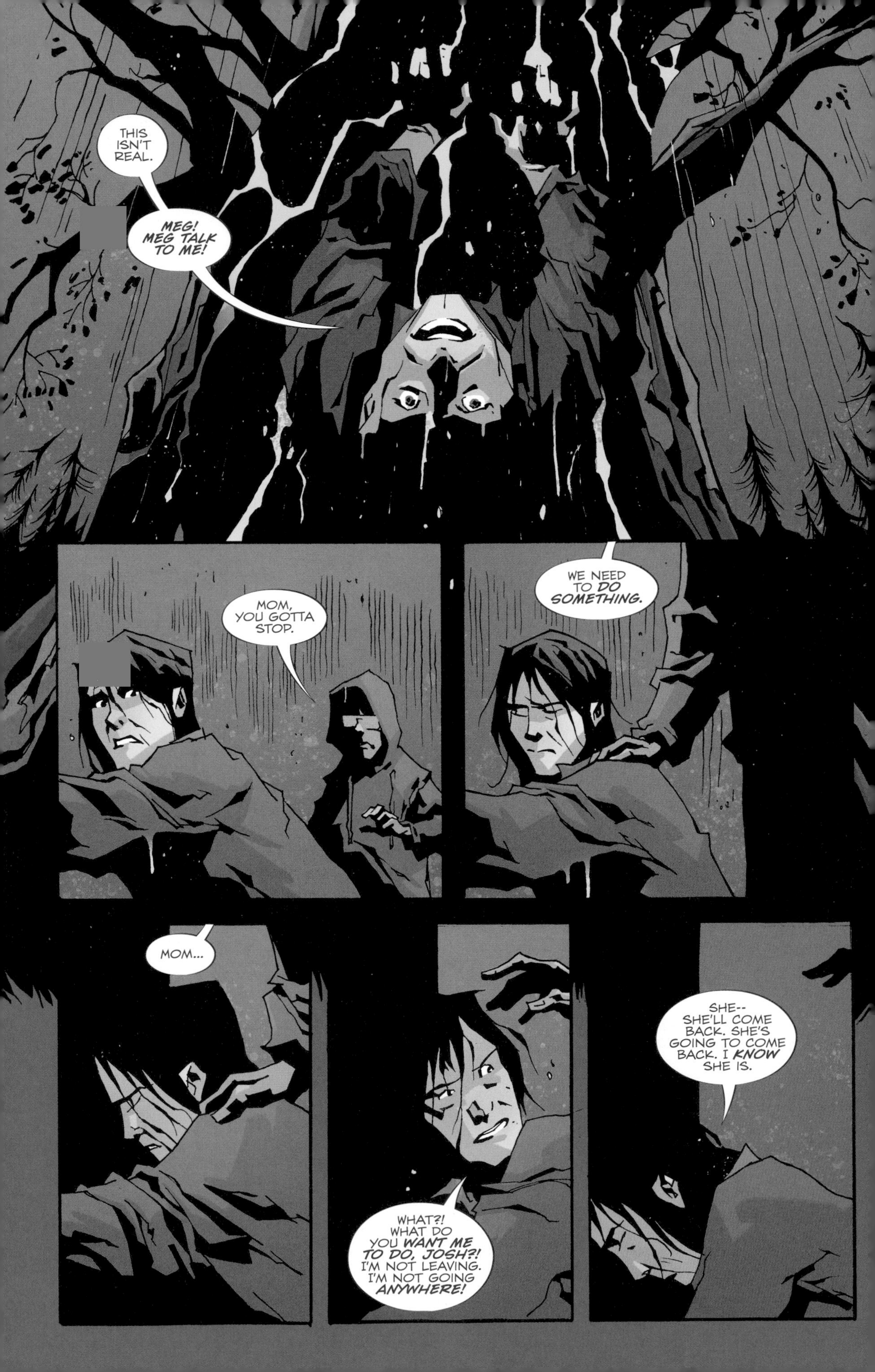
THIS ISN'T REAL.
MEG! MEG TALK TO ME!
MOM, YOU GOTTA STOP.
WE NEED TO DO SOMETHING.
MOM...
WHAT?! WHAT DO YOU WANT ME TO DO, JOSH?! I'M NOT LEAVING. I'M NOT GOING ANYWHERE!
SHE-- SHE'LL COME BACK. SHE'S GOING TO COME BACK. I KNOW SHE IS.

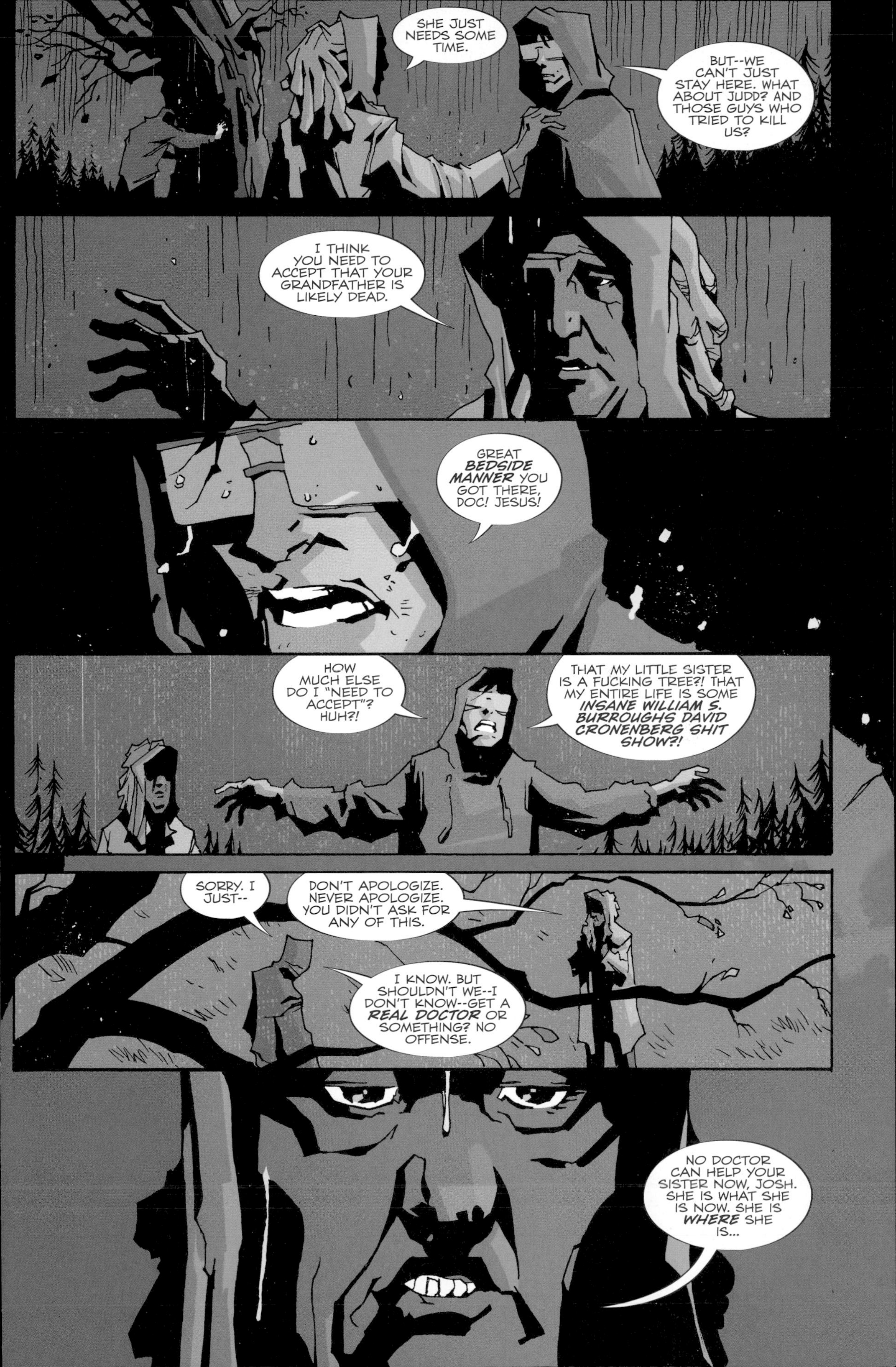
SHE JUST NEEDS SOME TIME.
BUT--WE CAN'T JUST STAY HERE. WHAT ABOUT JUDD? AND THOSE GUYS WHO TRIED TO KILL US?
I THINK YOU NEED TO ACCEPT THAT YOUR GRANDFATHER IS LIKELY DEAD.
GREAT **BEDSIDE MANNER** YOU GOT THERE, DOC! JESUS!
HOW MUCH ELSE DO I "NEED TO ACCEPT"? HUH?!
THAT MY LITTLE SISTER IS A FUCKING TREE?! THAT MY ENTIRE LIFE IS SOME ***INSANE WILLIAM S. BURROUGHS DAVID CRONENBERG SHIT SHOW?!***
SORRY. I JUST--
DON'T APOLOGIZE. NEVER APOLOGIZE. YOU DIDN'T ASK FOR ANY OF THIS.
I KNOW. BUT SHOULDN'T WE--I DON'T KNOW--GET A ***REAL DOCTOR*** OR SOMETHING? NO OFFENSE.
NO DOCTOR CAN HELP YOUR SISTER NOW, JOSH. SHE IS WHAT SHE IS NOW. SHE IS ***WHERE*** SHE IS...

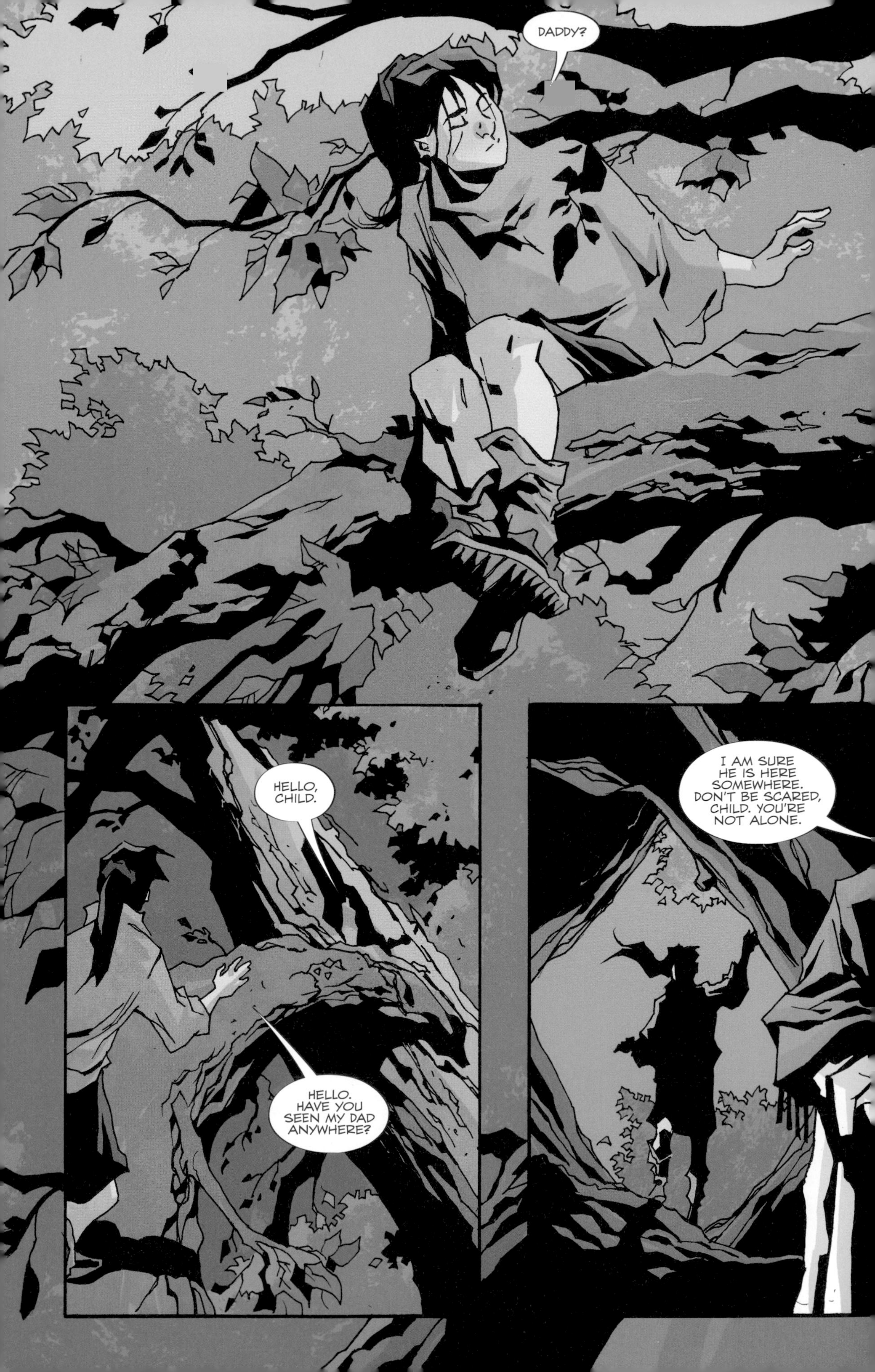
DADDY?
HELLO, CHILD.
HELLO. HAVE YOU SEEN MY DAD ANYWHERE?
I AM SURE HE IS HERE SOMEWHERE. DON'T BE SCARED, CHILD. YOU'RE NOT ALONE.

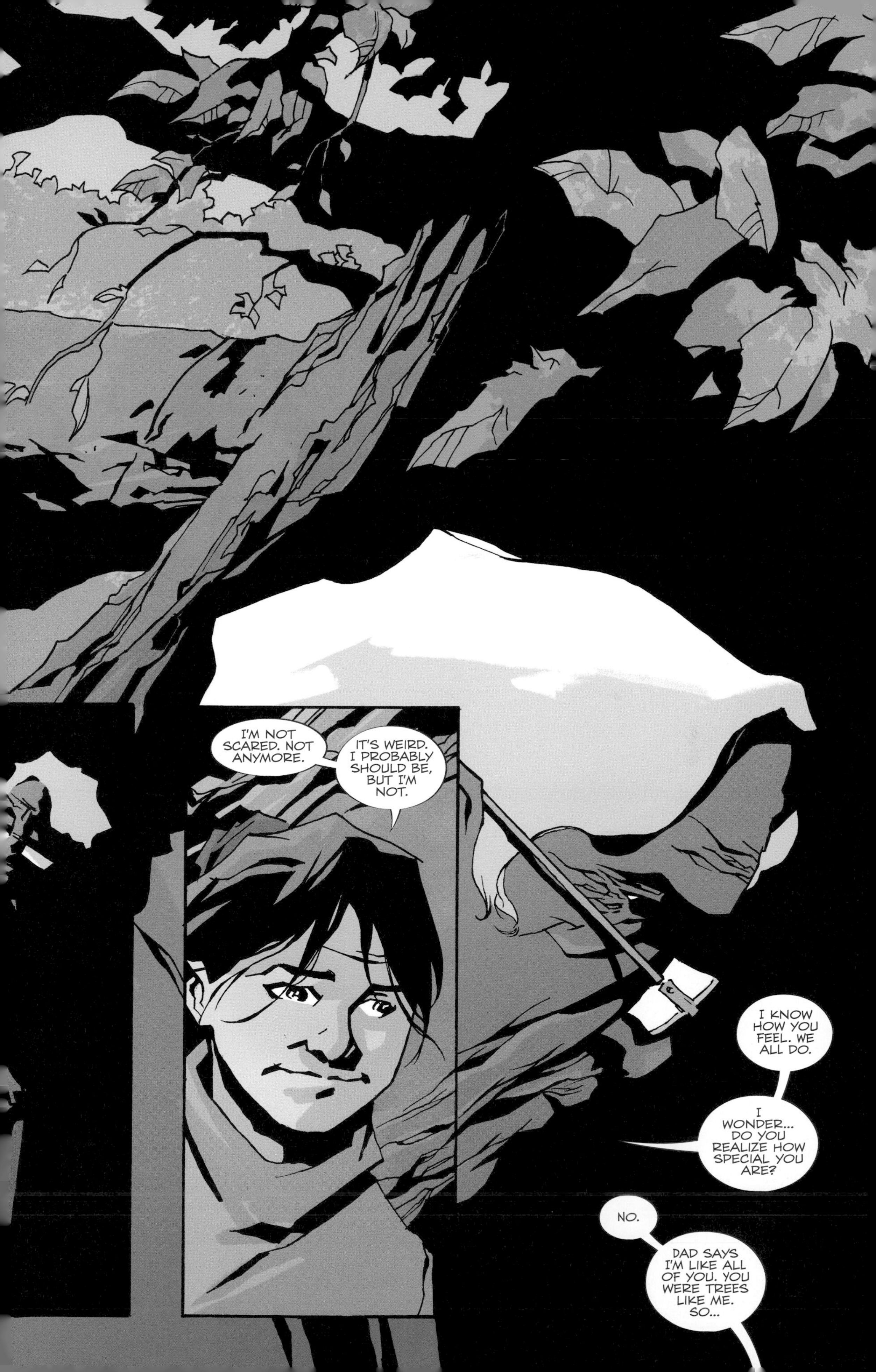

I'M NOT SCARED. NOT ANYMORE.
IT'S WEIRD. I PROBABLY SHOULD BE, BUT I'M NOT.
I KNOW HOW YOU FEEL. WE ALL DO.
I WONDER... DO YOU REALIZE HOW SPECIAL YOU ARE?
NO.
DAD SAYS I'M LIKE ALL OF YOU. YOU WERE TREES LIKE ME. SO...

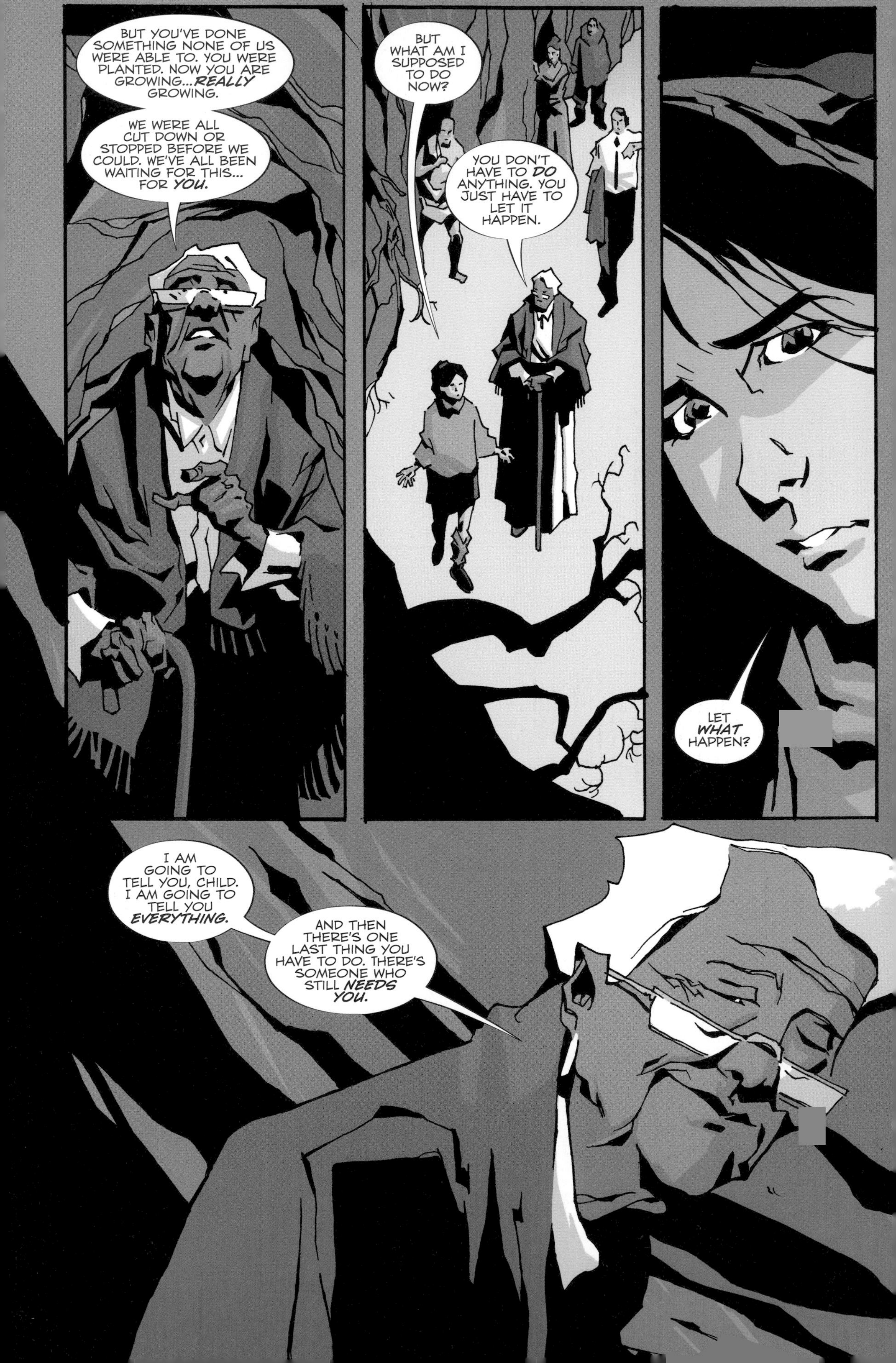
BUT YOU'VE DONE SOMETHING NONE OF US WERE ABLE TO. YOU WERE PLANTED. NOW YOU ARE GROWING... REALLY GROWING.
WE WERE ALL CUT DOWN OR STOPPED BEFORE WE COULD. WE'VE ALL BEEN WAITING FOR THIS... FOR YOU.
BUT WHAT AM I SUPPOSED TO DO NOW?
YOU DON'T HAVE TO DO ANYTHING. YOU JUST HAVE TO LET IT HAPPEN.
LET WHAT HAPPEN?
I AM GOING TO TELL YOU, CHILD. I AM GOING TO TELL YOU EVERYTHING.
AND THEN THERE'S ONE LAST THING YOU HAVE TO DO. THERE'S SOMEONE WHO STILL NEEDS YOU.

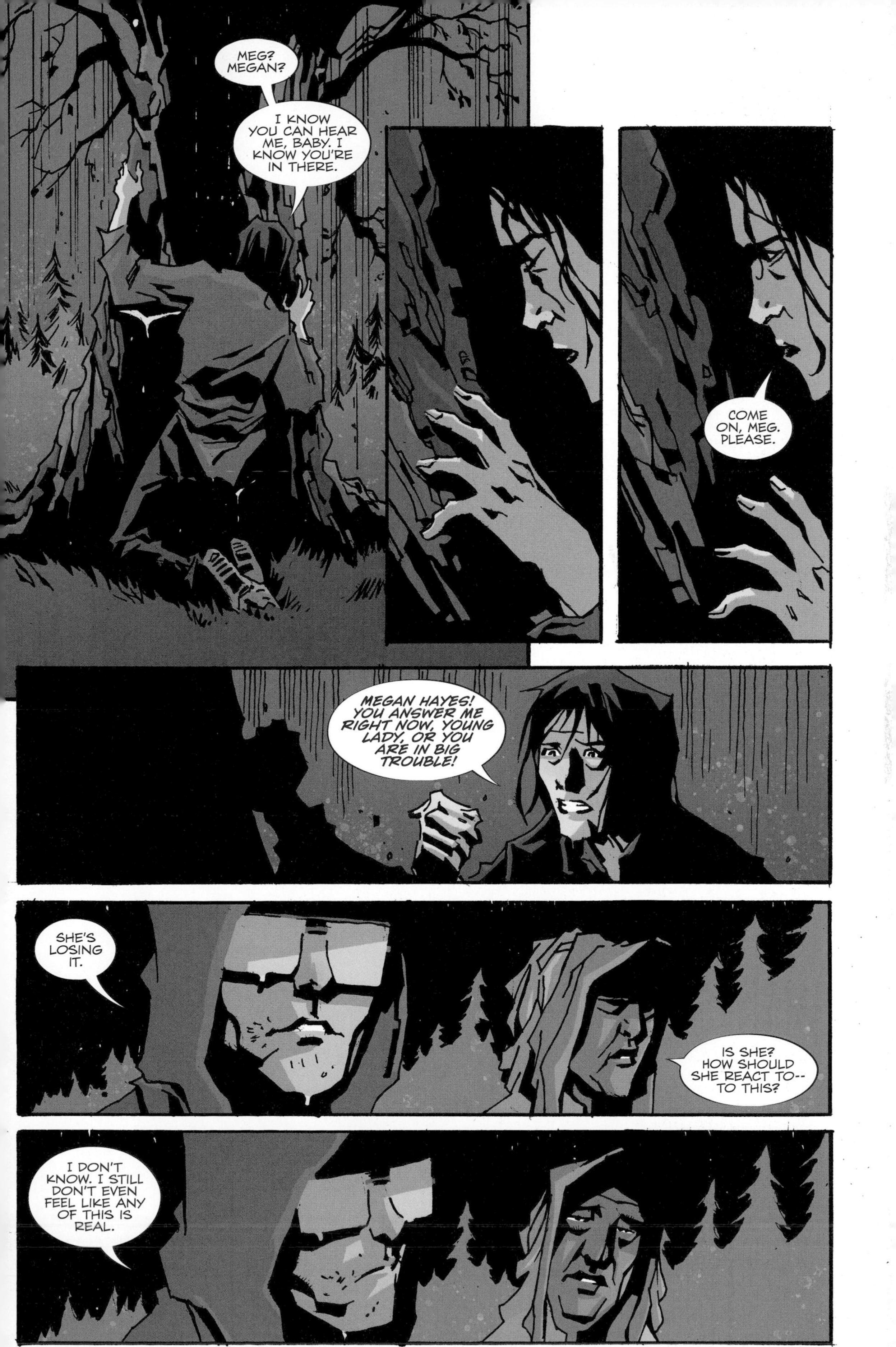
MEG? MEGAN?
I KNOW YOU CAN HEAR ME, BABY. I KNOW YOU'RE IN THERE.
COME ON, MEG. PLEASE.
MEGAN HAYES! YOU ANSWER ME RIGHT NOW, YOUNG LADY, OR YOU ARE IN BIG TROUBLE!
SHE'S LOSING IT.
IS SHE? HOW SHOULD SHE REACT TO-- TO THIS?
I DON'T KNOW. I STILL DON'T EVEN FEEL LIKE ANY OF THIS IS REAL.

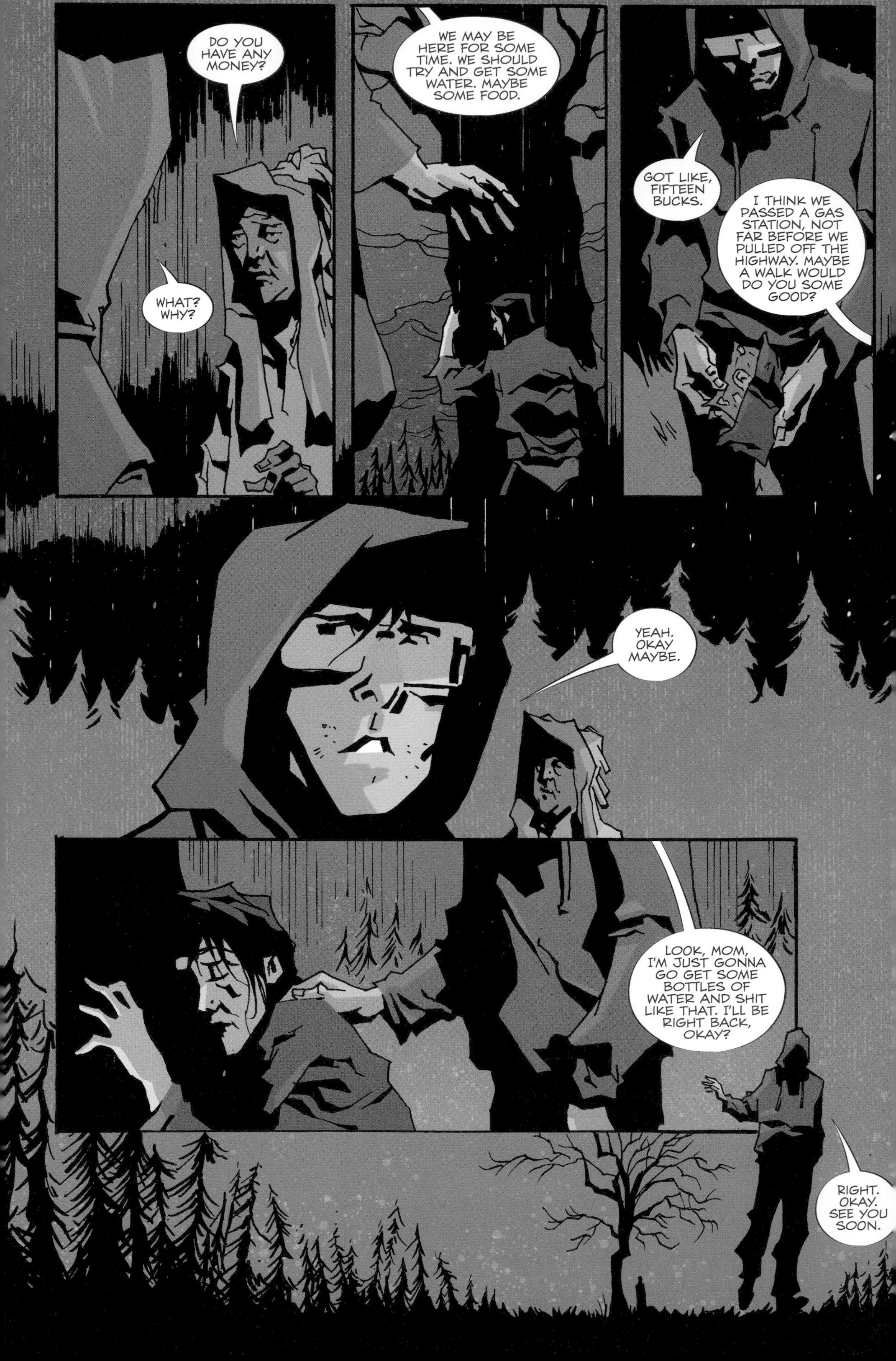
DO YOU HAVE ANY MONEY?
WHAT? WHY?
WE MAY BE HERE FOR SOME TIME. WE SHOULD TRY AND GET SOME WATER. MAYBE SOME FOOD.
GOT LIKE, FIFTEEN BUCKS.
I THINK WE PASSED A GAS STATION, NOT FAR BEFORE WE PULLED OFF THE HIGHWAY. MAYBE A WALK WOULD DO YOU SOME GOOD?
YEAH. OKAY MAYBE.
LOOK, MOM, I'M JUST GONNA GO GET SOME BOTTLES OF WATER AND SHIT LIKE THAT. I'LL BE RIGHT BACK, OKAY?
RIGHT. OKAY. SEE YOU SOON.

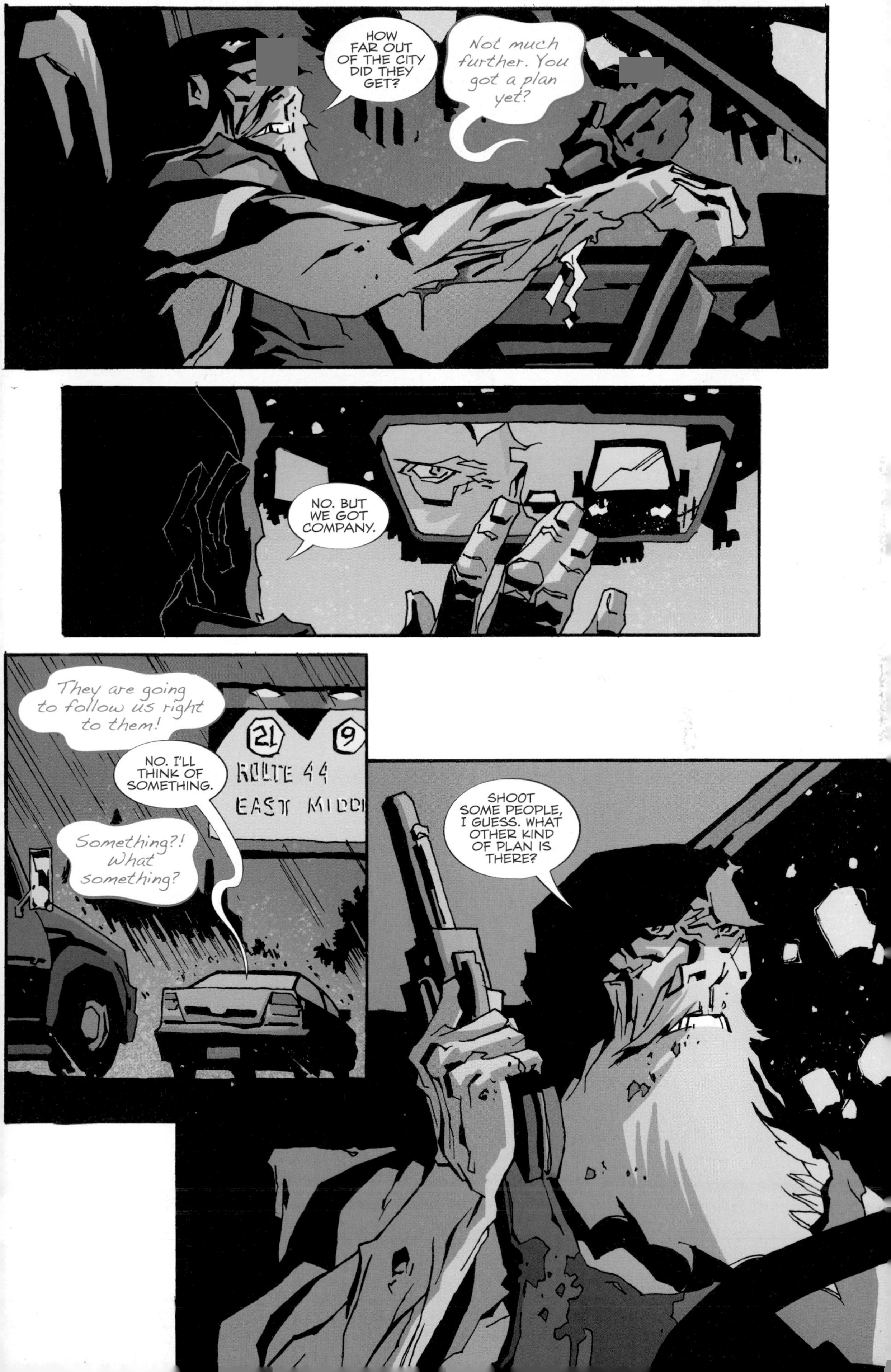

HOW FAR OUT OF THE CITY DID THEY GET?
Not much further. You got a plan yet?
NO. BUT WE GOT COMPANY.
They are going to follow us right to them!
21
9
ROUTE 44
EAST MIDD
NO. I'LL THINK OF SOMETHING.
Something?! What something?
SHOOT SOME PEOPLE, I GUESS. WHAT OTHER KIND OF PLAN IS THERE?

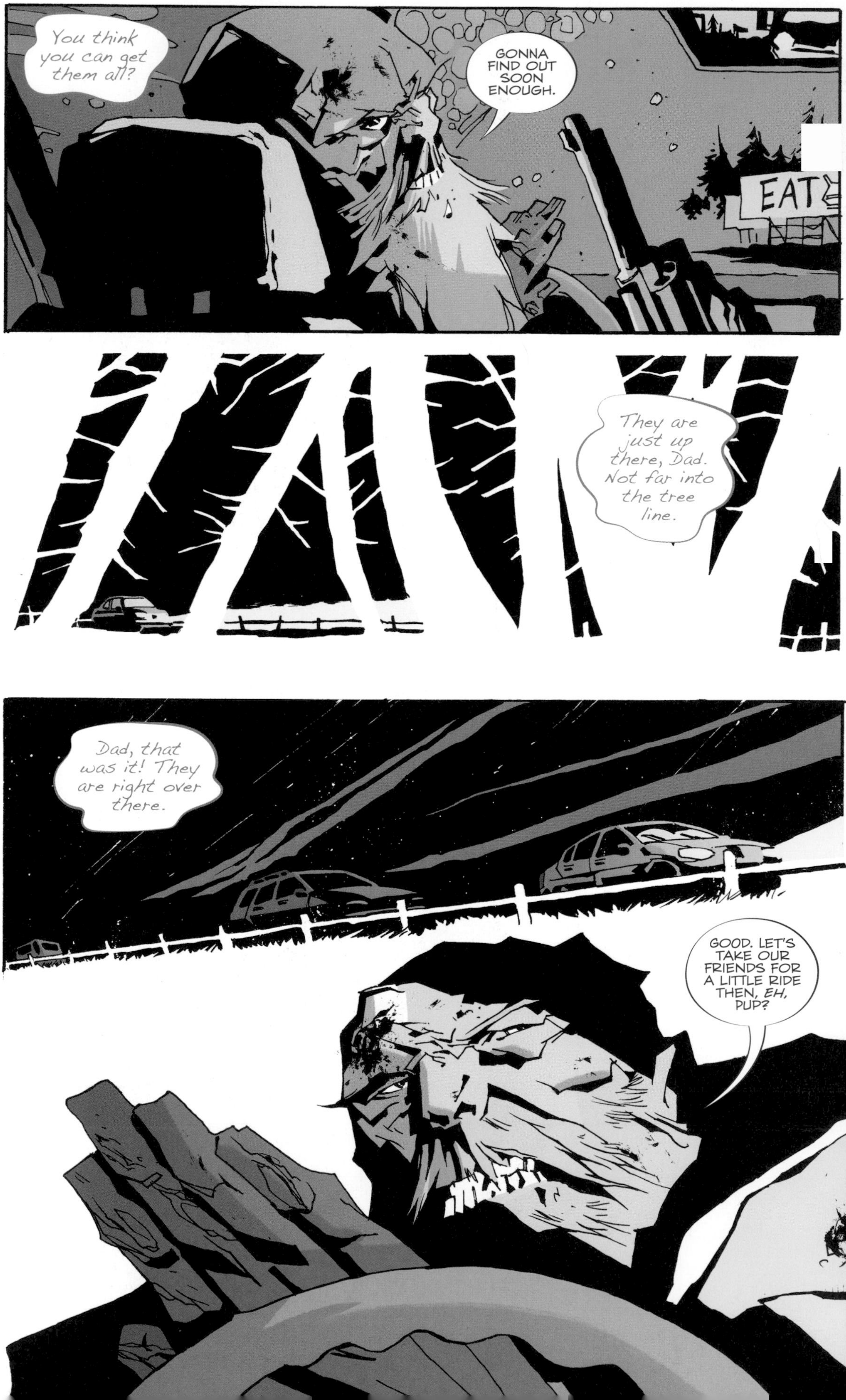
You think you can get them all?
GONNA FIND OUT SOON ENOUGH.
EAT
They are just up there, Dad. Not far into the tree line.
Dad, that was it! They are right over there.
GOOD. LET'S TAKE OUR FRIENDS FOR A LITTLE RIDE THEN, *EH*, PUP?

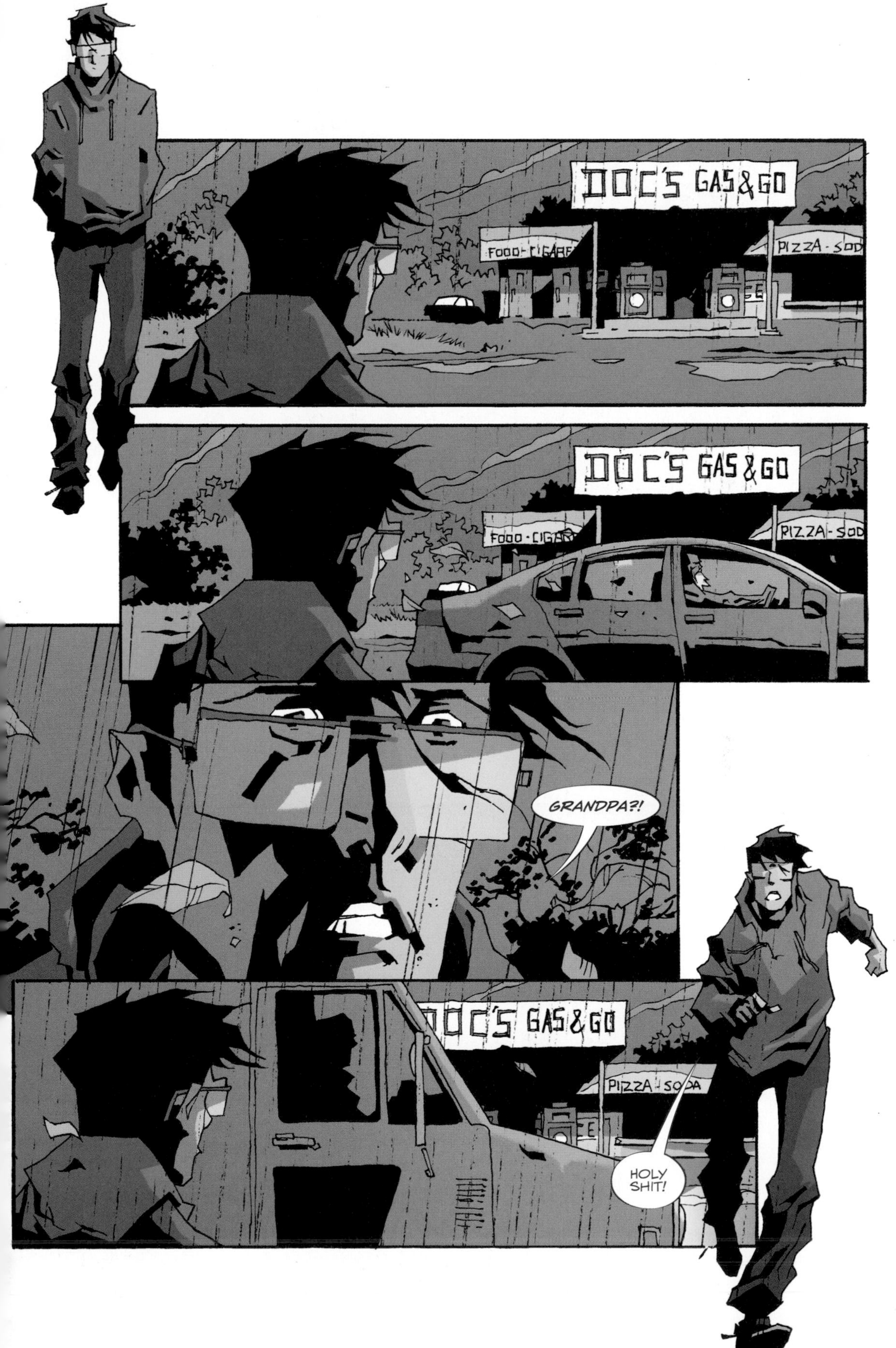
DOC'S GAS & GO
FOOD · CIGARE
PIZZA - SOD
DOC'S GAS & GO
FOOD · CIGAR
PIZZA - SOD
GRANDPA?!
DOC'S GAS & GO
PIZZA - SODA
HOLY SHIT!

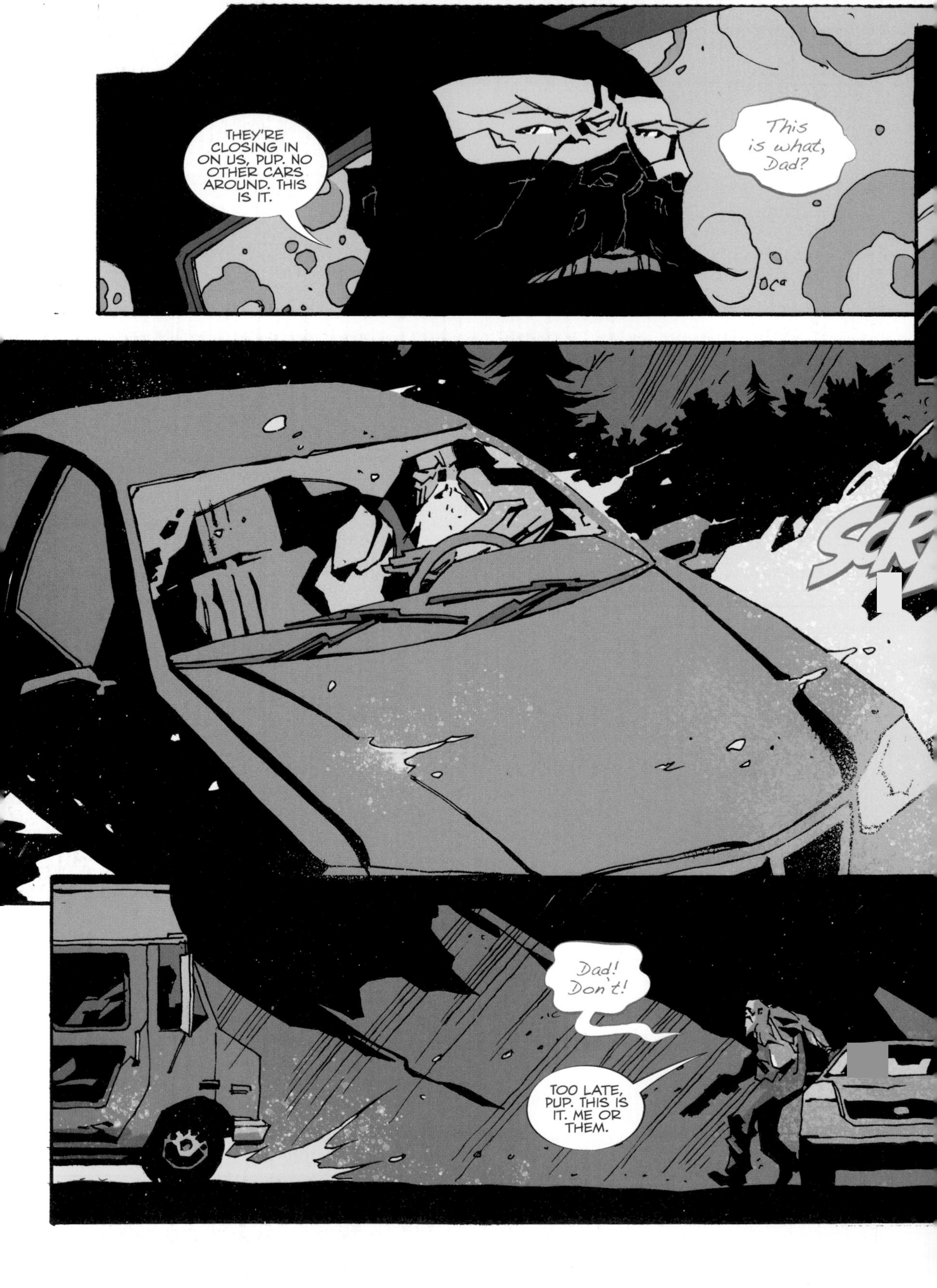
THEY'RE CLOSING IN ON US, PUP. NO OTHER CARS AROUND. THIS IS IT.
This is what, Dad?
Dad! Don't!
TOO LATE, PUP. THIS IS IT. ME OR THEM.

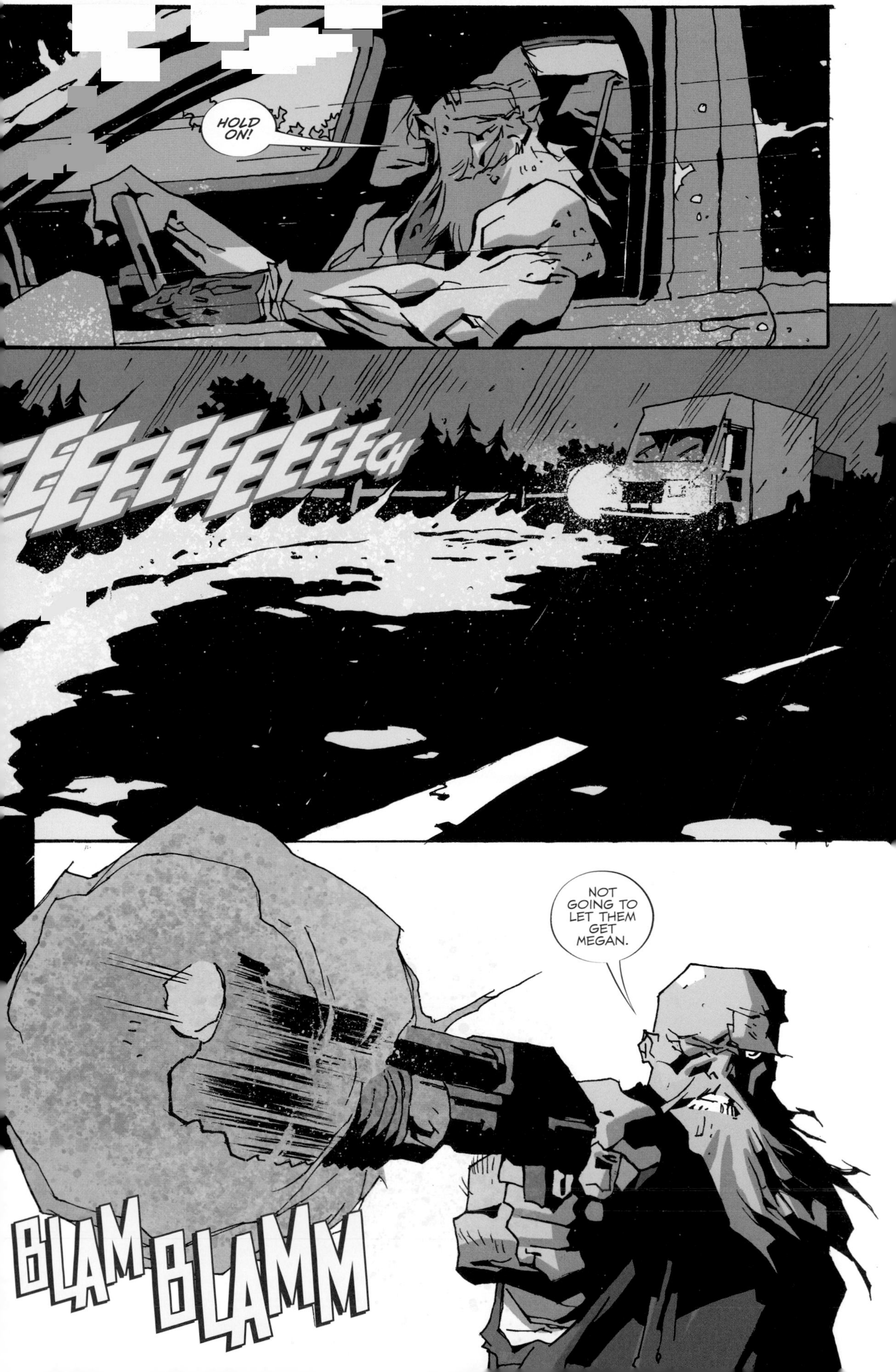
HOLD ON!
EEEEEEEEEECH
NOT GOING TO LET THEM GET MEGAN.
BLAM BLAMM

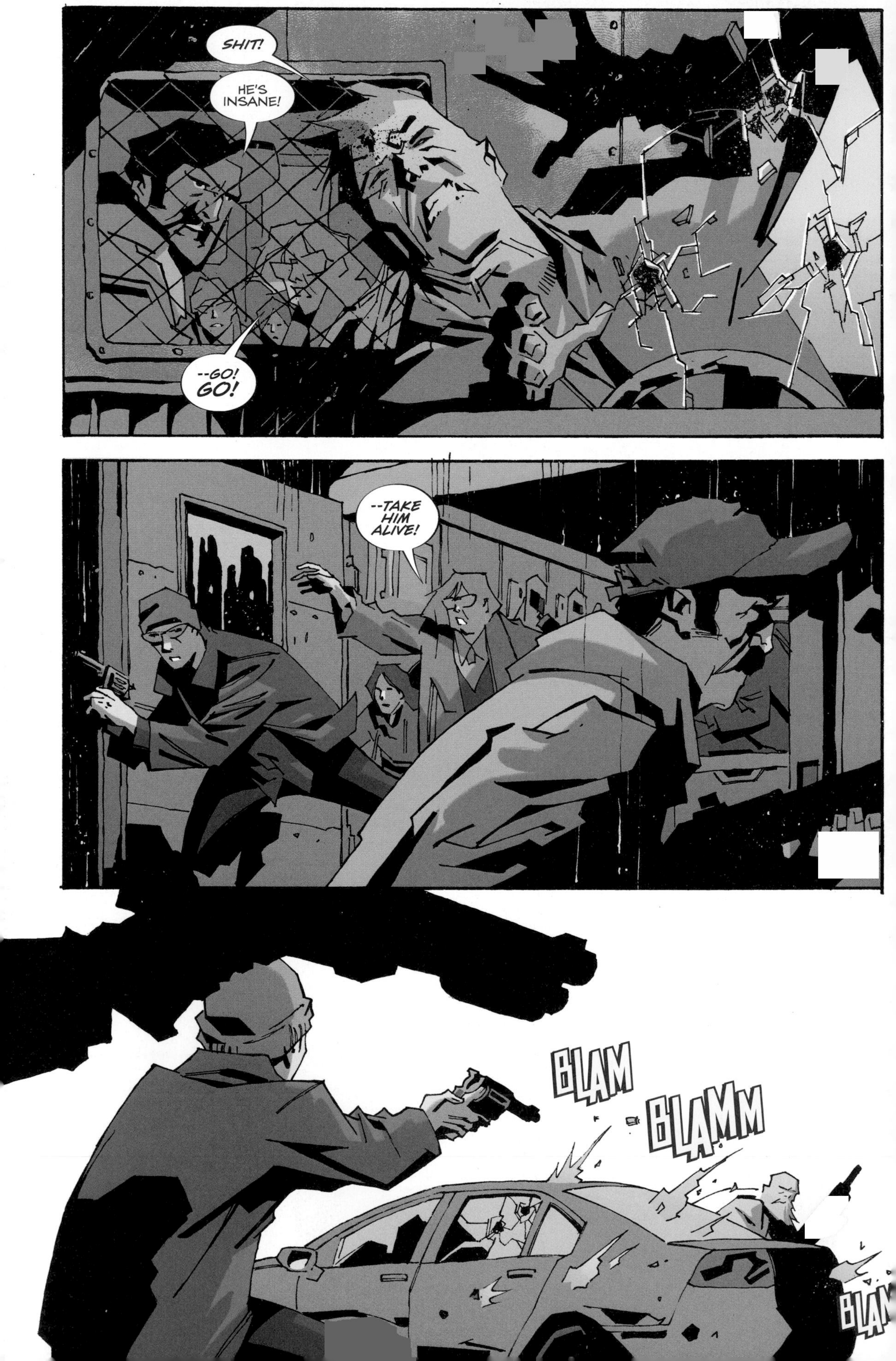
SHIT!
HE'S INSANE!
--GO! GO!
--TAKE HIM ALIVE!
BLAM
BLAMM

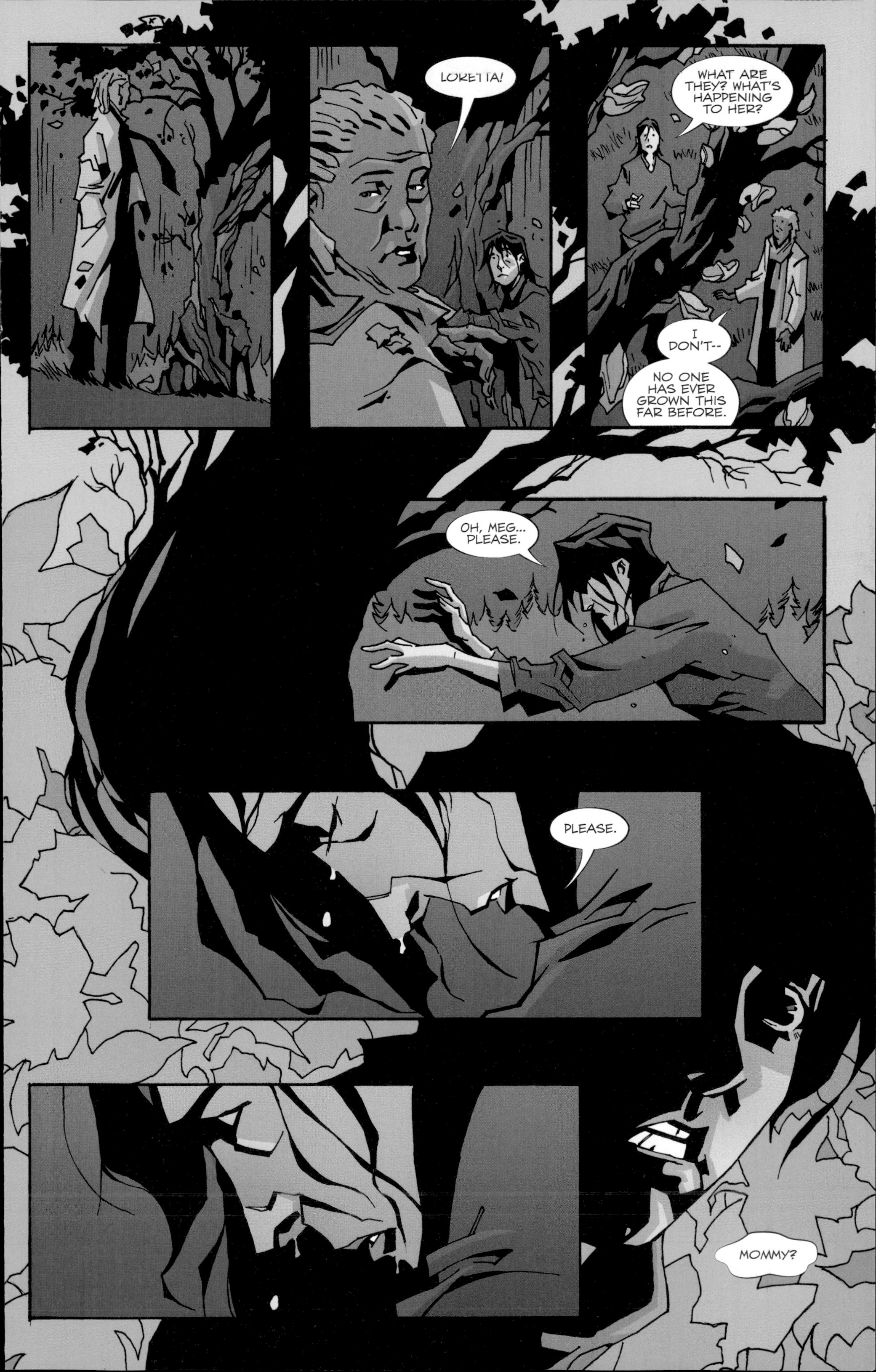
LORETTA!
WHAT ARE THEY? WHAT'S HAPPENING TO HER?
I DON'T--
NO ONE HAS EVER GROWN THIS FAR BEFORE.
OH, MEG... PLEASE.
PLEASE.
MOMMY?

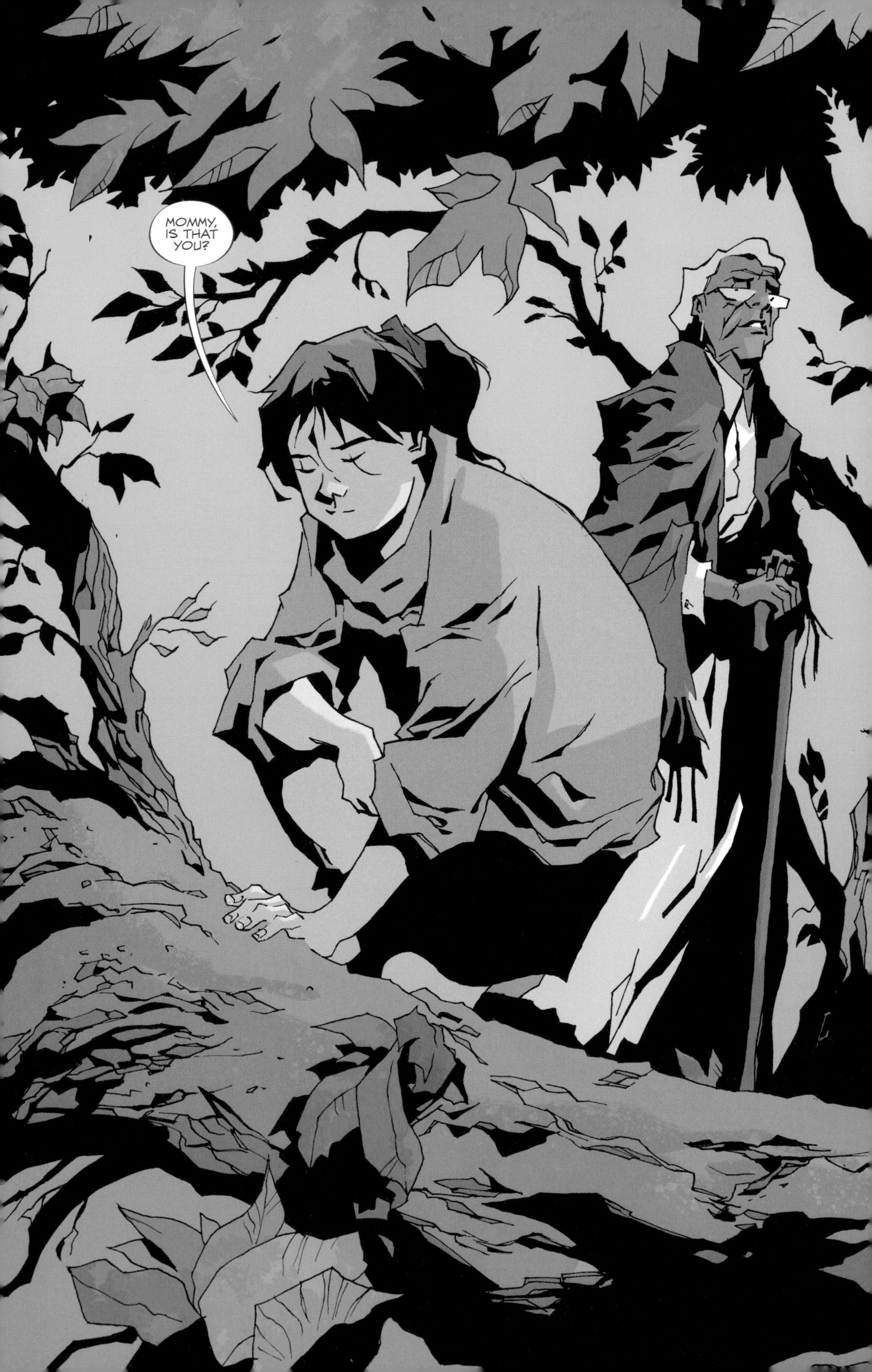
MOMMY, IS THAT YOU?

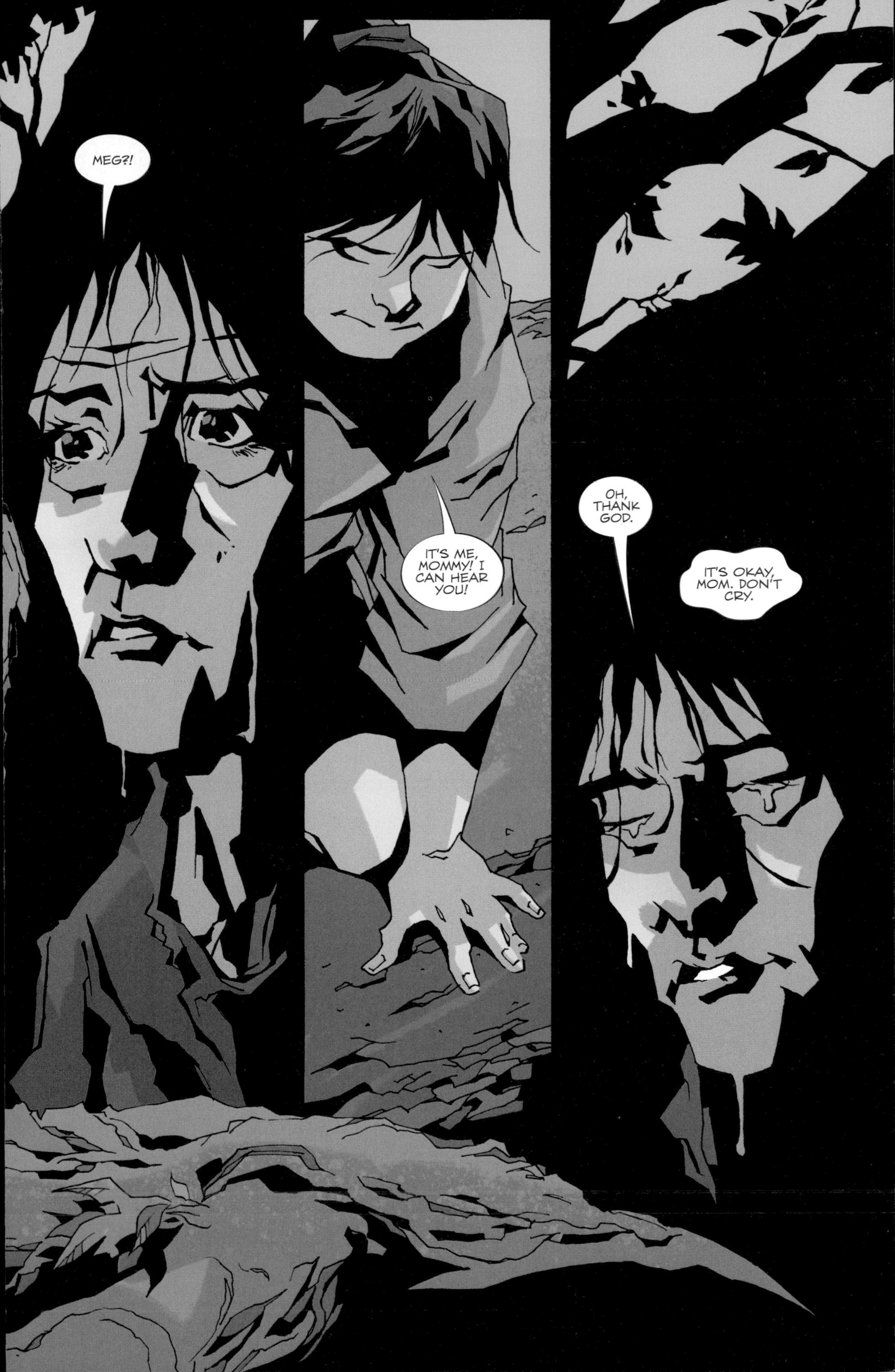
MEG?!
IT'S ME, MOMMY! I CAN HEAR YOU!
OH, THANK GOD.
IT'S OKAY, MOM. DON'T CRY.

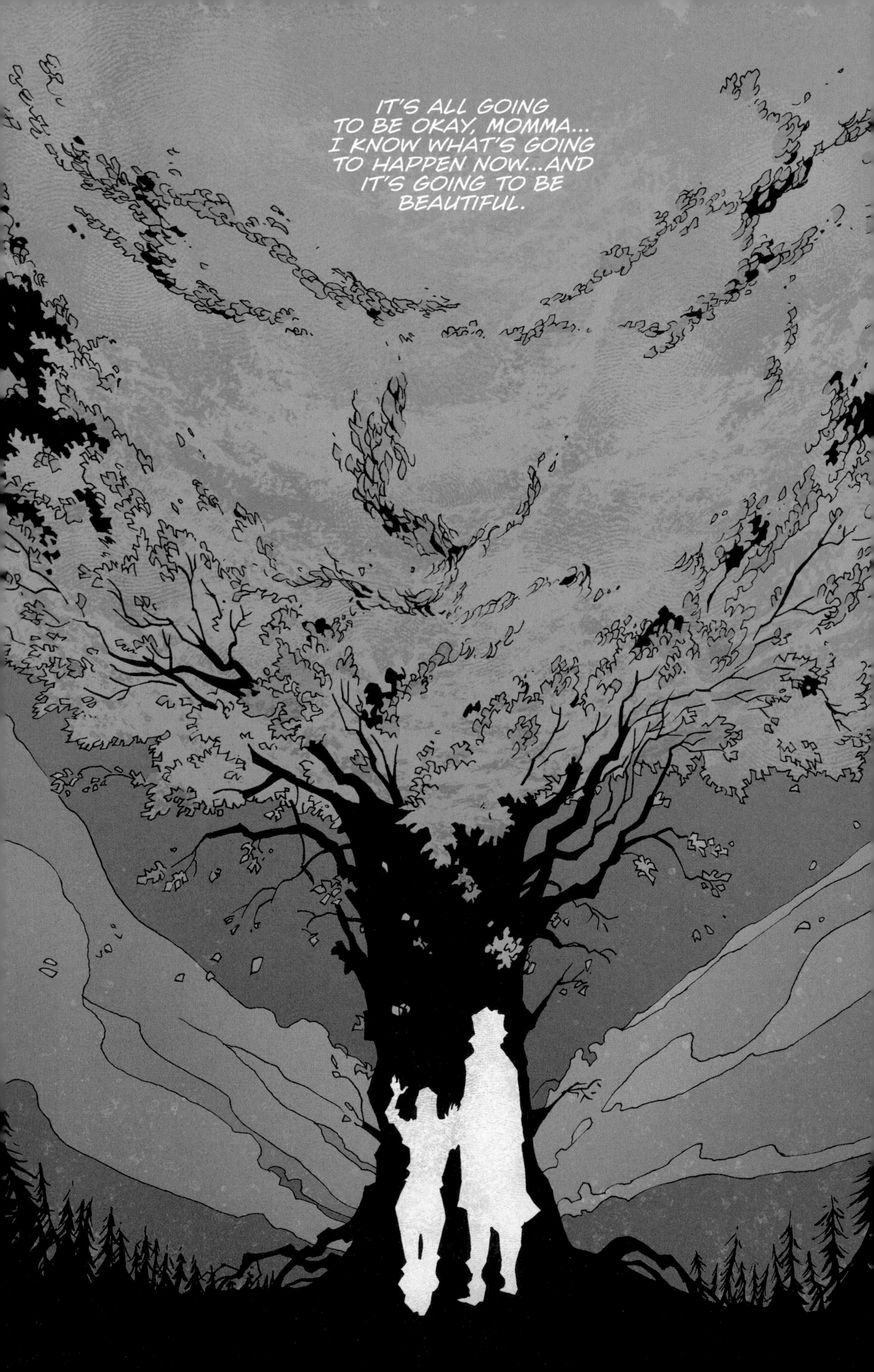
IT'S ALL GOING TO BE OKAY, MOMMA... I KNOW WHAT'S GOING TO HAPPEN NOW...AND IT'S GOING TO BE BEAUTIFUL.

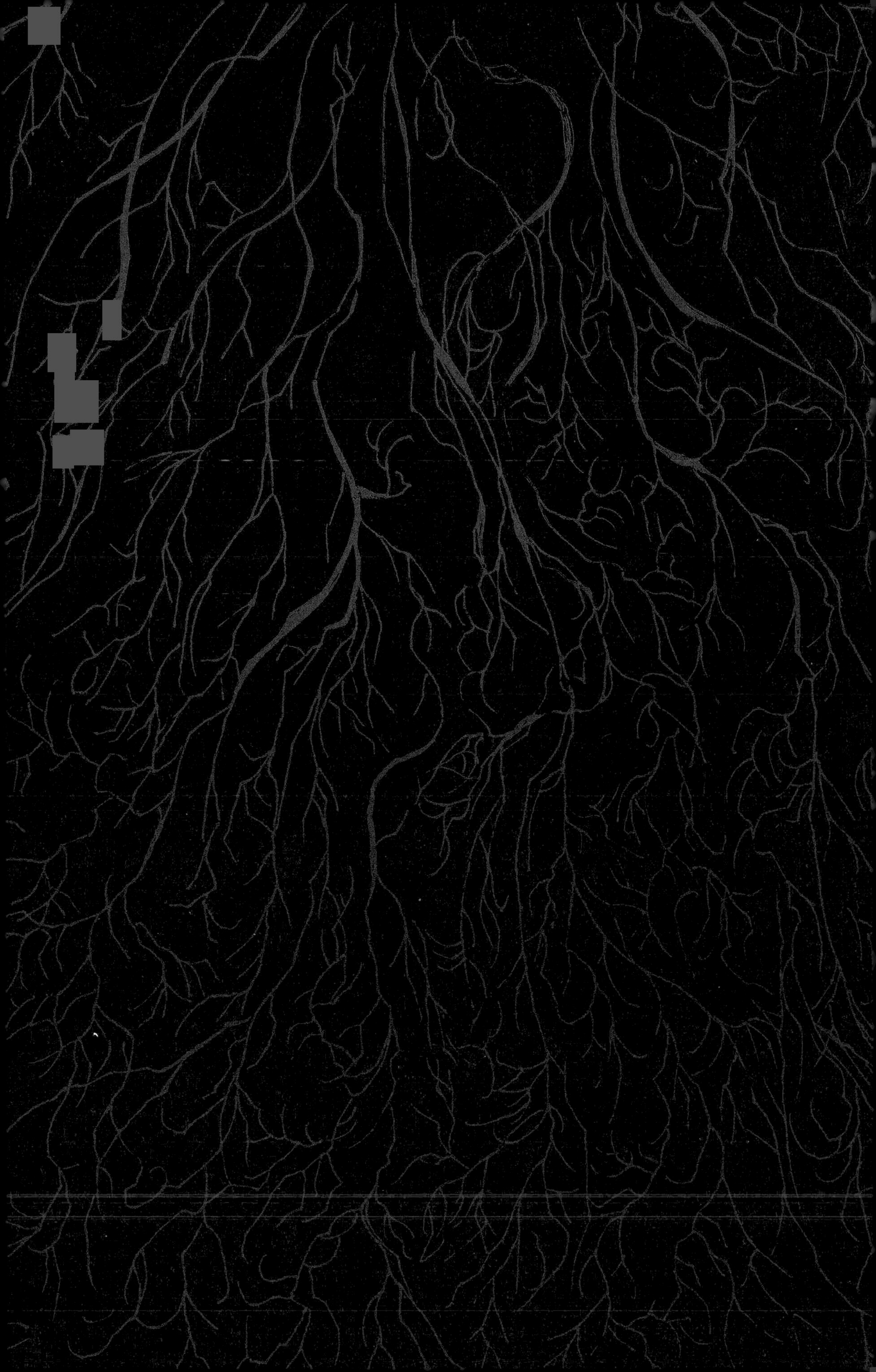

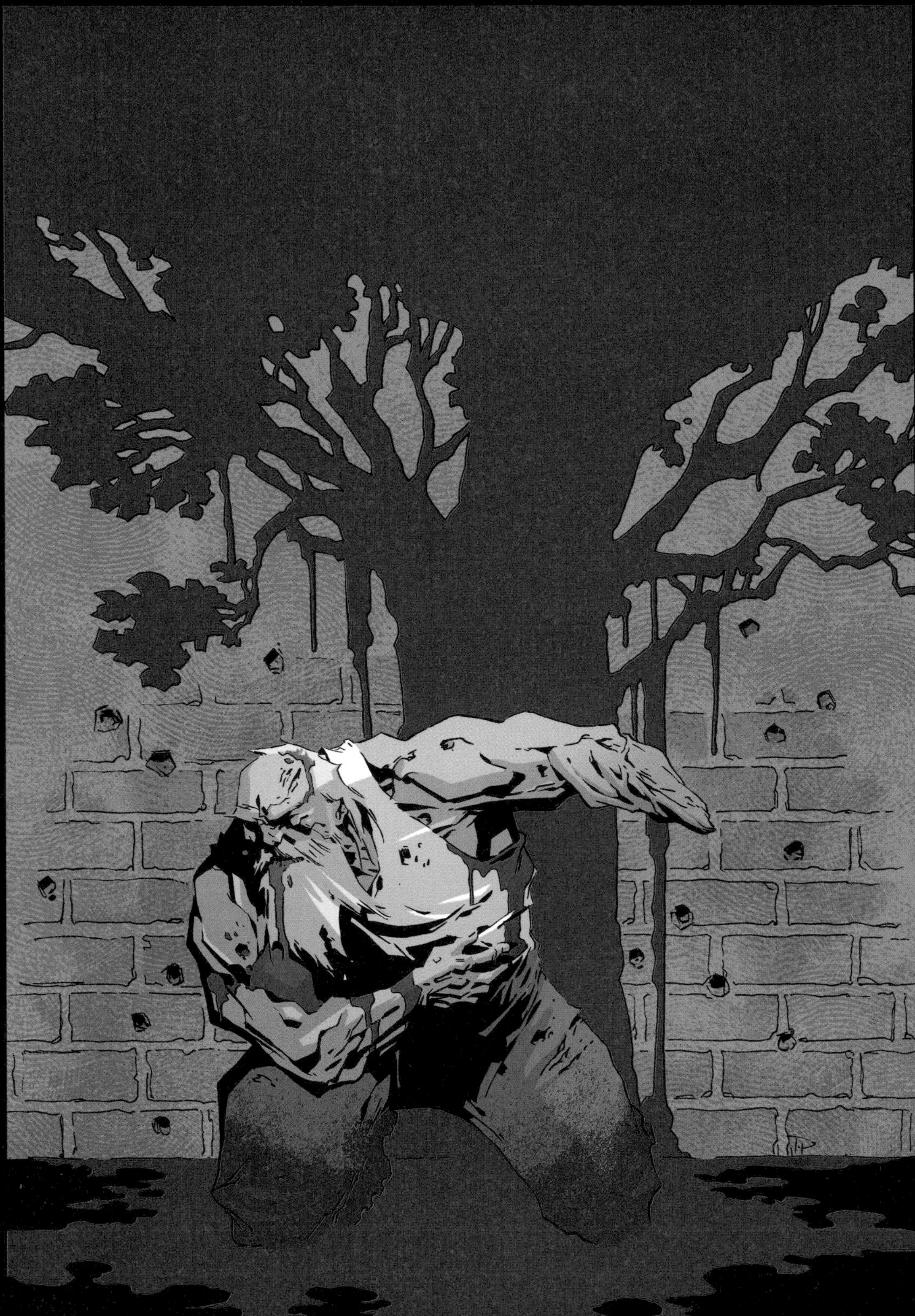

CHAPTER
EIGHT

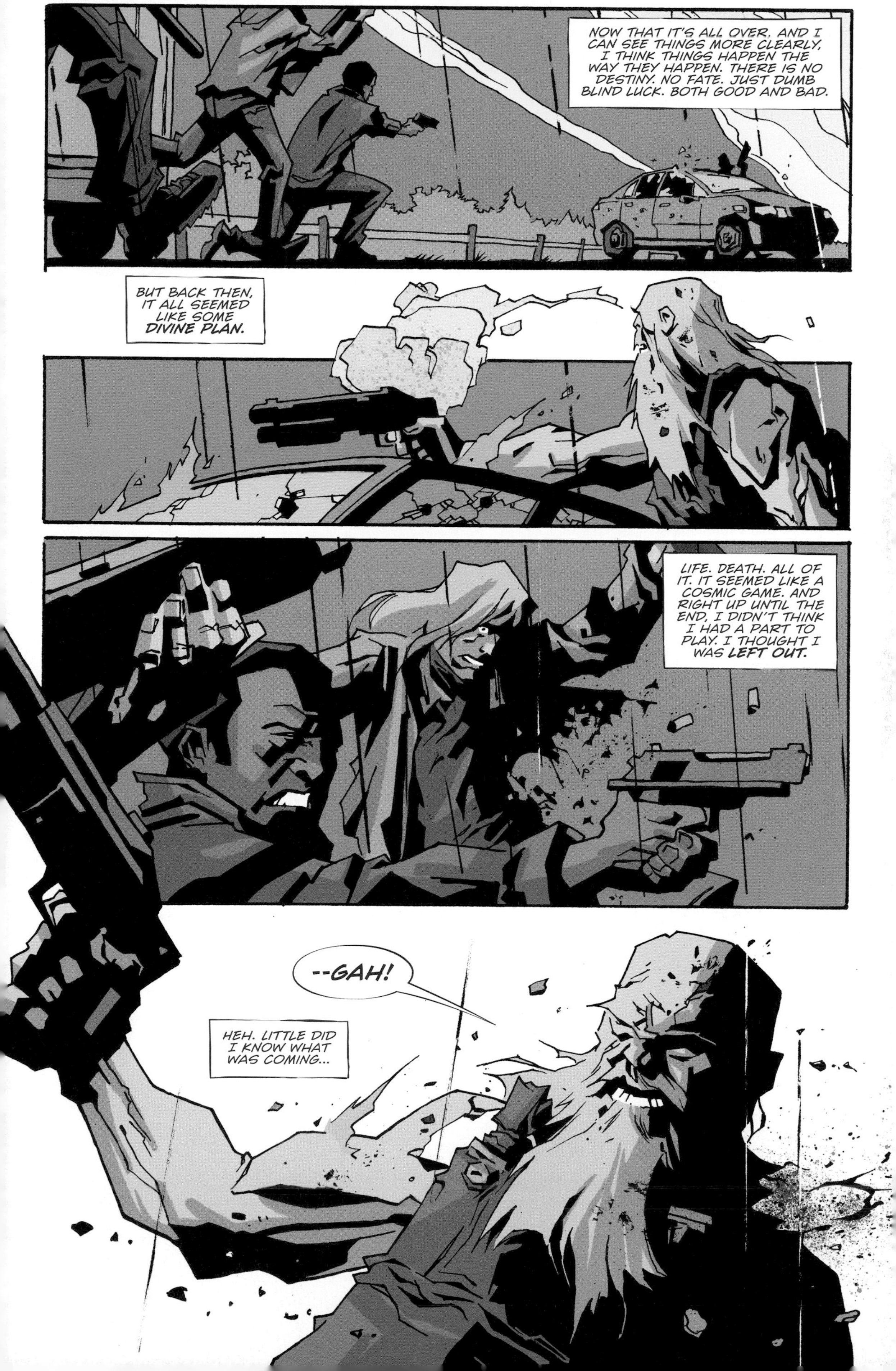
NOW THAT IT'S ALL OVER. AND I CAN SEE THINGS MORE CLEARLY, I THINK THINGS HAPPEN THE WAY THEY HAPPEN. THERE IS NO DESTINY. NO FATE. JUST DUMB BLIND LUCK. BOTH GOOD AND BAD.
BUT BACK THEN, IT ALL SEEMED LIKE SOME DIVINE PLAN.
LIFE. DEATH. ALL OF IT. IT SEEMED LIKE A COSMIC GAME. AND RIGHT UP UNTIL THE END, I DIDN'T THINK I HAD A PART TO PLAY. I THOUGHT I WAS LEFT OUT.
--GAH!
HEH. LITTLE DID I KNOW WHAT WAS COMING...

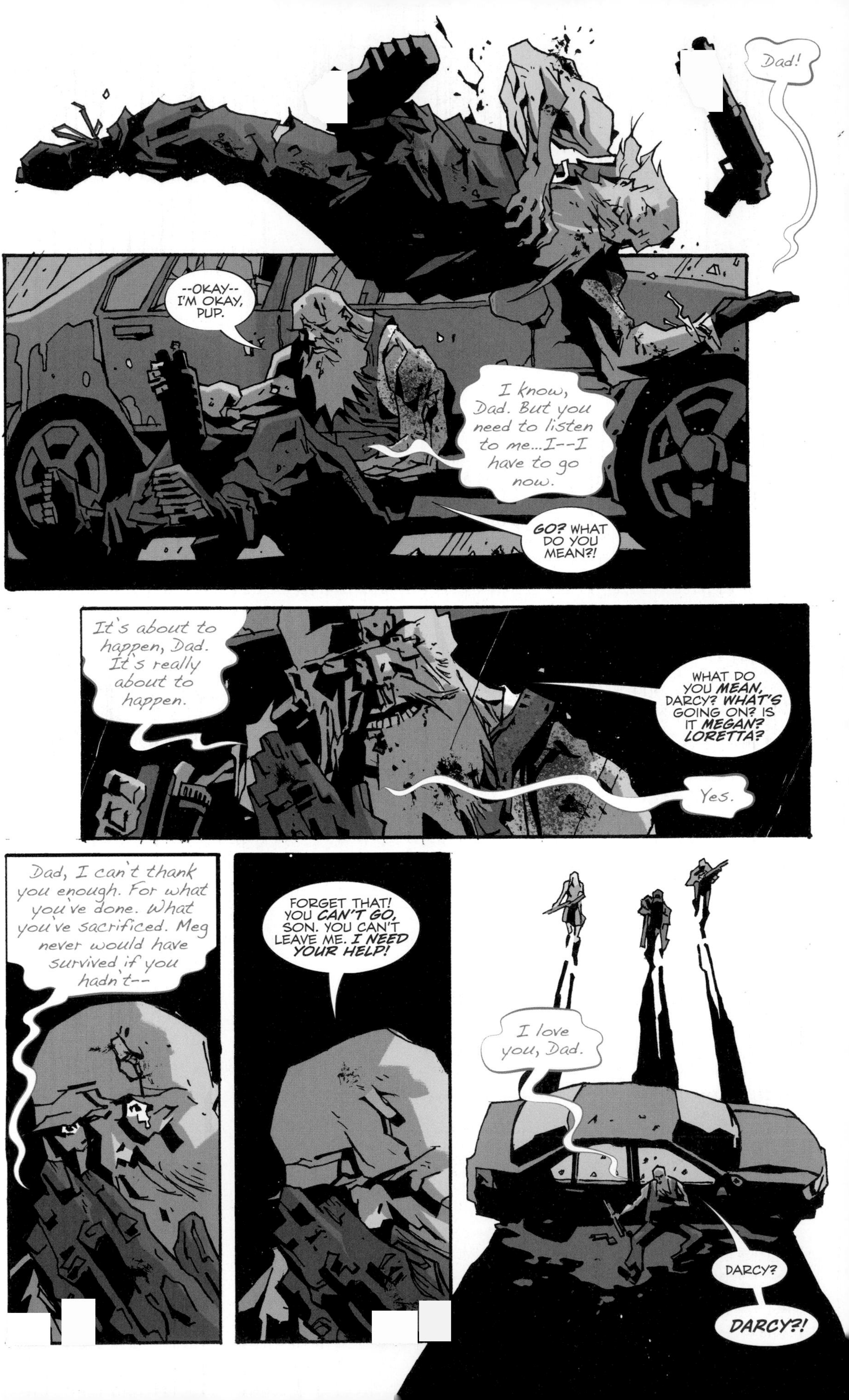
Dad!
--OKAY-- I'M OKAY, PUP.
I know, Dad. But you need to listen to me...I--I have to go now.
GO? WHAT DO YOU MEAN?!
It's about to happen, Dad. It's really about to happen.
WHAT DO YOU MEAN, DARCY? WHAT'S GOING ON? IS IT MEGAN? LORETTA?
Yes.
Dad, I can't thank you enough. For what you've done. What you've sacrificed. Meg never would have survived if you hadn't--
FORGET THAT! YOU CAN'T GO, SON. YOU CAN'T LEAVE ME. I NEED YOUR HELP!
I love you, Dad.
DARCY?
DARCY?!

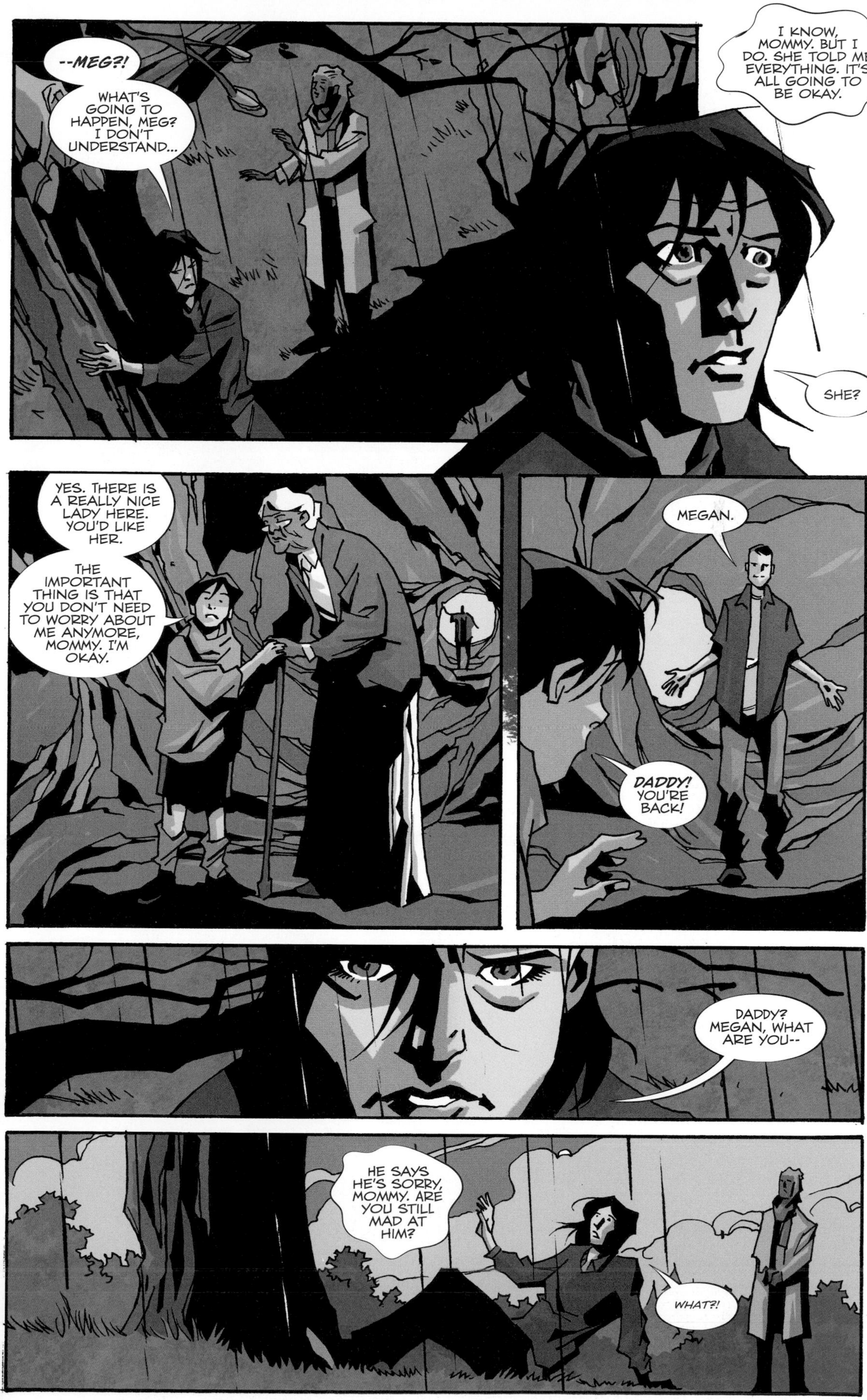
--MEG?!
WHAT'S GOING TO HAPPEN, MEG? I DON'T UNDERSTAND...
I KNOW, MOMMY. BUT I DO. SHE TOLD ME EVERYTHING. IT'S ALL GOING TO BE OKAY.
SHE?
YES. THERE IS A REALLY NICE LADY HERE. YOU'D LIKE HER.
THE IMPORTANT THING IS THAT YOU DON'T NEED TO WORRY ABOUT ME ANYMORE, MOMMY. I'M OKAY.
MEGAN.
DADDY! YOU'RE BACK!
DADDY? MEGAN, WHAT ARE YOU--
HE SAYS HE'S SORRY, MOMMY. ARE YOU STILL MAD AT HIM?
WHAT?!

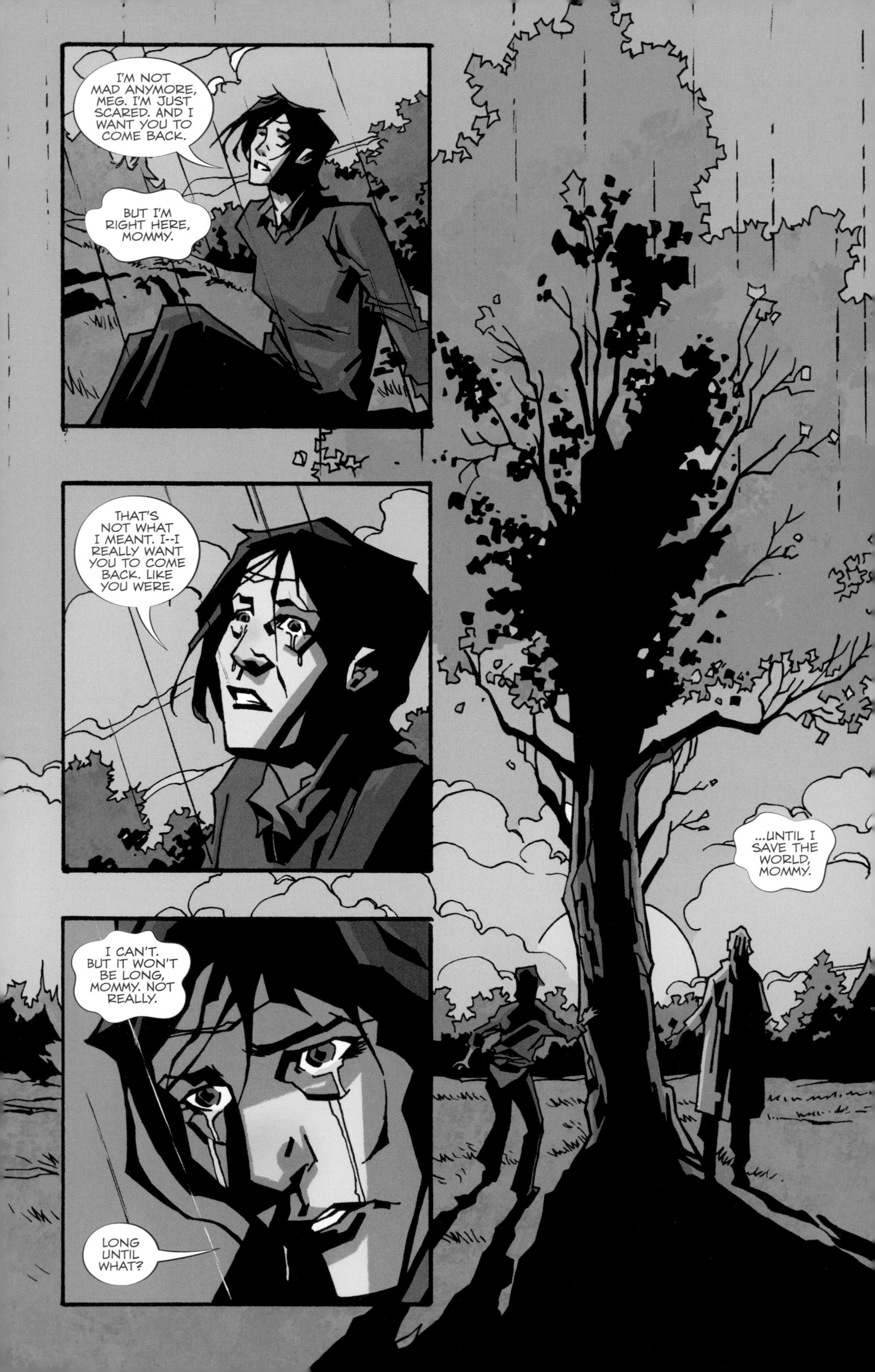
I'M NOT MAD ANYMORE, MEG. I'M JUST SCARED. AND I WANT YOU TO COME BACK.
BUT I'M RIGHT HERE, MOMMY.
THAT'S NOT WHAT I MEANT. I--I REALLY WANT YOU TO COME BACK. LIKE YOU WERE.
I CAN'T. BUT IT WON'T BE LONG, MOMMY. NOT REALLY.
LONG UNTIL WHAT?
...UNTIL I SAVE THE WORLD, MOMMY.

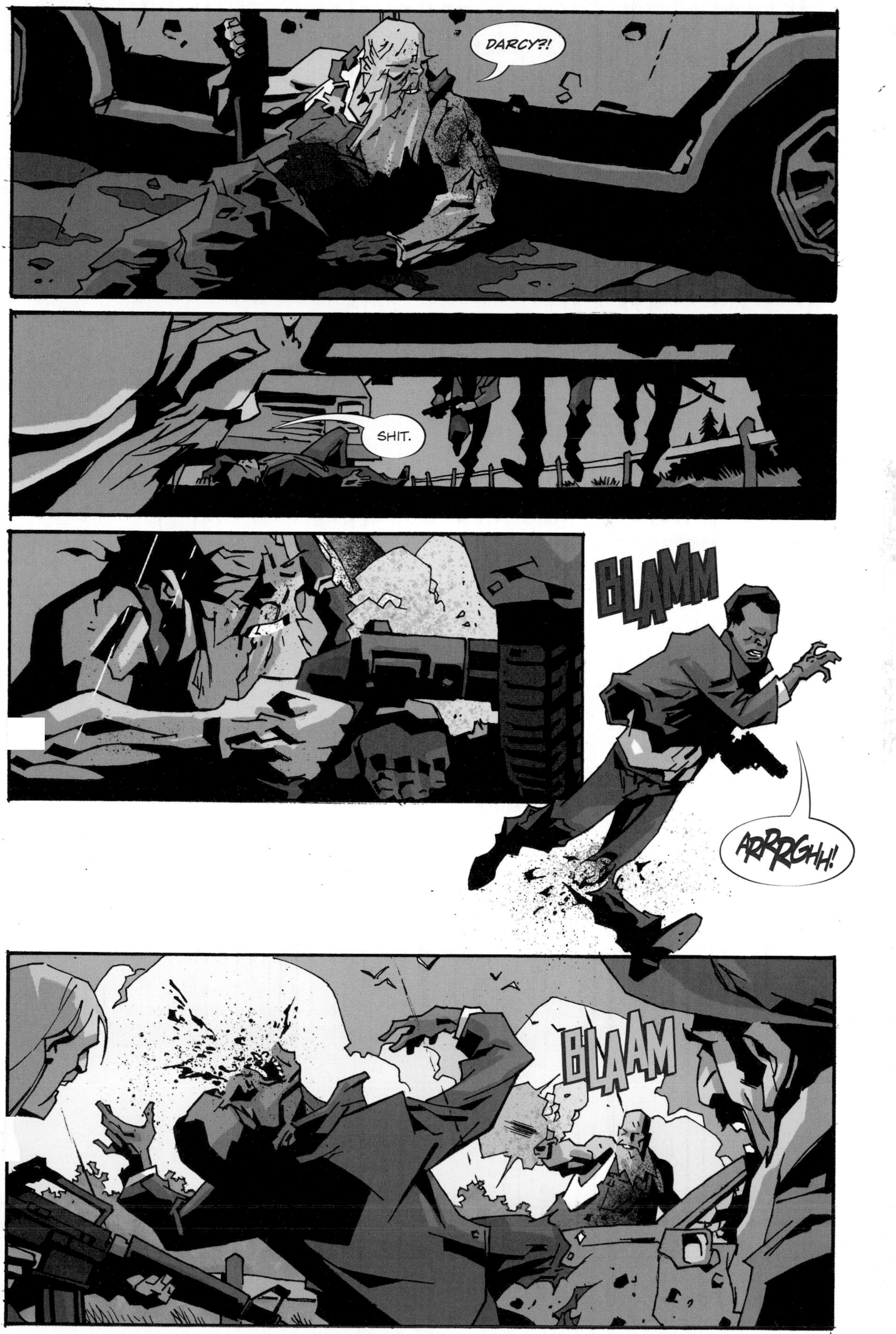
DARCY?!
SHIT.
BLAMM
ARRRGHH!
BLAAM

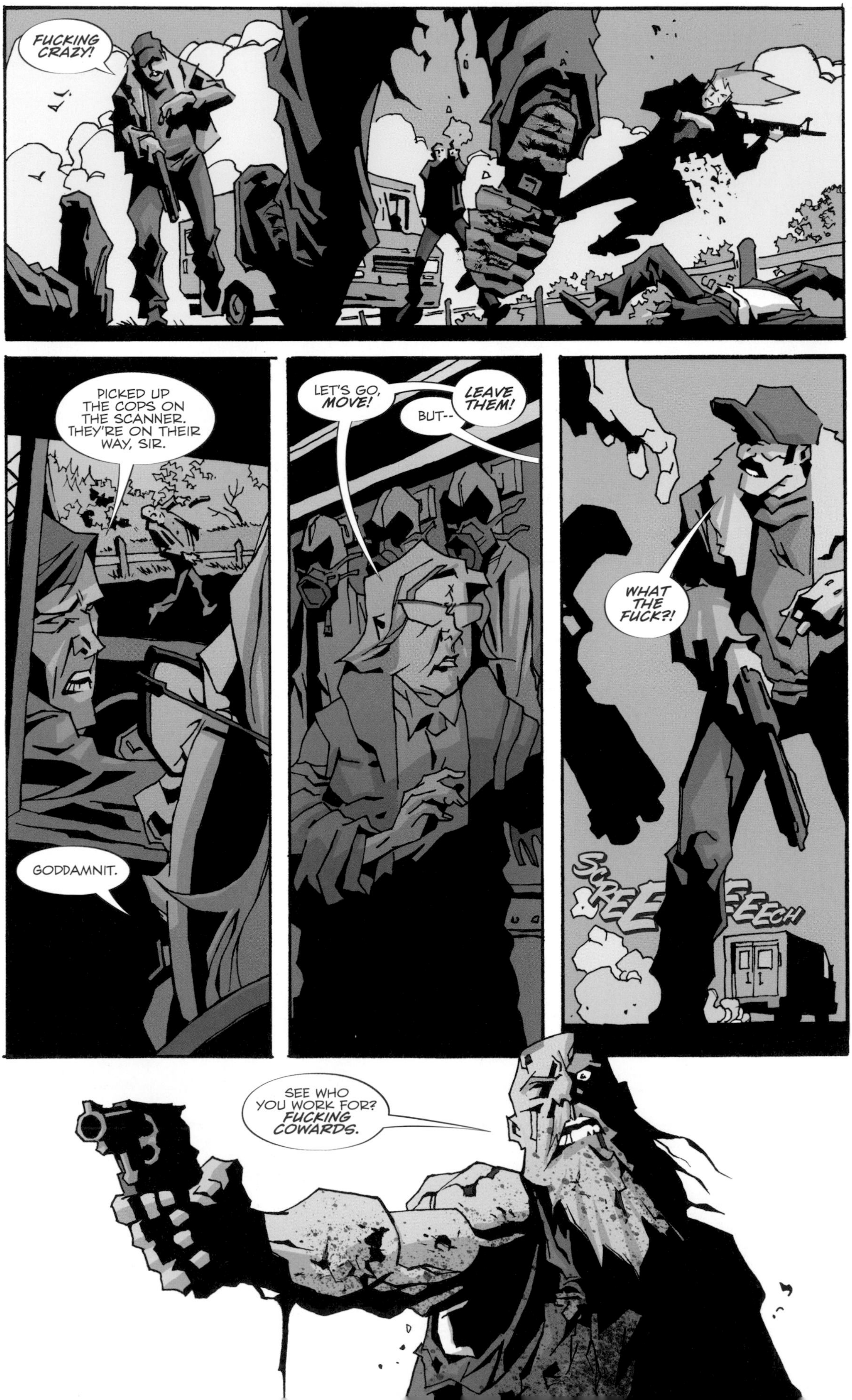
FUCKING CRAZY!
PICKED UP THE COPS ON THE SCANNER. THEY'RE ON THEIR WAY, SIR.
GODDAMNIT.
LET'S GO, MOVE!
BUT--
LEAVE THEM!
WHAT THE FUCK?!
SCREEEEEEECH
SEE WHO YOU WORK FOR? FUCKING COWARDS.

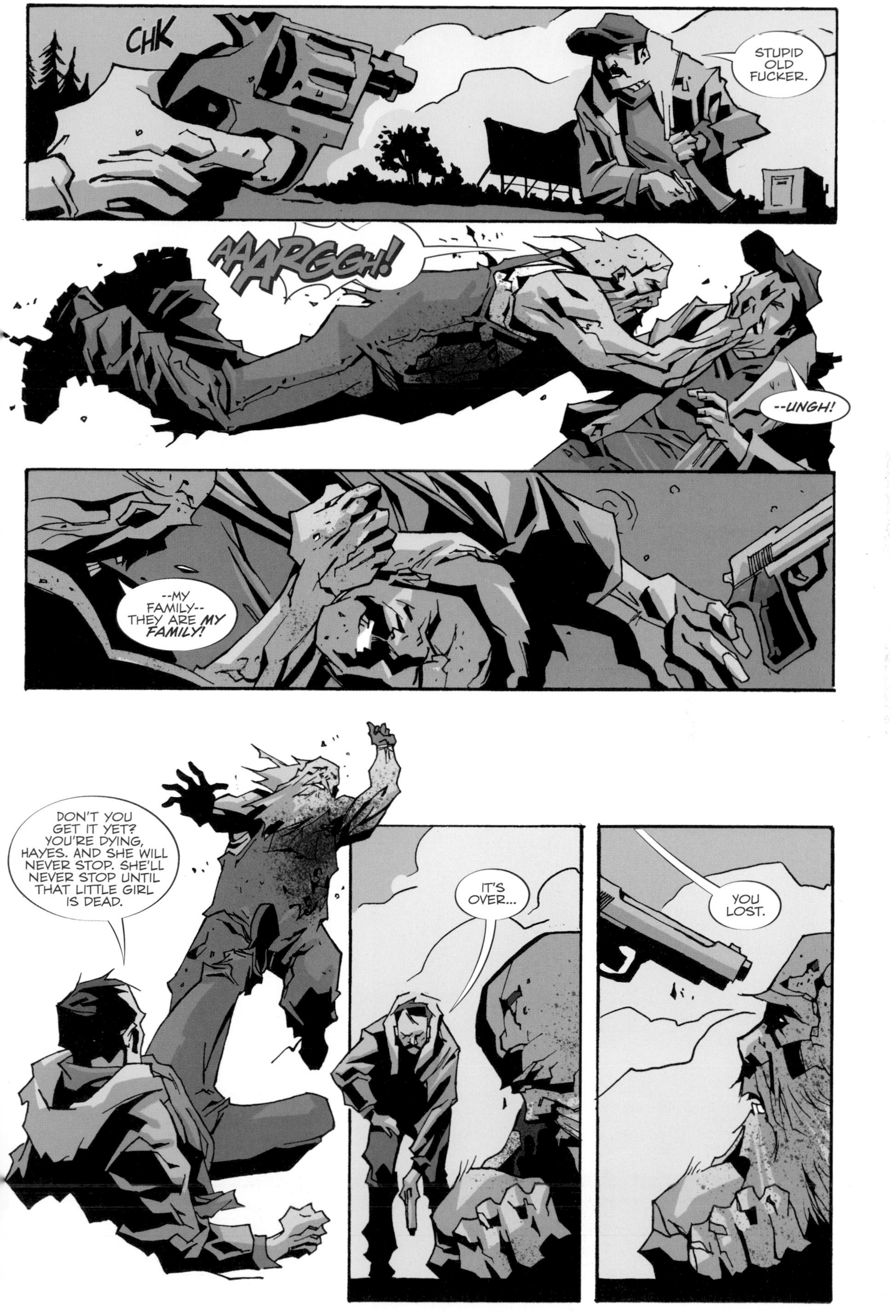
CHK
STUPID OLD FUCKER.
AAARGGH!
--UNGH!
--MY FAMILY-- THEY ARE *MY FAMILY!*
DON'T YOU GET IT YET? YOU'RE DYING, HAYES. AND SHE WILL NEVER STOP. SHE'LL NEVER STOP UNTIL THAT LITTLE GIRL IS DEAD.
IT'S OVER...
YOU LOST.

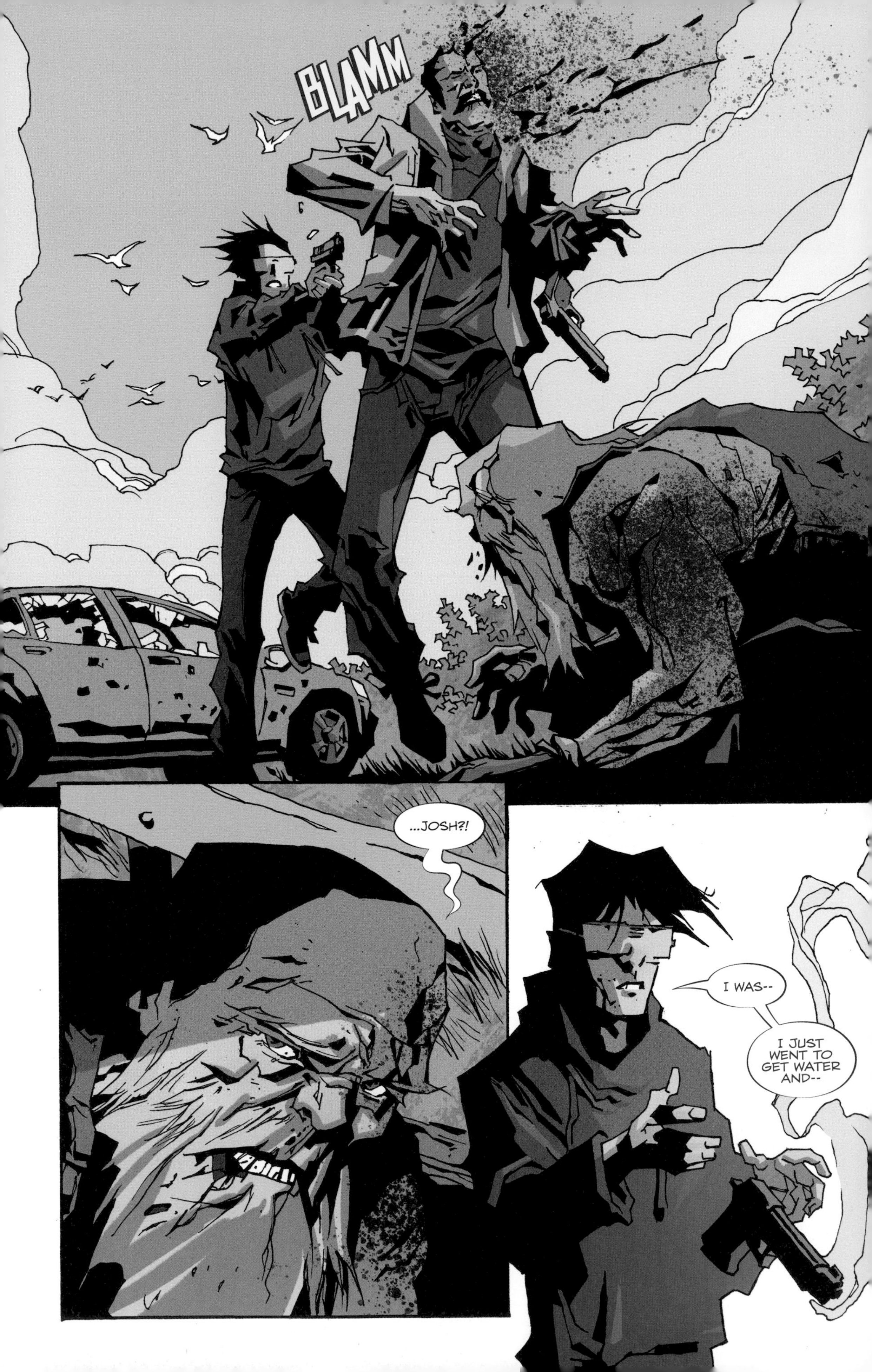
BLAMM
...JOSH?!
I WAS--
I JUST WENT TO GET WATER AND--

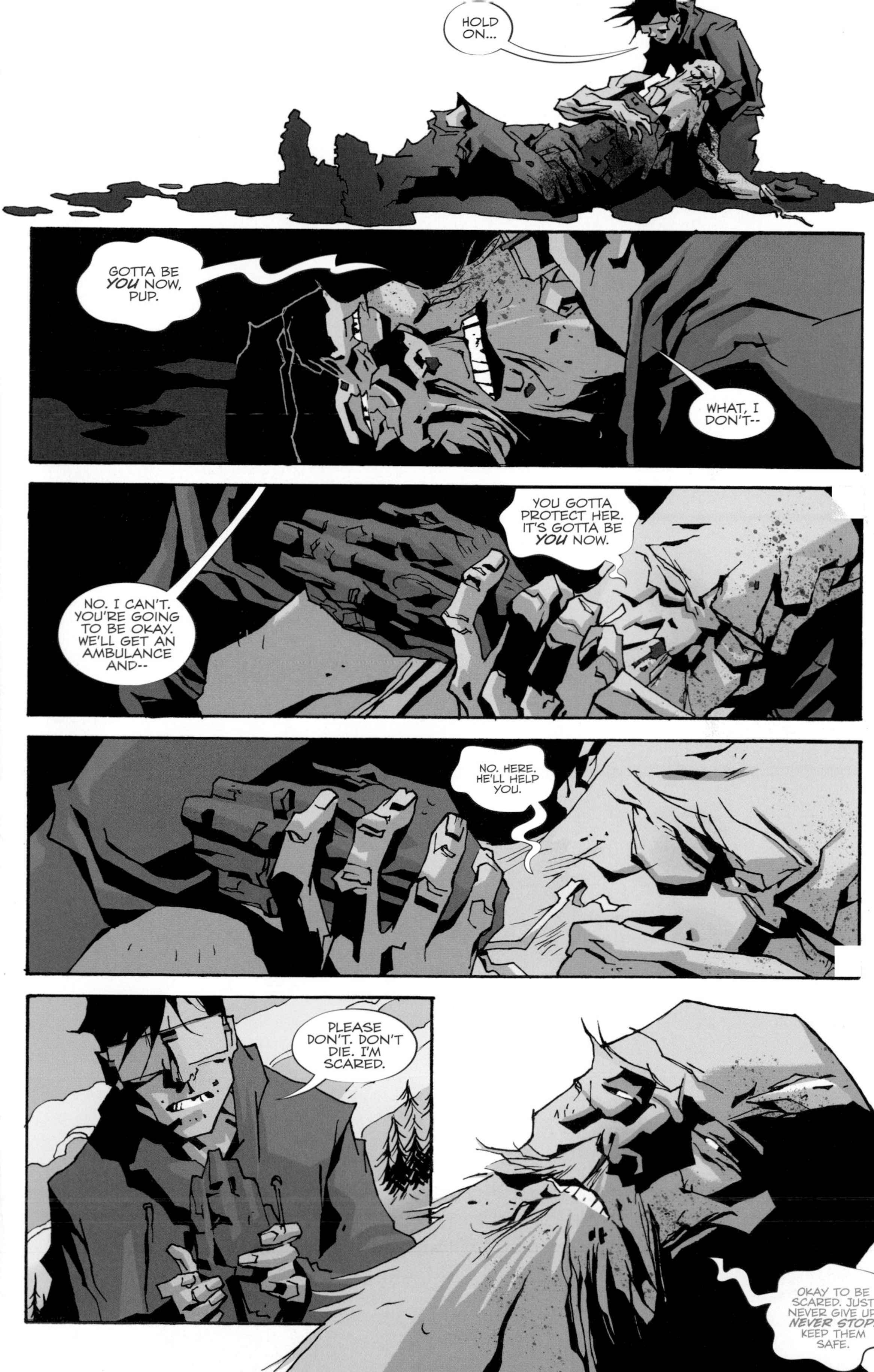
HOLD ON...
GOTTA BE *YOU* NOW, PUP.
WHAT, I DON'T--
NO. I CAN'T. YOU'RE GOING TO BE OKAY. WE'LL GET AN AMBULANCE AND--
YOU GOTTA PROTECT HER. IT'S GOTTA BE *YOU* NOW.
NO. HERE. HE'LL HELP YOU.
PLEASE DON'T. DON'T DIE. I'M SCARED.
OKAY TO BE SCARED. JUST NEVER GIVE UP. *NEVER STOP.* KEEP THEM SAFE.

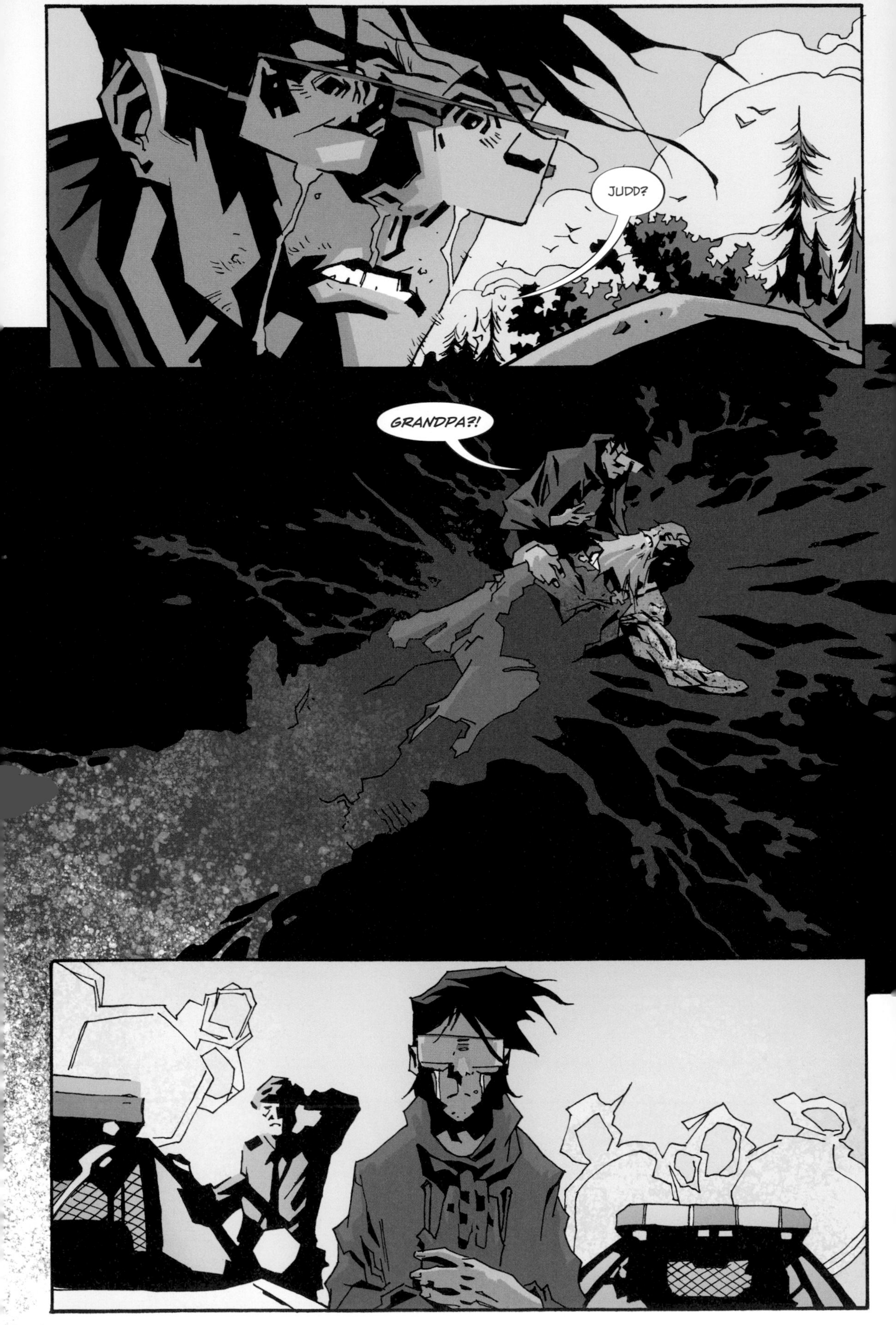
JUDD?
GRANDPA?!

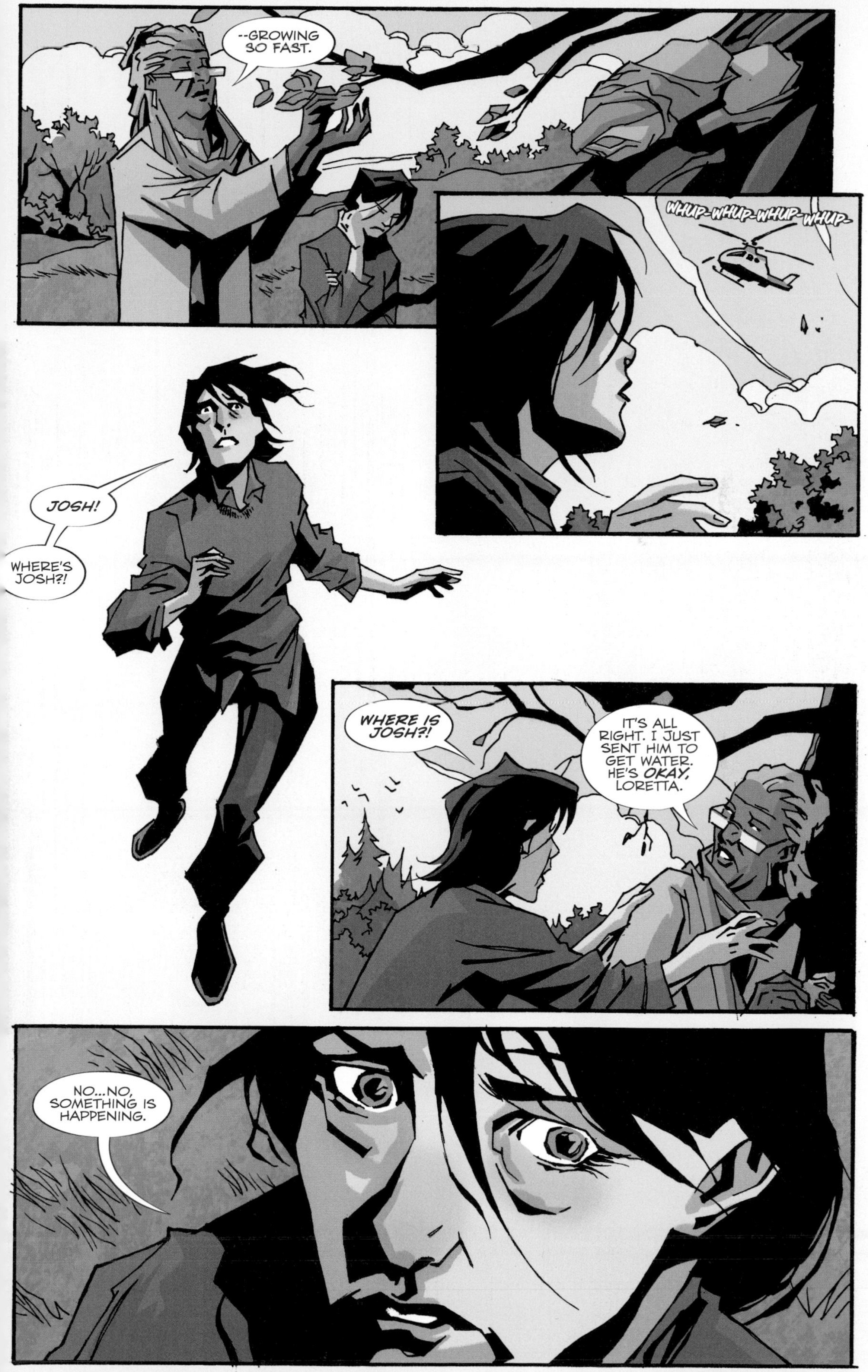
--GROWING SO FAST.
WHUP-WHUP-WHUP-WHUP-
JOSH!
WHERE'S JOSH?!
WHERE IS JOSH?!
IT'S ALL RIGHT. I JUST SENT HIM TO GET WATER. HE'S OKAY, LORETTA.
NO...NO, SOMETHING IS HAPPENING.

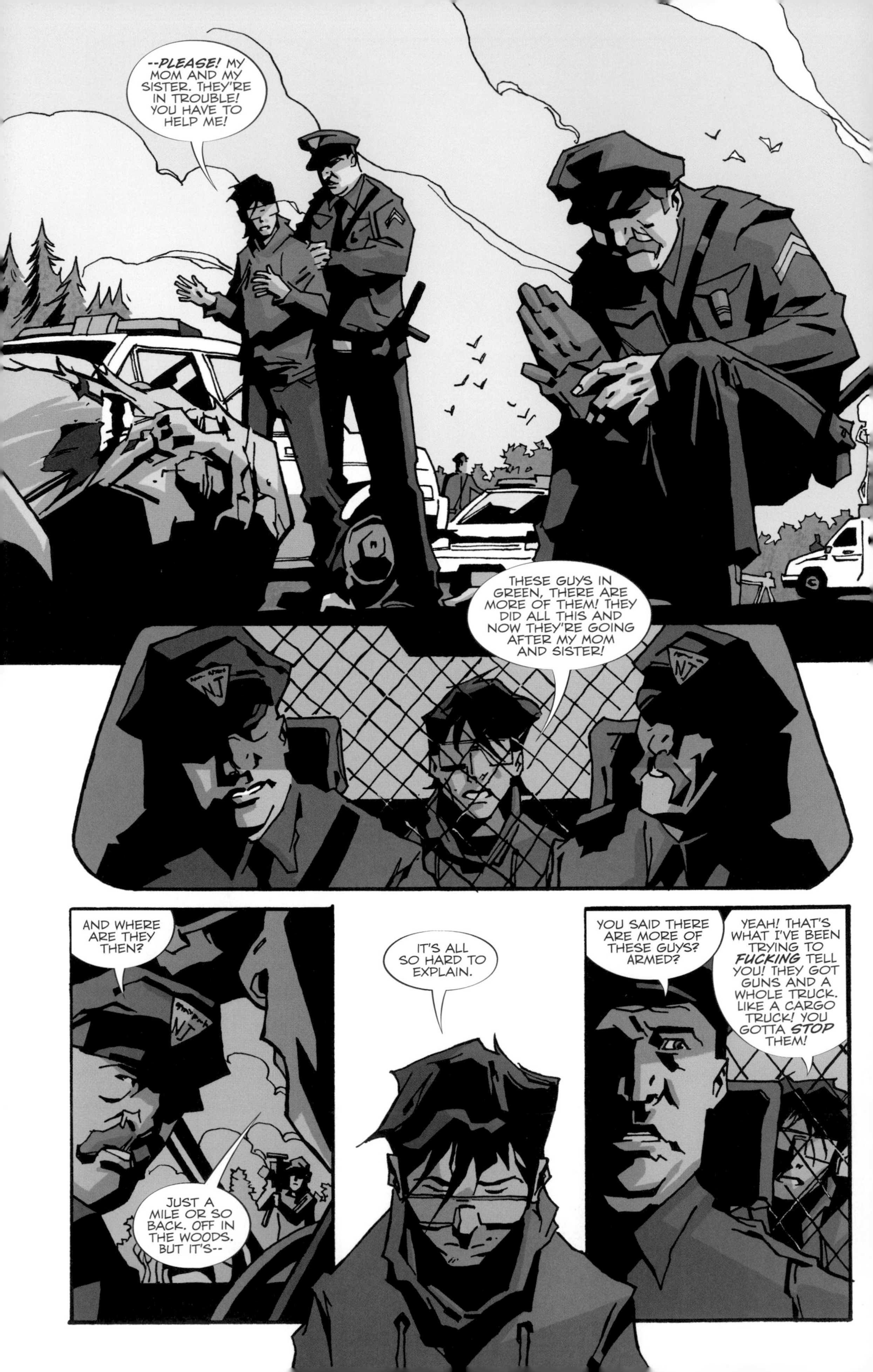
--PLEASE! MY MOM AND MY SISTER. THEY'RE IN TROUBLE! YOU HAVE TO HELP ME!
THESE GUYS IN GREEN, THERE ARE MORE OF THEM! THEY DID ALL THIS AND NOW THEY'RE GOING AFTER MY MOM AND SISTER!
AND WHERE ARE THEY THEN?
JUST A MILE OR SO BACK. OFF IN THE WOODS. BUT IT'S--
IT'S ALL SO HARD TO EXPLAIN.
YOU SAID THERE ARE MORE OF THESE GUYS? ARMED?
YEAH! THAT'S WHAT I'VE BEEN TRYING TO FUCKING TELL YOU! THEY GOT GUNS AND A WHOLE TRUCK. LIKE A CARGO TRUCK! YOU GOTTA STOP THEM!

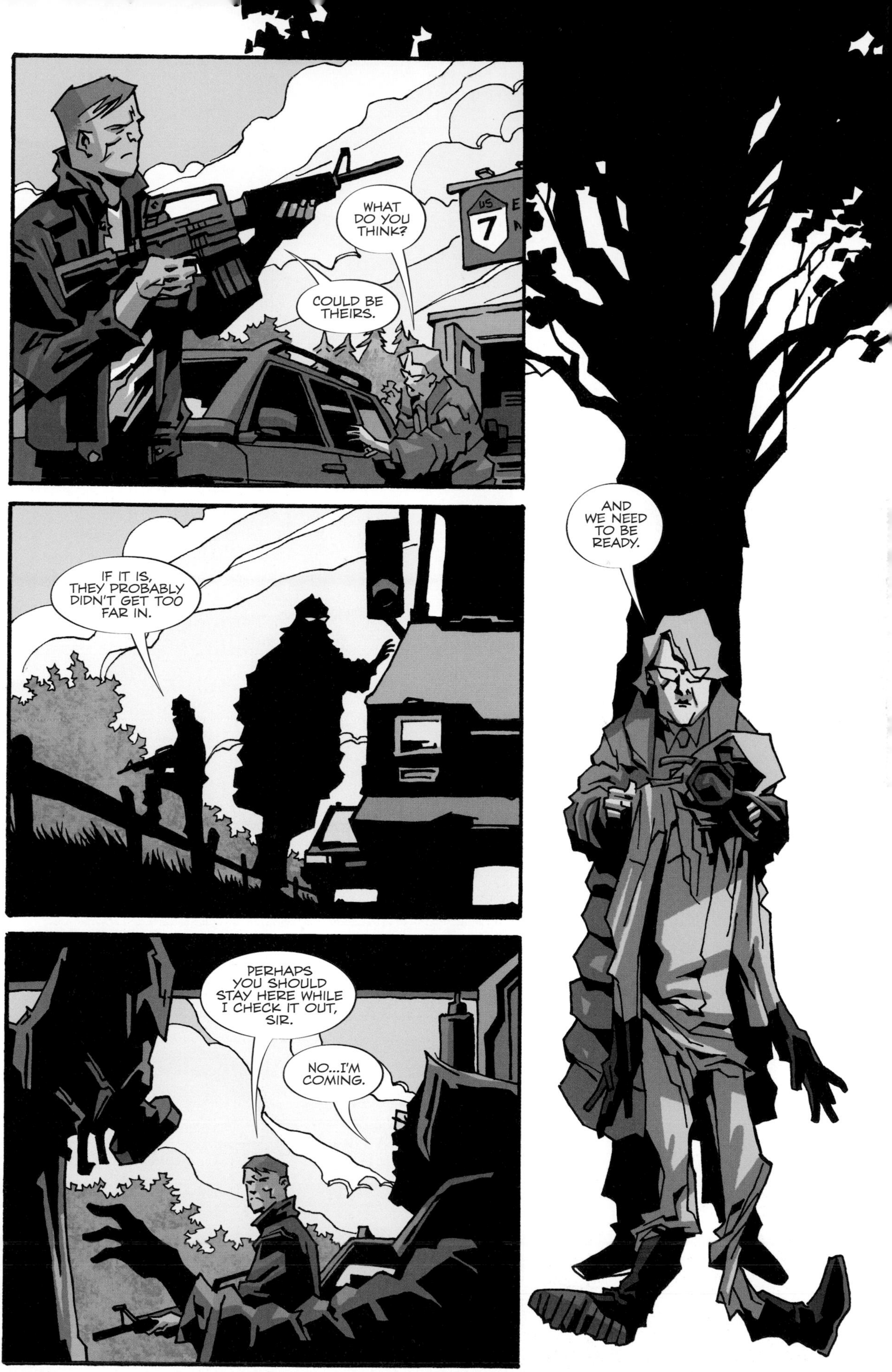
WHAT DO YOU THINK?
COULD BE THEIRS.
US
7
IF IT IS, THEY PROBABLY DIDN'T GET TOO FAR IN.
AND WE NEED TO BE READY.
PERHAPS YOU SHOULD STAY HERE WHILE I CHECK IT OUT, SIR.
NO...I'M COMING.

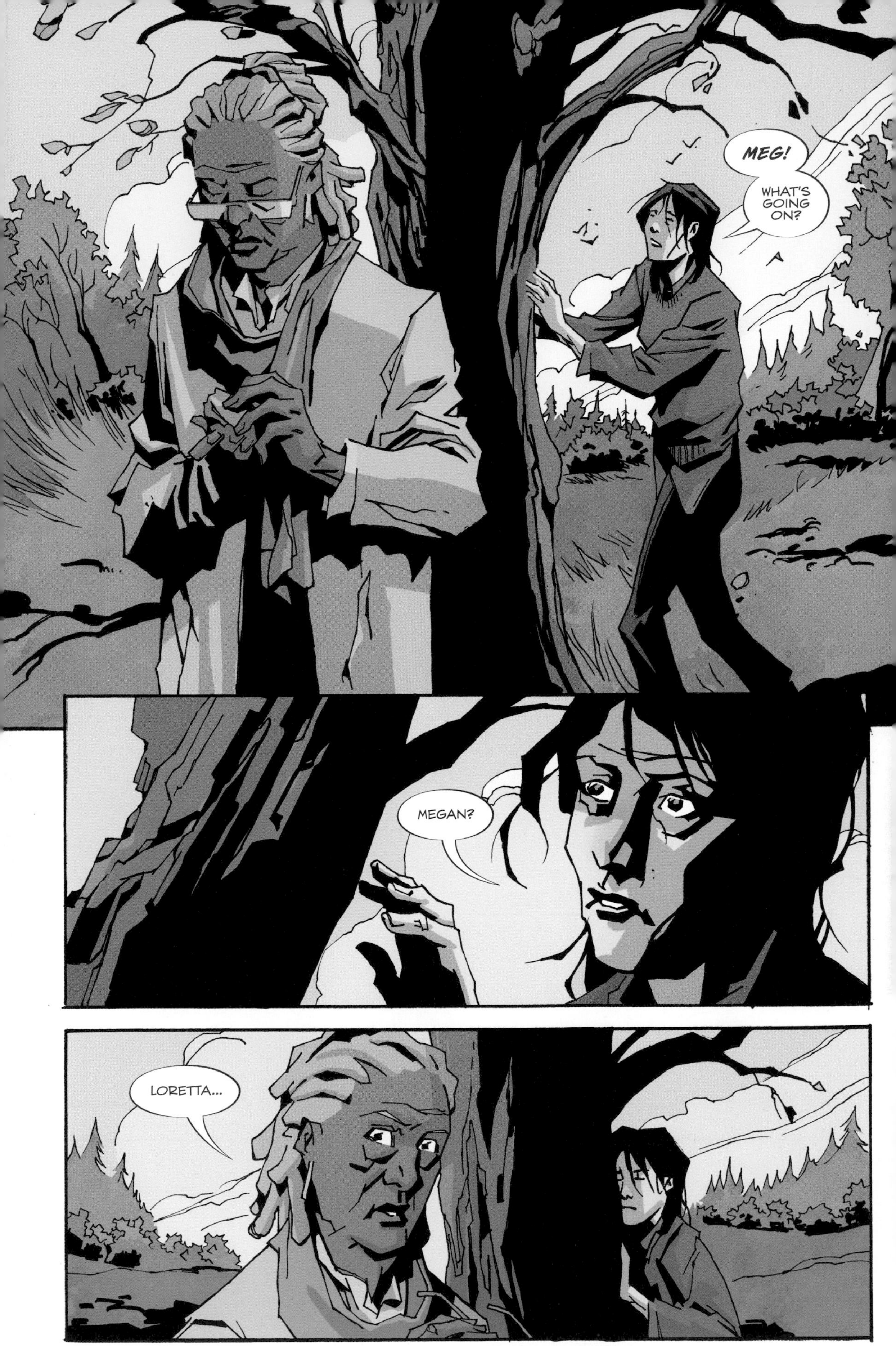
MEG!
WHAT'S GOING ON?
MEGAN?
LORETTA...

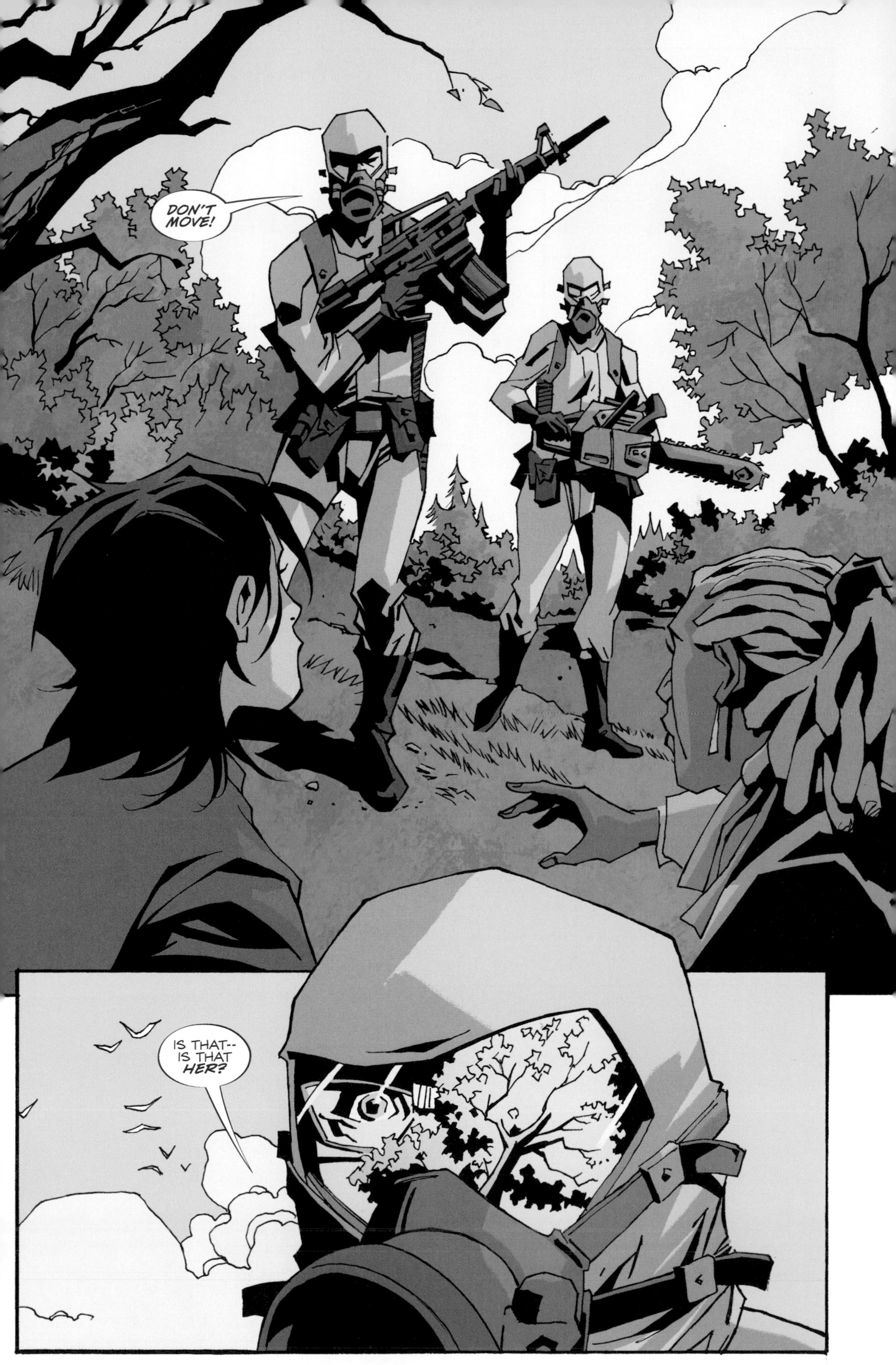
DON'T MOVE!
IS THAT-- IS THAT HER?

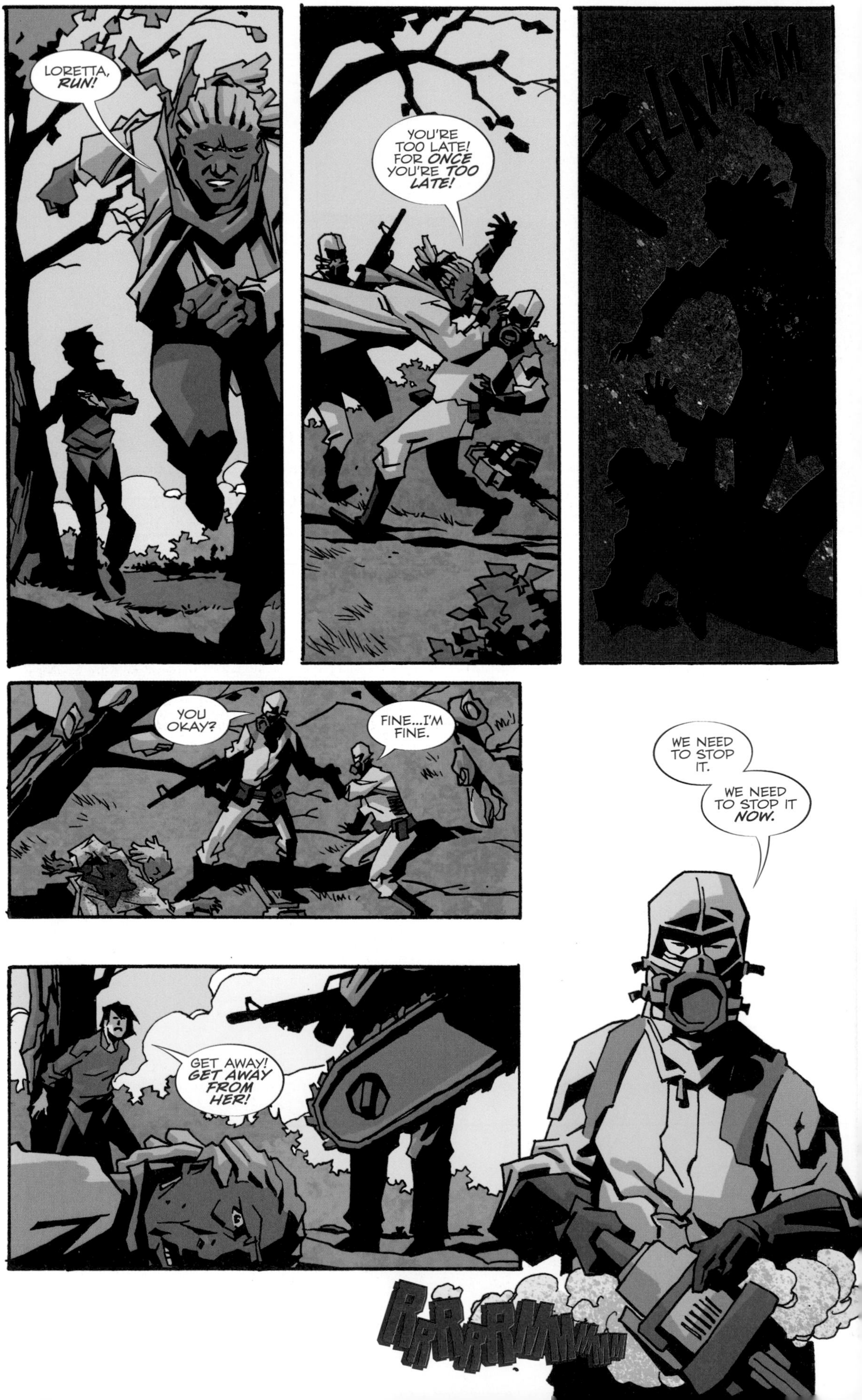

LORETTA, RUN!
YOU'RE TOO LATE! FOR ONCE YOU'RE TOO LATE!
BLAMMM
YOU OKAY?
FINE...I'M FINE.
WE NEED TO STOP IT.
WE NEED TO STOP IT NOW.
GET AWAY! GET AWAY FROM HER!
RRRRRMMMMM

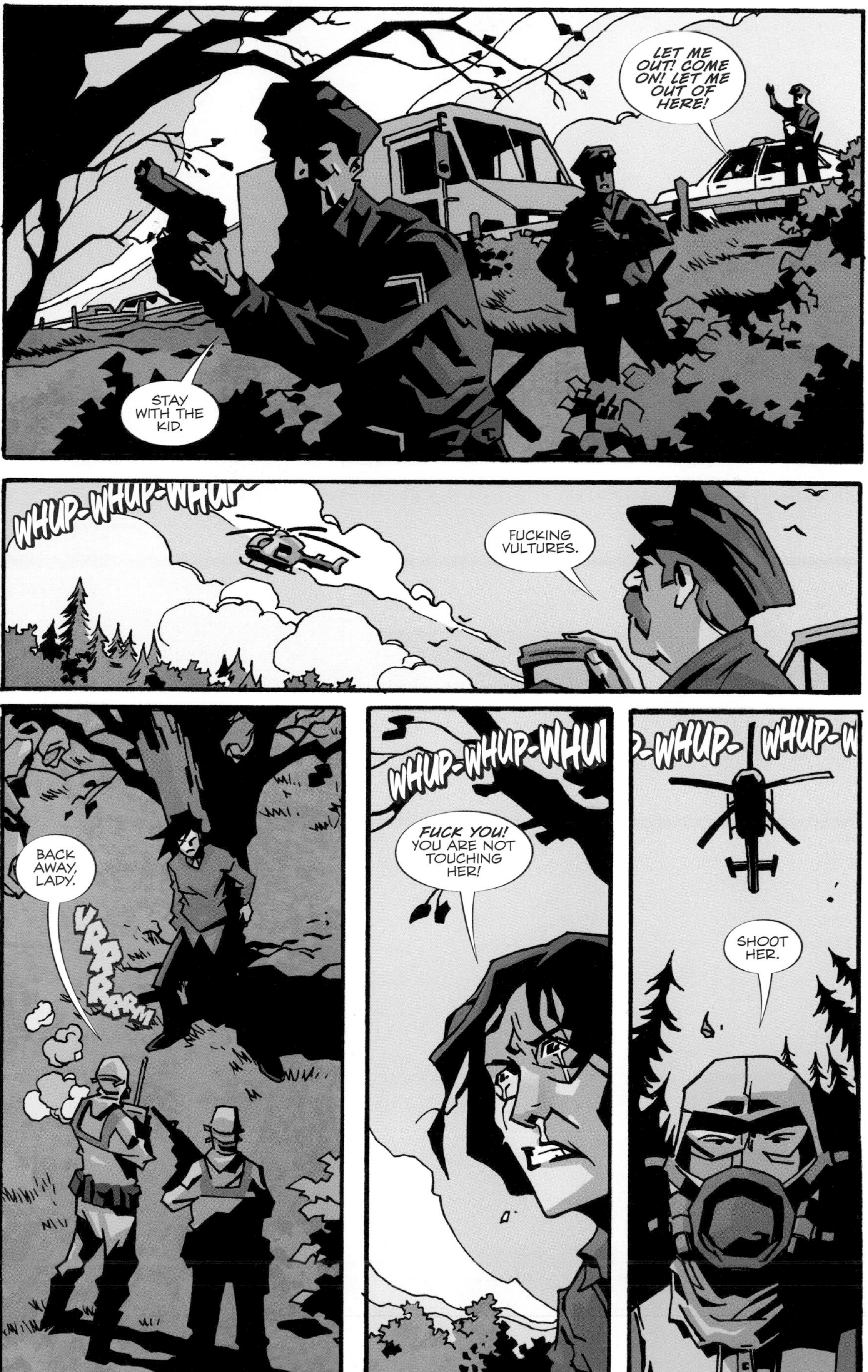
LET ME OUT! COME ON! LET ME OUT OF HERE!
STAY WITH THE KID.
WHUP-WHUP-WHUP
FUCKING VULTURES.
BACK AWAY, LADY.
VRRRRRRRM
WHUP-WHUP-WHU
FUCK YOU! YOU ARE NOT TOUCHING HER!
-WHUP- WHUP-W
SHOOT HER.

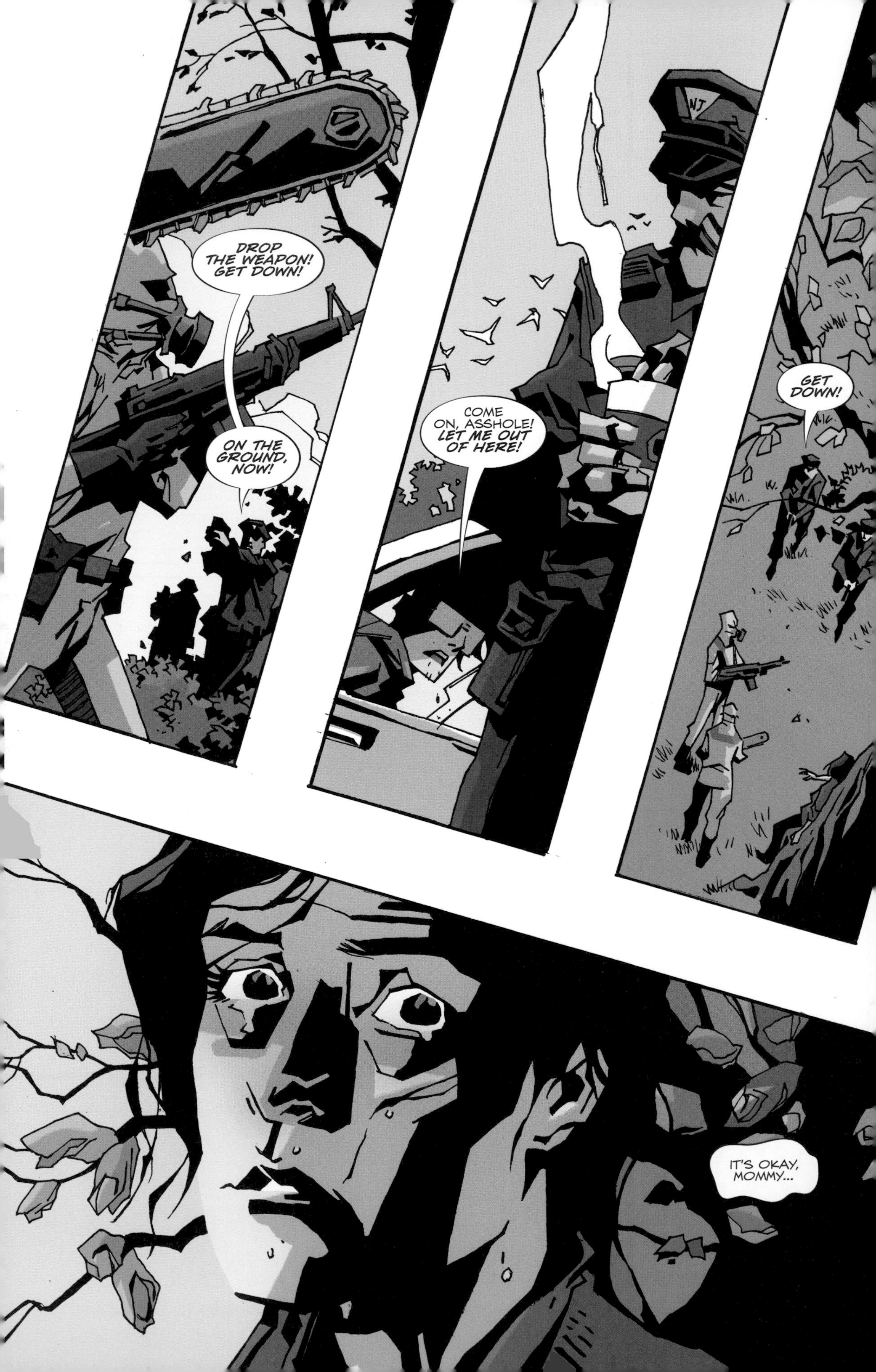
DROP THE WEAPON! GET DOWN!
ON THE GROUND, NOW!
COME ON, ASSHOLE! LET ME OUT OF HERE!
GET DOWN!
IT'S OKAY, MOMMY...

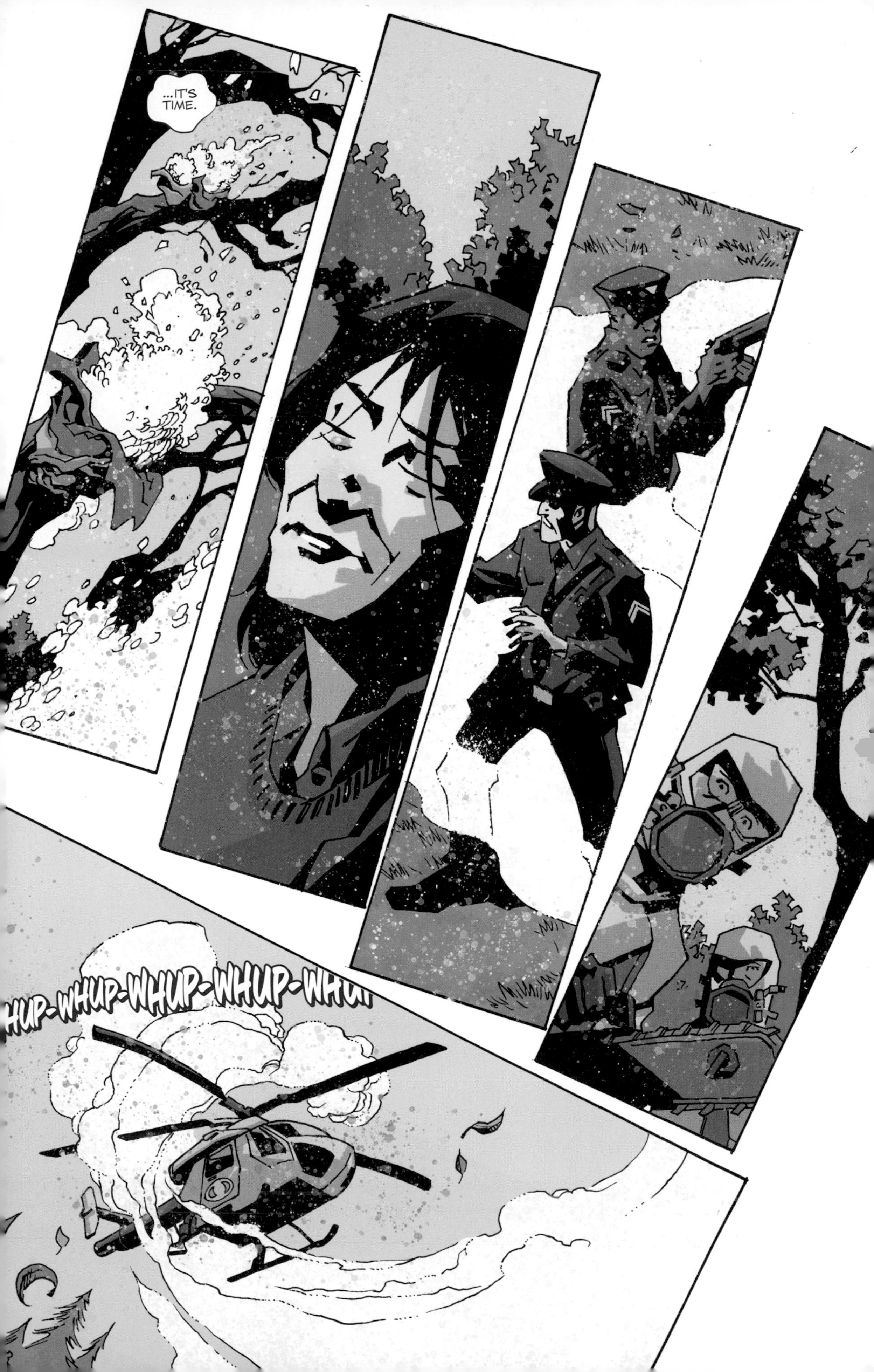
...IT'S TIME.
HUP-WHUP-WHUP-WHUP-WHUP

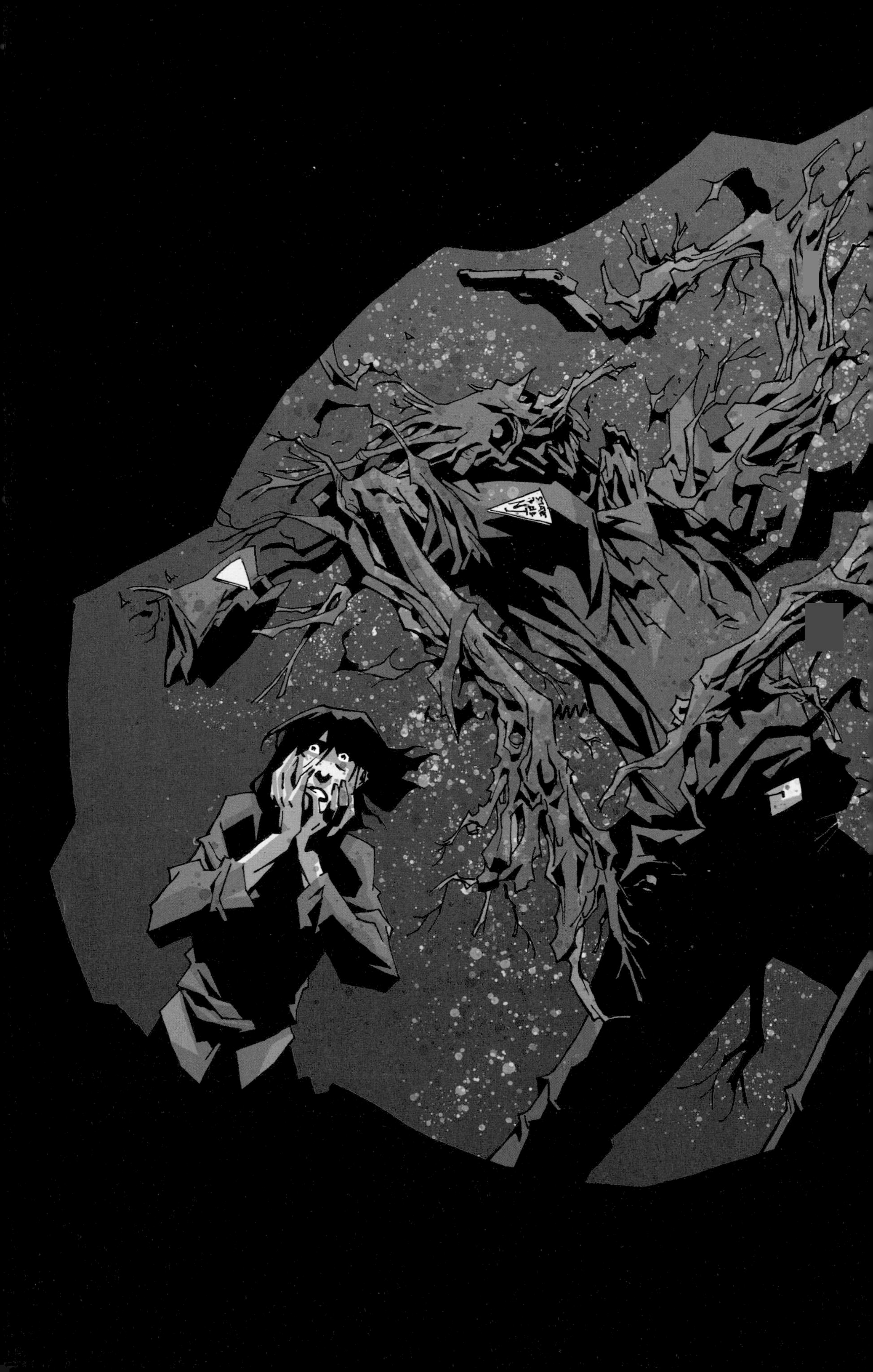

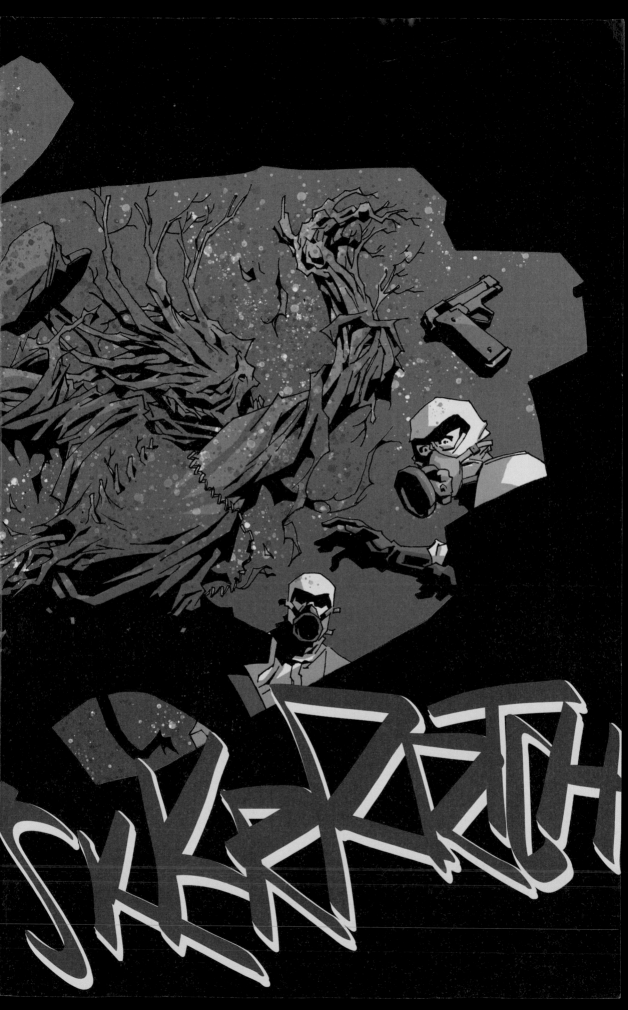

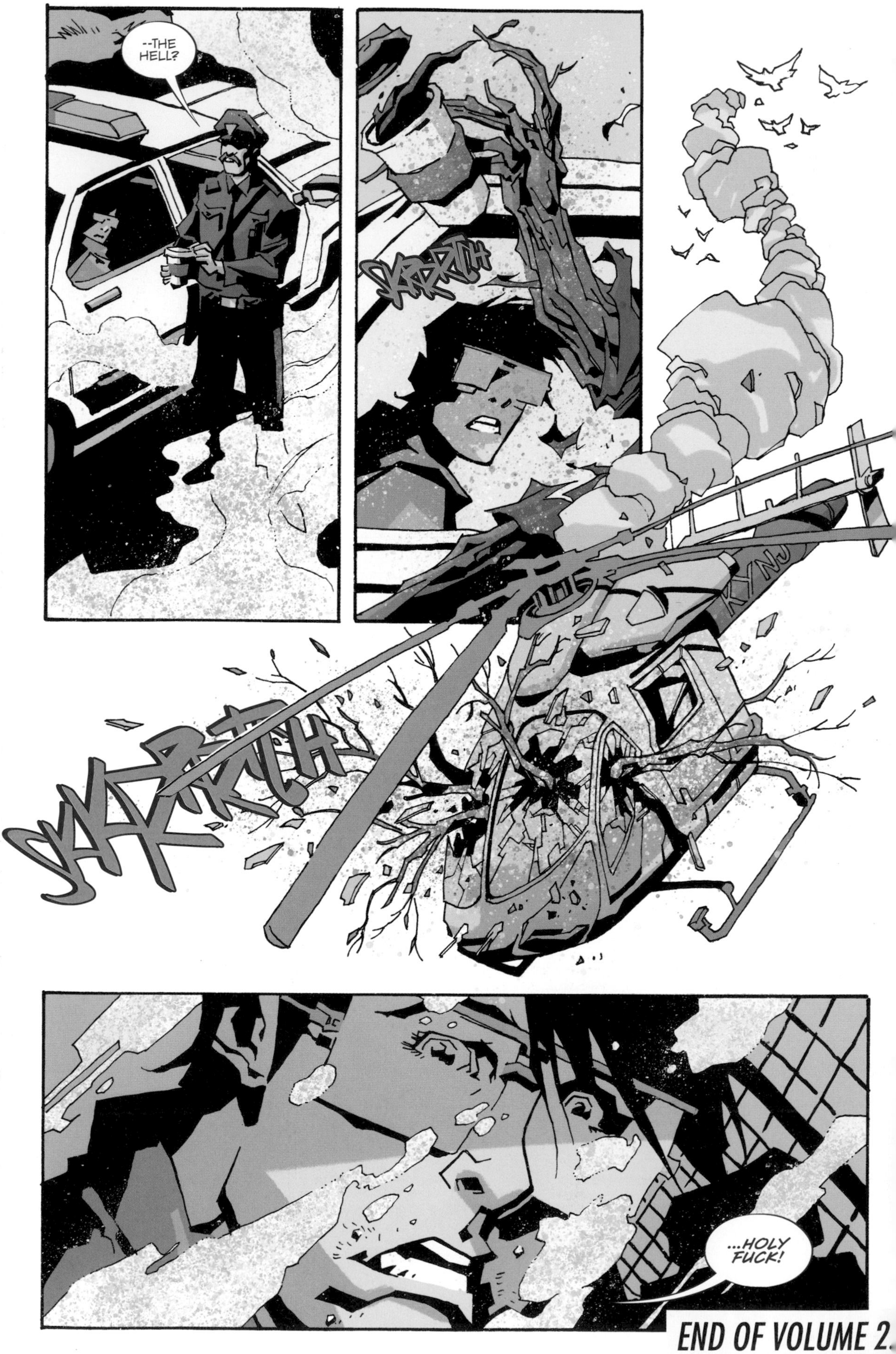
--THE HELL?
SKRRTCH
SKRRRTCH
...HOLY FUCK!
END OF VOLUME 2.